LEECH

GABRIEL RYVES

23 Ghosts · New York

ISBN: 979-8-9904069-0-2

eISBN: 979-8-9904069-1-9

Publisher contact:
gabrielryves@23ghosts.com
www.23ghosts.com

First edition 2024

LEECH

Gabriel Ryves

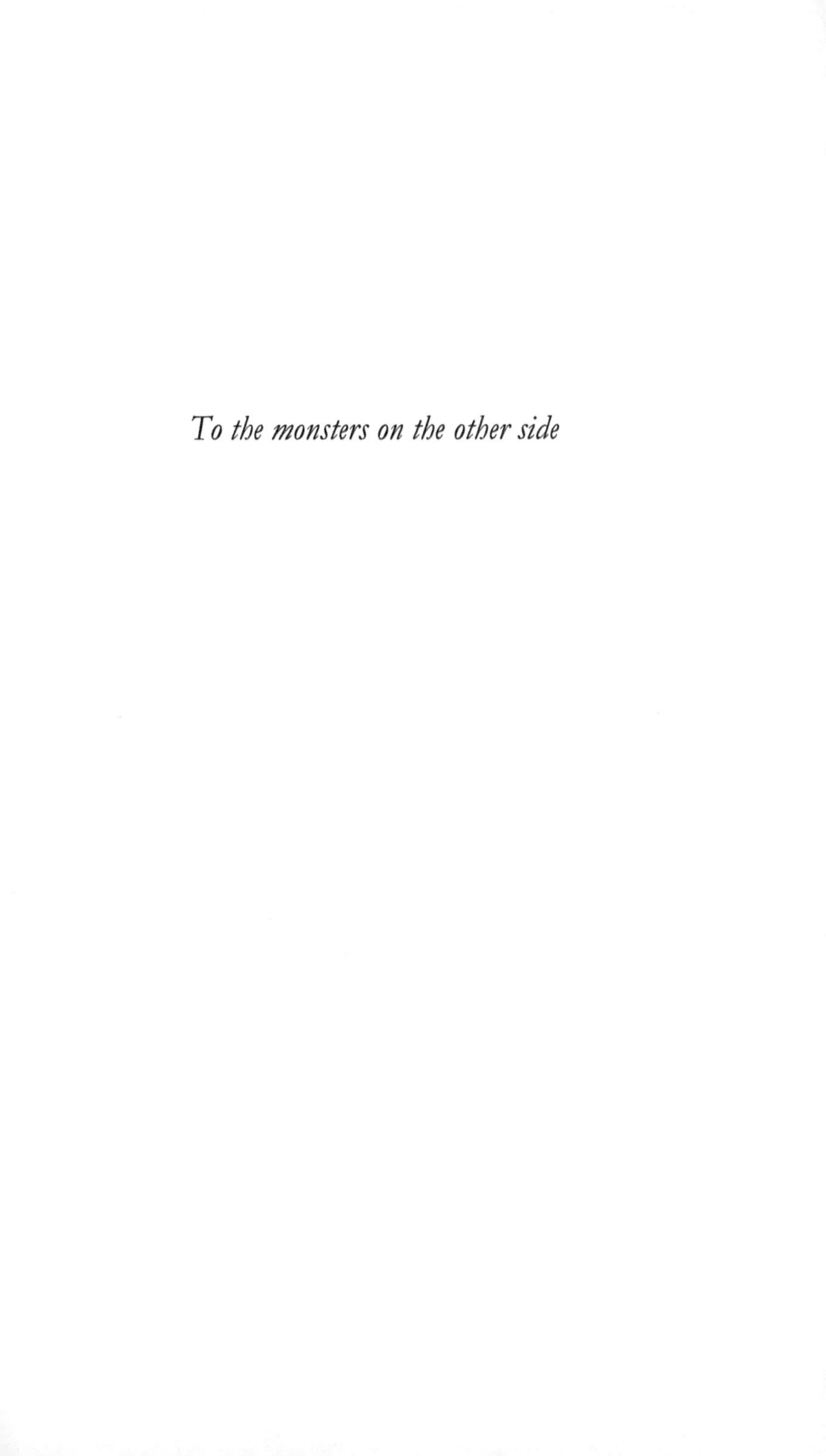

To the monsters on the other side

JUNE 6TH
1899

CHAPTER ONE

THERE WAS A MOMENT when Jasper thought he would die. The auto careened on two wheels, Leo sliding on top of him from the driver's seat as his pounding pulse screamed that he was about to be crushed. His blood would make mud in the dirt, and when they found him, he'd be no more than carrion.

The automobile landed, right side up on four wheels, with a thump. His teeth rattled. No blood spilled. Jasper folded over in relief, forehead propped on one hand while he wiped his eyes under his goggles. Grime, blown freely from the roads over the automobile's open carriage, mixed with sweat and dripped down his face. Leo's knuckles were clenched on the gear shift, but he laughed as if it had all been great fun.

"Scared you, didn't I?"

"Yes," was all Jasper managed, still feeling like the wind had been knocked out of him.

"Awfully sorry. There was rock in the road, practically a boulder. God knows they don't maintain anything up here."

They had been going *fast* too. It had snuck up on Jasper; the wind strengthened, the landscape blurred, and he'd felt a little spike of fear. He'd never gone so fast, not even in an auto. How could you in Manhattan? But it was easy enough on this void of a road. Nothing but dirt, dark on the cloudy day, surrounded by trees thick as a net and mountains waving over each other. Jasper had never seen any of it before. Beautiful, but discomfiting; he couldn't tell whether he felt trapped or too exposed. It was different in the city, where buildings hugged close and the view changed every minute. Here, the same peaks followed them for miles. One grew bigger, greener—must be what they were driving towards.

"Is this your first time in an automobile? How do you like it?" Leo asked.

Jasper's fingers were still dug into the seat. He thought a moment before answering. "It's fantastic."

A smile crept onto Leo's face, and Jasper basked in its delight. It wasn't his first time, but he didn't bother making the correction. Leo was always happy to impress, and the auto was his latest tool. He'd been positively gleeful when he announced they would be driving up in the car, almost as much as when he had invited Jasper to the castle in the first place.

"When I was a boy, I was in a carriage accident," Leo said. One hand, sheathed in a cream suede glove, held the wheel. "Something spooked the horses, and we crashed right into the post on 30th and Park. Or Lexington. 30th definitely, because I remember the sign. We had to crawl out through the luggage trunk."

"Were you hurt?"

"No." Leo's other hand reached into his vest for a silver cigarette case. "Don't mention it in front of Mother. She'll have a fit."

Jasper doubted he'd make small talk with Mrs. Lambert or any of Leo's family. He was along for their vacation, but the invite came with a stipulation: officially, he was here as a servant. He wondered if he should light Leo's cigarette. That was probably too much. Rich people lit their own smokes, didn't they? He had no clue. His only concept of what a valet did was seeing black-suited men flit down hallways in expensive townhouses. Certainly not a job he was qualified for, but the role was just a guise to sneak around Leo's family. Jasper wasn't really here to work.

Gloved fingers fiddled with the case, less interested in the steering wheel.

"Here." Jasper took it out of his hands. He had a drag for himself before handing the cigarette over. Tobacco cut through the mulchy air. Clouds rolled down, obscuring the bony edge of a hill. The fog was descending, about to cover the trees too. Branches reached for them as they turned onto a mountain path. Jasper craned his neck up towards the peak, trying to spot anything that might look like their destination. It was a *true* castle, Leo had insisted, brought over from Europe brick-by-brick. His real estate mogul father had gotten ahold of it, and the whole Lambert family was moving in for a few months' country getaway.

Not an experience Jasper ever thought would drop in his lap. He probably would have agreed to go no matter who offered, but for it to come from Leo Lambert was ideal. There would be plenty of time together, Leo treating him to fancy pleasures as always. And this incredible place to explore: thrones and armor and dungeons, he imagined. Getting paid on top of that, and for no real work. He just had to fetch a few meals.

His mother had thought it so grand an offer she became suspicious and showed her displeasure by bragging. *My Jasper's leaving me to become a knight. My last child is moving into a castle.* She said it to every neighbor and street peddler, who'd look at him funny until he talked it down. *It's just a job. Ma exaggerates.* She didn't understand how he had managed an opportunity like this, and his a-friend-got-it-for-me explanation wasn't enough detail for her. In her defense, it wouldn't make sense to anyone else. Jasper was a handyman who did the occasional job around the Lambert house, and as far as anyone knew they were strangers. More than strangers; Leo wasn't supposed to acknowledge Jasper's existence, and Jasper shouldn't expect him to. Of course, it didn't add up to his mother. She thought he was being scammed or hiding something from her. Which he was, he supposed, not that he liked it that way. Oh, well, no use dwelling on it. The road was getting narrow.

"Where do you suppose the last person we saw was?" Jasper asked.

"Back on 59th St. Ha!" Leo's cigarette swelled bright orange. "Though truly it must have been that soldier outside Camp Townsend."

"Do you think there's a dun—"

The car skidded to halt, nearly thrusting Jasper out of the seat.

"God—!" He bit his tongue to stop from cursing at Leo. A scraggily man bent under a sack had appeared out of the trees. Unhurt, he loitered in front of the auto with a wide-eyed glare.

"I say!" Leo exclaimed, equal parts relief and irritation.

The woods where the man had come from were dense as anything, but it was sparser on the other side. Jasper saw wheat and the hint of a farmhouse. Closer to the road, moss-covered gravestones languished between trees. Leo noticed the graves too—he was staring at them with a noticeable grimace—and the man laughed.

"You fear 'em?"

Leo snapped his head. "I feared running you over. You're a bit old to have so little sense."

The man's face fell into a glower. "What're you doing with this thing way up here?" He spat at the car. Leo's chest puffed, struggling to remain a gentleman.

"My family owns the castle on this mountain."

"*Oh*," the man said with a jeer. "Heard about that."

"Quite so. Then you must know this is practically our land."

"Prac-tic-al-ly." The man sang each syllable as his boots crunched down next to the graves. Leo's frown followed him until he had disappeared into the woods.

"Loony hick farmers." Leo jostled the stick, and the car sputtered to life. Spoked wheels chewed gravel as the fog rolled in and out. The path steepened, mud slowed them, and with each crest and hairline turn, they grew more anxious to get to their destination. Hard to tell at times whether they were still on the road at all. Staring into the forest, Jasper wondered how far in he'd have to go to become irrevocably lost. Trees bent into each other, forming a maze of tunnels; the ground wobbled with rocks, holes, and dead leaves. Not far.

Leo forced the auto up a final craggy hill onto a plateau. Deep in, hidden until the very end, was the castle. Jasper's jaw hung open. Stone ascended fifty, eighty, a hundred feet. Higher at the three towers, two stretching out from the back corners and third out from the center, each ending in a pointed spire. Arched, narrow windows mottled the walls, dark and hollow. No flags hung. It was flat gray, no variation apart from stains on the weathered stone. Earlier, he'd wondered if the castle would have a dungeon. Now, he was sure of it.

They were parked on roots before a wrought iron gate, beyond which the castle ground sprawled. A wall bordered them, though how far it went exactly, Jasper couldn't tell, since past the center gate its stones disappeared under a mesh of vines. Difficult to tell what grew on the wall and what grew next to it. The thicket surging around it extended from the woods.

Leo was out of the auto and doing stretching exercises on the grass. Bent, touching his toes, he announced: "Welcome to Kasteel Verlossen!"

"What?" Jasper said.

"That's the estate's name: Kasteel Verlossen."

Jasper peeled off the driving goggles and removed his cap, shaking his hair out. "It has name?"

At the gate, Leo yanked on a hefty padlock.

"First ones here," he said. "You know Florence called the auto a wasteful purchase?"

Florence, his sister. She was the older one; there were two, and the younger sister was called Elsie. That's all Jasper knew of them, besides that Elsie's bout of scarlet fever last winter had prompted this entire thing: doctors said she needed country air, and now the family was taking an extended vacation in a mountaintop castle.

Specks of dead insects from the drive littered Jasper's jacket. He tried in vain to pick them off as Leo shouted over the vacant grounds to be let in.

"This should be unlocked for our arrival," Leo said, face between the bars of the gate. He rang a brass bell that hung perilously from the wall.

"Is there a groundskeeper?" Jasper asked.

"There most certainly ought to be." Leo folded his arms. "And a housekeeper and however many others. We only needed to bring a limited staff, and the rest would be here. That's what father arranged for. I do say, you won't be the only one serving me Jasper. Just the, ah, primary one. So to speak." He gave the bell another try.

"None of the other staff your family brought..." Jasper twisted his lips. "No one who would recognize me, right?"

It was the butler, not members of the family, who had hired him. The Lambert's house staff knew him as a handyman, not a gentleman's valet. How odd for him to be clearing gutters in April and by the Lambert son's side in June. What if it led them to suspect a relationship? Leo had presented his plan for them to stay at the castle so confidently, Jasper hadn't thought any of this through.

"It won't be an issue. I'm allowed to hire whoever I wish for my personal valet," Leo said. "Perhaps there's another gate. One short enough to hop. You go that way, I'll go this."

He pivoted left. Jasper was sure he'd detected a frown and hoped he hadn't put Leo in a mood. If Leo said it wouldn't be an issue, he supposed he should trust it. He went right, following the wall.

The sky was monochrome gray and Kasteel Verlossen grim. He considered how far to fudge the truth when he wrote his mother. He didn't want to add to her stress. She had been left in their dingy apartment, crammed next to the Cappellis and a few other stray boarders. No family with her. He was the only one of her children who had both survived into adulthood and still talked to her, and now he'd left too. But he had promised her letters, and he'd keep his word. Besides, it was only a few months. She could make it that long, couldn't she?

Jasper ducked low branches and dragged against clumps of weeds. Leaves twisted around each other, some with long hairs; some flat and oily, reddish, curled; and some with prickers that stuck to his clothes. There was a fruit that could be a blackberry, except the shrub it attached to was wrong. Jasper picked one but thought better about eating it.

He stopped to catch his bearings, realizing he'd wandered several yards into the woods. The brush around the wall was too thick; it had pushed him between the trees. If there was another gate, he'd need a saw to get through it.

Branches snapping sounded like firecrackers. His head whipped, and he caught a silhouette moving deep in the forest.

"Hey! 'Scuse me!" Jasper called. He was met with silence. "Anybody there? We're the new people at the castle." What was it called? "Cats steel. Cast steel—"

The something sprinted away. Could be a deer for all he saw.

"Who's there?" Leo said, jogging towards him from the brush.

"No one. Or nobody who wanted to talk to me," said Jasper.

"Ah, I see!" Leo faced the woods. "*Hello!*"

"You didn't find a gate?" Jasper asked.

"Oh, I quit that. One can barely follow the wall, it's so overgrown. And, mmm…" Leo looked sly and scooped an arm around him. "I regretted having split up."

He squeezed his shoulder. Jasper returned the gesture and let himself relax into Leo's arms. It always calmed him, being held like that. The soft leather of Leo's jacket warmed him against the day's chill.

"There has to be a caretaker, because nothing is growing on the castle," Jasper said, pointing through the trees. Leo gave him a look. "I mean, there're vines everywhere, you can't even see the wall, but there's nothing growing on the castle itself. Who's cleaning it off?"

"So, you're right. Even the towers are clean." Leo peered at them for a beat before shifting his gaze back to Jasper. He sat on the ground, blue eyes inviting, and took his cap off. His hair was in place, dark and slicked neatly over his skull. There was still some shine to it, even in the gray. Jasper nestled down next to him.

"Quite secluded 'round this way," Leo said and kissed him. Suede brushed the back of Jasper's neck, and a lump in his throat grew.

They held each other, sticks and pebbles digging into their legs, until they became wary. Being in the open air like this was a first for Jasper, and he suspected for Leo too. Maybe if they hadn't both just bellowed into the woods, they could risk more. Side by side, they stared at the castle while holding hands that would be easy to pull apart. Their view was bordered by dewy branches. The old stones were crunched together, sliced by opaque glares off narrow windows.

"Appears more run-down then I expected," Leo said. "Still, properly living there will be…quaint? No. Droll? Not quite. What's the word…"

"What do you think the inside looks like?"

"I've no idea. None of us do. Father bought it on good faith from one of his associates. Whimsical! Yes, a *whimsical* place to stay. Do you know anyone else who's lived in a castle?"

Leo was looking coy. Jasper gave a slow cluck of his tongue.

"Probably. One of my other employers, I'd think."

"But you don't *know* them." Leo cupped Jasper's shoulder, and they grinned in between kisses. "Are your neighborhood friends jealous?"

Hell's Kitchen wasn't fawning in envy, if that's what Leo imagined. Jasper didn't have friends like that, anyway. His mother had told more people than he had.

"Are they?" Leo pressed. Jasper shrugged in response, and Leo seemed disappointed, but that mood soon passed.

"My hope for the summer is to sport," said Leo. "It wouldn't be improper for me to play with my valet, on occasion, as we are removed from polite society. And the only other person to play with is Flo, and I simply will need a reprieve from her. Do the lower classes play tennis?"

"I don't," Jasper said.

"Fine with me, I don't mind beating you. Ha! Oh, and hikes, we'll take lots of hikes. Though this place is so gigantic it'll be easy to avoid the scullery maids and other riffraff."

"When they get here."

"Indeed!"

Leo made a sweeping gesture towards the castle and landed his hand on Jasper's knee. Jasper leaned into him but couldn't help stealing glances behind them. It was foreign to him to see nothing but dense forest, no path, no lantern, no sign of humanity. The trees were so tall he couldn't see one fully, looking at the trunks and then up at the canopies.

From the road, they heard wheels and clopping hooves. Leo sprang up, clearing his throat. There was a last forlorn look between them before he walked back towards the entrance. Jasper followed, keeping his distance, because he wanted nothing less than to be front and center when they met the rest of the Lamberts. Besides, it probably looked servantly to trail behind.

They rounded the corner to a party of carriages. A group of men huddled around the gate's padlock while others milled by neighing horses. Drivers and servants, Jasper noted. The four other members of the Lambert family idled apart in the mud. He had only seen them before in passing, in a window while thatching a roof or heard through Leo's bedroom wall. But it wasn't hard to pick them out. Mr. Lambert, bald and dressed for cold weather, scrutinized the men trying to break the padlock from afar. His wife was next to him, covered in jewels. She would be glittering head to toe if the sun were out. The daughters were by one of the carriages, coils of their Gibson poofs flopping over their foreheads. The younger sister, Elsie, was straw blonde, her head poking out from a swath of fabric. Florence, the eldest dressed in a tight button jacket, had amber hair and Leo's same long face. They both got it from their father, Jasper saw.

"I say, I beat you all, didn't I?" was Leo's cheerful greeting as he embraced his family.

"There is a problem," said William Lambert, lumbering in a mink overcoat to his son, "No one is here! No groundskeeper. No guard. They did not even open the gate, and I wrote that we would arrive today."

"Yes, I rang the bell and no one answered. I was searching for another entrance, but no luck there either. You don't suppose we're at the wrong medieval castle?" Leo grinned. His quip went unacknowledged.

"We're having to break the lock like common thieves." William glanced at the men fighting with the padlock.

"But we've *bought* it. We *own* it," Cordelia Lambert said, as if in an argument with someone. Her husband nodded, producing a set of keys which he held righteously in the air.

"I was handed these at sale!"

Leo frowned.

"And you've tried *those* keys in *that* lock?" He pointed. That annoyed his father, but he diffused it by giving his mother a supportive pat on the shoulder. Behind him, Florence and Elsie grimaced under plumed hats.

"The air is giving me a cough!" Elsie said, followed by a pointed cough. "It's supposed to be fresh up here. For my *health*."

"Well, it's raining, darling." Mrs. Lambert shifted to her youngest. A woman in a white nurse's cap appeared from around the carriage, hovering near Elsie.

"Takes a while to hack up all the Manhattan smog," Leo said.

Florence leaned against the carriage, brushing a pelt scarf which looked to be from the same animal that made her father's coat. Her eyes scanned over Jasper. He shrunk towards the thicket. Not that there was reason to, he told himself; he was supposed to be here. Was there something else he needed to be doing besides standing? The other servants were stretching their legs. She wasn't looking at him any longer.

A clink and a satisfied cry told them the lock had been cracked. Leo sauntered with the rest of his family through the gate while the others—the limited staff, Jasper assumed—scrambled to unpack what luggage they could. The butler, Mr. Thorley, directed the staff. Jasper felt himself starting to sweat, anticipating the butler noticing him and asking, *Why are you here?* Some of the others were faintly familiar. He remembered the chef, a man named Proulx who looked like a boxer and sported a thick waxed mustache.

They were looking his way. What was wrong? He had been standing here too long. The butler caught his eye, but instead of launching an interrogation, Mr. Thorley motioned for Jasper to help with the luggage. Jasper breathed out, chiding himself. So worried about what would happen when he was recognized, he forgot he was supposed to be working. He fell in with them and was handed two suitcases and a hatbox to carry. He figured he should be carrying Leo's luggage, not that he would know what it looked like anyway. Didn't matter; he was overthinking it. The best thing was to follow the others' lead.

The staff grumbled as they trailed after the family. A driver worried about the condition of the stables. Mr. Thorley needed tonic but had already drunk his supply dry. One of the maids, who seemed to be Florence's, bemoaned the whole trip. The doctors had steered the family wrong, she said, and the parents were taking things out of hand.

Cobblestones, slippery in the fog, led them inside the grounds. The path was wide but overgrown, and weeds nipped at their ankles. Farther in rose the massive thicket, coiled shrubs so dense they completely obscured the wall. The party trudged on, now silent. Jasper gazed over the grounds, trying not to look too long at the members of staff, lest they look back. He hadn't expected to be thrown in with them so suddenly.

They weren't total strangers, but that was worse, wasn't it? Wouldn't they all think it odd: a kid who had done the occasional job around the Madison Avenue house had reemerged as one of the Lamberts' trusted staff? They were suspicious; they could tell. His heart dropped thinking about it.

A man with a patchy mustache cocked an eye at him.

"You that guy who was around a while ago? Clearing the gutters?"

Jasper nodded, hoping his expression didn't betray his anxiety.

"They didn't bring you here to clean the leaves off the roof, huh?" he grinned, pointing at the hulking central tower. Jasper smiled back.

"I'm working for –"

Elsie cried out, snapping their attention. She had slipped, caught by her father and brother before the fall. Patchy mustache shook his head.

"I dunno where everyone is. They better not expect *us* to do all the," he waved his hand in the air, "*work*. For this place. I mean, I'm a sous-chef, that's my job. I work with Monsieur Proulx, I'm a sous-chef, and sous-chef only."

Jasper thought of something to say but decided against it, wanting the conversation to end. Cobblestone changed to wood planks. It was a drawbridge, he realized, still hinged to the castle and laid over grass. The bridge might not have been raised for centuries. It led to four wide steps and hefty double oak doors. Their wood was strapped by corroded metal bands, and where the doors met a single circular handle rested above a lock.

Mr. Lambert paused at the top step and faced the others. His eyes shifted deliberately over each family member, then his staff, and his luggage. He looked about to give a speech but instead simply turned one of the keys in the lock. Iron scraped against iron. The door stayed shut as he pulled vainly on the handle. Leo skirted around his father to try a push, which cracked it open. Another heave, and the castle doors thrust apart.

CHAPTER TWO

COLD AIR WAVED OVER the crowd. The nurse blinked furiously as if her eyes were agitated.

"Oh, hoorah!" Mrs. Lambert said with a light clap of her hands. The children and servants smiled only when Mr. Lambert looked at them, though Leo had covered his face with a handkerchief. Jasper was sure he was smirking underneath. It was Elsie who went inside first, bouncing over the threshold. The rest folded in after her.

The staff watched the family disappear into the maw of the entrance, frozen on the drawbridge. After a moment, the butler moved forward, and the others followed him, muttering to each other with luggage in tow. The doors opened to a stone vestibule which they all filtered through, ducking their heads under the grimy, low ceiling. Jasper remembered a time he and a neighborhood boy had snuck into a tunnel by the river, freshly dug, that was being laid with pipes. It was the smell that triggered his memory. Cold, damp, newly exposed dirt. There was a musk that only came from things that never saw sunlight.

The family squealed from deeper in the castle. At the end of a cramped path, an archway opened into an expansive room around which the Lamberts scurried. Woven red and purple tapestries hung interspersed with portraits of rich men. None from later than a century ago, Jasper guessed. A particularly large painting hung above a gaping mantle. Light came from windows well above their heads, and he saw empty sconces meant for candles, not gas. There were a few scattered doors, each arched like miniatures of the entrance and latched shut. In the center, a heavy table that could seat at least two dozen stretched over the slate floor.

The others set down what they were carrying to explore, careful to give the family space. Jasper followed suit, dropping the luggage gently so it wouldn't risk making a sound.

"I hope he has keys to those," Mr. Thorley said to Proulx, jiggling the handle of the one of the doors. Jasper walked past them, avoiding Leo and taking in the paintings. He ended up in front of the largest, standing behind William and Cordelia Lambert. Mr. Lambert turned around and he jumped back, blushing, certain he had gotten too close. But the man spoke to him genially, tapping the frame.

"Pieter Van Hoensbroeck. This was his," William Lambert said. In the portrait, a sallow-faced man rested an arm on a table next to a silver cup, to the other side of him a saltshaker and tub of yellow powder. A green snake had been painted slithering from the salt to the arm. Pieter Van Hoensbroeck stared ahead, unconcerned with the viper at his fingertips.

"He built this castle?" Jasper asked, feeling as he said it that he shouldn't have talked.

"No, lad, he brought it over from Holland." Mr. Lambert at least did not seem offended by Jasper's presence. "It was first constructed in 1235. Burned and rebuilt a few times before the Dark Ages ended. But these stones are at least four hundred years old. Van Hoensbroeck had them brought over *brick* by *brick*."

"Is that his son?" Cordelia scooped her husband's shoulder and pointed to another portrait.

"Maybe. Although if he did have children, they didn't live here," said Mr. Lambert. He began to explain the history of the property, how it moved from banks to the occasional occupant to different banks. He soon forgot about Jasper, demanding all the attention for his story from his wife. As she listened, she stood with shoulders angled and hands folded, like an illustration from a catalog. Jasper slipped away.

"Eureka!" The exclamation turned everyone's attention to Mr. Thorley, who had opened a door to the right of the archway. They congealed around him to see where it led. The new room was neither as grand nor as stark as the hall. It looked more modern—at least the furniture did, especially the plush sofa and armchair set arranged around a fireplace, just as they might be in a proper sitting room.

"Oh, thank god," Florence said as she strolled in.

"Elsie, come and see!" Mrs. Lambert called. There were other rooms leading off from this new one: three bedrooms, a study, small dining room, and, thankfully, a Spartan water closet. All fully furnished and barely dirty. It was warmer too, with plaster walls, rugs, and heavy red curtains. No gas lamps, but otherwise a decently livable apartment. Florence declared as much while her mother inspected the furniture.

Jasper stood clumped with some of the drivers and the sous-chef by the entrance, watching the others poke around.

"Maja, start the fire." Mrs. Lambert pointed at one of the maids. "Please. Elsie, come here!"

"The last owners must have lived here," Mr. Thorley said. William Lambert looked silently relieved.

"The wood's wet," Maja said, crinkling her nose at a dusty log.

"Have everything brought in here," Mr. Lambert said to the butler. "The girls will bunk together."

"Father—" Florence protested.

"One of you get to chopping, then." Mrs. Lambert fanned her fingers towards the men. The sous-chef turned to the drivers, who turned to Jasper. He stared blankly back. Get to chopping where? She was fixated on him, peeved. Her husband and daughter bickered behind her.

Mr. Thorley turned from them to her. "We'll get right on it ma'am, but," he said, "without the castle staff present, we of course don't know our way around."

Jasper nodded. Leo had long since disappeared into one of the bedrooms.

"We can't have no fire!" Cordelia grimaced. "There are no lamps, no other lighting to speak of, and what's more, it's *freezing* all the way out here in the country. You know Mr. Lambert detests freezing."

"Of course. We'll figure everything out." The butler pulled Jasper aside, brow flustered. "There must a woodshed. Find it, and if you have to, get an axe and chop down a tree."

"I've never chopped down a tree," Jasper said. The few wrinkles on Thorley's face were deep ridges, animating as he grit his teeth.

"Well, there are plenty to choose from, if you have to. Watch it doesn't fall on anything important. But I'm sure there's a woodshed. And if you get lost…don't get lost." He clapped Jasper on the back and pushed him out into the hall.

Another of the doors had been opened, this one close to the mantle on the other side of the massive table. It led immediately to a stone staircase, from which Elsie Lambert came bounding down. She was jubilant as she ran to her mother.

"There's a bedroom in the tower!" she called. "It's mine, I'm sleeping there. I'll be like a princess!"

Jasper slipped back under the archway and out the way he'd come.

Alone on the steps of Kasteel Verlossen, Jasper was unsure where to go. On the other side of the gate, horses whinnied in the damp. Nobody had unhitched them yet. Where would they lead them? The stables were *somewhere*, just as the woodshed was *somewhere*. The overgrowth made it hard to see far into the grounds.

He looked straight down the path through the gate, past the carriages, and over the tree line. Two mountain peaks rose like the wings of a hawk. Streaks of deep emerald emerged from under mist, morphing as the peaks grew into bare rock that struck against a hidden sun. He shivered—he could not imagine looking away, knowing that even if he tried his hardest to remember the sight, his memory would never do it justice. Clouds grew thicker. He shook himself loose. A woodshed. There would be plenty of time to stare at nature later.

That furnished apartment was on the right side of the castle, so he turned left. He had the feeling that, if he looked again after turning his back, the mountains would be closer. To humor himself, he glanced behind, but already fog and brush obscured the view.

There was no path, just tall grass between the castle wall and the trees. He sneezed. The air certainly was different.

Hopefully that was enough to heal Elsie, whatever she needed. Leo hadn't said much about her illness, just complained vaguely about his sister and assured Jasper that they'd be here no more than half a year, tops. The senior Lambert would not last long doing business by mail only.

Monotonous gray stone stretched in front of him. The back of the castle was in sight, but he couldn't seem to get closer no matter how much time passed. He remembered an old job that had him ferrying crosstown, over the same street east to west and back again. Walking and walking and never getting there. At least in the city, the buildings varied; there were people to look at. Activity. It did smell better up here, he had to admit. He sneezed. No woodshed. It wasn't raining, but the wet air stuck to him. He wiped the back of his neck as he finally turned the corner.

The property stretched back as far as he could see. Untamed grass, then the thicket, and beyond that, who knew. Leaning against the wall, he rubbed his fingers into the mortar. He was at the base of one back tower, the other on the opposite corner, each casting shadows over the other.

Not far back, a section of the grounds was circled off by a stone wall. Hard to judge on first glance how large or small. Seeing it against one of the towers, it looked only a few yards, but he was underestimating either the size or distance, because as he got nearer, it was plain that the enclosure was far bigger. It might run the length of a small house. The wall was about six feet high, a mesh of branches brimming over the top. It looked as if, rather than cut down this part of the thicket, someone had simply fenced it in. A round green fruit hung over the side—an unripe peach. A break in the wall marked an entrance; he went in and was hit with the scent of fresh flowers. A garden. It hadn't been tended anytime recently, but whatever had been cultivated still bloomed. Peonies, honeysuckles, irises, ferns. Weeds lived harmoniously beside them. Blue round berries hung from a bush with stalks of a violent pink color. Fruit trees that had been planted along the wall formed the mesh, insulating the place. He could almost forget there was a castle next to it.

It was sticky here, and as he drifted further in, his shins tore up spiderwebs that had been weaved across the garden path. He ended at a lily pad-dotted pond buzzing with mosquitoes. A frog hopped; something stirred under the water where the reeds sprouted. He plunged a stick in to judge its depth—at least two feet. The stick came out with a fat leech curled around it, and he tossed the whole thing back with a splash.

Wood. He needed to find it; he didn't want to be freezing cold any more than William Lambert did. One winter, his family had burned all their chairs to keep the fire going while it snowed through a broken window. He had to remember to write his mother a letter.

Roses had been planted on the other side of the pond, and their thorns had long since taken the path over. He went out the way he came. Facing the back of the castle, he saw rows of battlements that ran between the towers. From up there he could spot the woodshed instead of poring over the grounds, able to see over the brush and how far the property went. Maybe he'd have to be higher up for that. The clouds were thinning as he walked under a tower. He craned his neck to see up it, peering into the window at the very top. A trick of the light in the shape of a man rippled past. He shuddered.

There it was again. Startled, he looked away, fixing his eyes on the peach tree.

"Jasper!"

He heard his name as an echo. He spun back to see Leo waving from the tower.

"Come up here!" Leo shouted, voice faint.

Jasper cupped his hands over his mouth. "How?" he yelled back.

Leo only motioned with his arm, an animated silhouette.

There was a door at the base of the tower, stuck but not locked. A good push opened it. Stairs circled up. Hopefully they went all the way to the top, or Jasper would have no idea how to fulfill Leo's request. Anyway, he would be able to get a good view of the grounds from up there, though maybe not the shed. Plus, he knew Leo would keep him a while. The butler wouldn't like that, but Leo was the one he was supposed to obey, right? That was his job. He took a breath before ascending.

It was a dreary climb. He passed a few landings, a fork in the stairs, but still kept scaling the uneven steps. More than once, he had to catch himself from falling. There was gravel under his nails as he knocked, panting, on the door at the staircase's end.

Leo greeted him with a big smile. One sleeve was unbuttoned, his jacket and vest strewn on a plain bed behind him. He ushered Jasper in, closed the door, and said, "You're sweating."

Jasper held his knees, still winded, but managed a grin. Last September, after a particularly grueling job around the townhouse, Leo had offered him some brandy. Ever since, Jasper had been sneaking up to Leo's bedroom, whether he had work at the house or not. He could feel himself being looked at now.

The bed creaked as Leo sat on the edge. "I'm quartering here," he announced. Jasper laughed. The room was dusty and narrow, more like an attic. Leo Lambert had a canopy bed; he had velvet curtains and a cabinet solely for liquors kept in ornate crystal decanters. This room had exactly four pieces of furniture. The contents of a suitcase spilled out from on top of an armless, straight-backed chair. The desk and dresser were simple too, resting on an unvarnished wood floor. All the light came in through three, deep-set windows. No gas in here, either. Not even a candle holder.

He cocked a blue eye at Jasper. "I know what you're thinking, *but*," he said, "what's fascinating about this particular room is that it is—by my estimate—the furthest possible distance from where my parents are."

"You're just like Elsie," Jasper teased. Leo swatted at him.

"You have sisters, right?" Leo lit a cigarette.

"Yeah."

"Good, you understand how obnoxious they are." He hooked a finger around Jasper's suspender, guiding him to the bed and offering an inhale. Jasper sucked in enough smoke to satiate himself for a while, eyes falling over the thatched beamed ceiling.

"Your family really owns this place?"

"The bank was selling. Billy bought it. I suppose I should be planning what to do with it when he croaks. Excuse the morbidity."

Leo leaned on his elbows, one hand smoking while the other flicked Jasper's suspender band like a fiddle string.

"Is there food?" Jasper asked.

"Hm?"

"Your dad expected a staff, but nobody's here. The wood wasn't good to burn. Is there food?"

"I think Proulx is on it," Leo said with a squished little frown. His eyes ran down the walls. "There's no servant bell in here. That's fine. You'll come up here on the hour, three times a day. Let's say, breakfast at eight, lunch at noon, and a nightcap after dinner. Ten or eleven."

Leo was met with a blank stare.

"So, I just…bring you those things? At those times?" Jasper was sure there was something his friend-employer was forgetting to mention. And he couldn't picture himself carrying a meal up those steps without spilling it. Would the trays be silver?

"Yes. It's all very simple. Oh, you'll have to come tell me when dinner is ready too, so, four times a day. And fetch me if father needs me. Or don't. Ha. But that's all there is to it." Leo rested his chin in his palm. "Look, I'm not really working you, Jasper, but you do have to do *something*. You won't have to clean. Or dress me. Quite the opposite."

The band thumped against Jasper's back, and he let himself be pulled down. The bed was ratty. He'd actually gotten used to the Lamberts' smooth linens. When they were done, Leo handed him a cigarette, as always, and they smoked together. Jasper had never taken to tobacco, but he'd always had the cheap stuff before now. He took Leo's whenever he could. If he were wealthy, Jasper figured he would be addicted to everything.

Gray daylight came through the window. It made him uncomfortable that it was uncovered, no matter how high up they were, or how remote. He curled up, and Leo's embrace covered him like a shell. He puffed away, letting his brown hair be scattered. The massage of Leo's fingers over his scalp, the light tug of his hair being waved to and fro, melted Jasper into the bed. He heard Leo's voice like piano scales. Fragments floated in—something about a tapestry Leo had seen on a trip to someplace.

Jasper stared at his own arm, stretched over the scratchy yellow sheet, letting his eyes lose focus. He loved this, the warmth and weight of the man holding him, while all he cared about was bringing the cigarette back and forth to his lips.

On Madison Avenue, Leo would sweep him into the bedroom, and for the next few hours, Jasper wouldn't have to work or think or worry. Now that they were here, that could go on longer. Whole days of it. A true vacation. Not really working—Leo would take care of him.

They would barely have to sneak, since Jasper had reason to be in Leo's bedroom now. Not that anyone would be around the back tower to watch where he went. He bet no one could hear them, either. He thought of saying that, getting Leo excited again. Not now. Leo's hands were tracing his body, and he didn't care to move. A pinch brought him out of his thoughts. Fingers at the side of his waist. There was a nearby town Leo was talking about visiting, as perhaps there would be somewhere to sport, both he and Florence being concerned with badminton at the moment. Jasper told him about the garden.

"But no gardener," Leo sighed.

"What do you think happened?"

"Who knows." Leo twisted a tuft of Jasper's hair. "Perhaps everyone will be here tomorrow because father got his dates wrong. Wouldn't be the first time."

The panes of the window opened with a latch; Leo flicked his cigarette ash out. Jasper followed, catching a pale blue mountain in the distance. He looked down, hoping to spot the woodshed, but if one was there, it was hidden under treetops. He saw the round garden wall, the cross of the paths inside it, and a dark green circle in its middle—the pond. He still couldn't see a back gate, but the trees were, somehow, thicker past a certain point. Beyond that, the hills grew.

He dressed, olive pants and brown work boots, suspenders digging into a new shirt. Mrs. Cappelli had sewn it and sold it to him cheap. As he buttoned, Leo rummaged around for a robe. The silk one. He looked like something out of a myth as he showed Jasper out.

"Oh, the uniform!" Leo pivoted, producing a folded cube of cloth. "Wear that. At least when you're serving me. Usually, valets have to pay for it themselves, but of course I bought it for you."

He smiled, so Jasper smiled back.

CHAPTER THREE

O N HIS WAY DOWN, Jasper took a different route where the stairs forked. He found himself on a narrow landing that stretched out parallel to the battlements, across the back length of the castle. On one side, the stairs continued down into an expanse of dark empty stone below. It was a huge chamber, taller than the tapestry-covered hall. He did not hear a soul. Hooks covered the walls in batches, a handful of lone weapons hanging from them. Real ones. A sword, an empty crossbow. Suits of armor, some missing parts, lined the corners. He imagined the racks full, soldiers rushing to arm themselves.

Instead of going down or out to the battlements, he walked along the landing, hearing the clack of his own footsteps. It dawned on him that he had never been so removed from other people in his life. He felt like a spirit, slipping uninhibited through the castle. At the other end was an identical staircase, which must lead to the third tower. He wondered if it had a bed in it too. Maybe he'd sleep there, hundreds of feet between him and anybody else. He deserved that, once in his life, before going back.

He turned up the stairs. The climb felt easier, more natural than the hike up to Leo. Maybe he was getting used to the place. It needed a groundskeeper, didn't it? He could become that. The woods, he hated to admit, frightened him. But they were just new. The most he had seen of country before this were marshy oyster farms off the flatlands. Of course he felt uneasy. Once time passed, he'd get used to them. He would learn the woods and the castle, what their upkeep required. When the Lamberts went back to the city, they'd hire him to care for it permanently. Leo would visit for a while and then be on his way. Decades from now, with William long dead, Leo would realize he didn't care to own a castle and leave it all to Jasper.

The door to this tower was much the same as the other. He knocked, just in case some other Lambert had settled in there. Silence. He fought with the latch for a minute, but it gave, and he stepped into darkness. He could just make out the shape of shutters. Cautious walk over, he pried them open. Enough light shone in that he could see the other windows, and soon the room was almost bright.

There was no bed but a desk and, to his delight, a rotund iron cauldron. He couldn't help laughing: it looked like something off a Halloween card, resting on top of an old fire pit. Cobwebbed bottles and books lined shelves along bare stone walls. Behind the cauldron, an ornamented desk collected dust. Three sides were flush to the floor, all carved with petals, laurels, lion's heads. A stately chair was tucked behind it. There was an ink stand on top, antique by now, next to a single tome that seemed almost fused to the mahogany. With the edge of his index finger, he lifted the cover. Dust billowed up into his mouth. The pages were waxy, handwritten in a script that was nearly illegible and interspersed with bizarre runes. So, it really was a witch's cauldron.

Smile cracking, he turned pages while imagining midnight Sabbaths. He wondered who was the last person before him to open this. It might have been hundreds of years, and who knew what it contained. One of the strange sigils could probably summon the devil. Studying it, he felt rather intrepid.

None of the words were recognizable, even when he could parse out the letters. He brushed off the claw-foot chair and sat. It was comfortable, with curled armrests and a wide back he could lean into. It felt sturdy. No termites or rot had gotten to it over the years. The book was open in front of him, and beyond that, the cauldron. He turned more pages, but finding nothing he could understand, ran his eyes over the shelves. A memory of some childhood game floated through his mind. Played with a brother who hadn't lived long. A sister had played too; she was married now. She probably had kids, though he wasn't certain. He should write her. She wouldn't contact him herself unless she thought he had moved away from their mother.

She lived down by one the piers, sixteen or seventeen, and he thought he remembered the husband's name. He'd never met the guy. Their mother had dug up something about him being a gambler, but that might not be true. She only wanted fodder for her unremitting disapproval of every person any of her children were with. Jasper had heard her give variations of the same complaint his entire life. Each kid was a fool who picked a terrible spouse and was destined for a life of disappointment and woe. Almost funny, unless you were on the receiving end. In that light, it was okay he had to keep himself a secret. Next time he wished he could tell her, he would remind himself of that.

He rested an elbow on the desk as if he were working. This could be where he'd do business when he became the groundskeeper. His office, and he would quarter in the other tower. His guests could stay in the apartments; surely Leo would let him invite his family, if just to visit. He must have nieces and nephews who would be delighted by this. Hoping there would be a quill pen, he fiddled with the drawer, but it was locked.

Just like that, he felt himself deflate. Silly to play pretend, as if he were someone who would have a desk to do business, much less from a castle. He hopped up from the chair and meandered, focusing on the vials, books, and trinkets on the shelves as he circled the room. He stopped when a draft hit his ankles.

Nothing but wall in front of him. The door was on the opposite side, the windows shut. His eyes flitted over and down. The seam between the wall and the floor looked darker in one spot. Crouched, almost flat on the stone, he saw the gap. No more than a quarter inch. He traced it up, able to needle the tip of his nail through a break in the rock. The crack ran six feet up, over three, and down again. A door. It must be.

His heart pumped. A secret door in a castle. Pressing his ear to the wall, he pushed until he heard a click. Yes, it was real. He decided then that whatever was behind it, he wouldn't tell the Lamberts. Not even Leo. Air gasped out as the stones slid behind the true wall.

The smell of earth billowed into the room. On the other side was a plank staircase leading down a tunnel of packed dirt, braced open by wooden beams. They lined it like a rib cage. From a shelf, Jasper shook loose an old lantern, half a candle still in it. It crackled as he lit it, centuries of dust burning as it hissed to life. Holding out the hazy light, he embarked into the tunnel. The planks made for high, uneven steps, and the slope down was steep. He had to contort himself so as not to hit his head. Finally at the bottom, he could stand upright. Looking back, he struggled to glimpse a sliver of the tower room. He had descended farther than he thought. There was nothing he could see before him except more tunnel.

He had to know what was down here. There had to be something worth finding. He pressed on, breathing in the dirt. The earth had been forced open into a wide, even path. Gaps just big enough to squeeze through led off from the main stretch. He shone the lantern down a few but, seeing nothing, kept straight. Exposed roots snaked out from the walls. Running his fingers over them, he thought that this must be what worms feel like.

What would someone hide under here? Maybe it was gold. A pirate's chest. That seemed almost likely, given everything else. He would sneak the treasure away right before they went back to the city. Turning it into cash would be tricky; he'd have to be smart. Pawn it somehow. If he looked like himself, they'd try to screw him over or assume he was a thief. To fit in, he'd wear Leo's clothes. It wouldn't be a problem getting them, now that Jasper was his servant. Then it was only a matter of keeping the money safe. He might have to open a bank account.

The first thing he'd buy was a house. If it was really a lot of treasure, something three or four stories. His mother would have her own floor. It would be better that way, with so much space, not having to sleep in the same room as each other and the strangers who happened to be boarding, hearing every neighbor plus whatever was going on in the street. She would be less tough in a house. And, of course, she would be grateful to him. She would have to be, at that point. They'd buy nice clothes; he'd start caring about badminton or whatever it was. Get a car and a telephone. Thinking realistically, he may need to leave New York altogether to avoid suspicion about his sudden fortune. So, he would travel. He imagined himself holed up in a fancy hotel, taking a local man out for a night. It would be fun, not like the pitiful alley fucks he'd had before Leo. Enjoyable, romantic. He would hate to leave Leo, though. Maybe he would get the man to come to him. Meet each other halfway across the world, and it would be so fantastically fun that Leo wouldn't mind where Jasper had gotten the money in the first place.

He stopped at a split in the tunnel. It bent to the left and right, while the path directly ahead curved up. He went up. It was a low slope at first but got steeper as it went, leading to another set of rickety board-stairs. Those in turn became a ladder, as the dirt gave way to stone.

Looking up was like staring up a chimney, except he saw no sky. His shoulders slumped. How much had he already climbed today? He tugged at the ladder, which felt secure. It occurred to him that if he fell from it, he would certainly die, and that people didn't really hide gold in their walls. Or, if they did, people like him didn't find it and get rich.

No sooner did he think of turning around than curiosity began to gnaw. Why build a secret door if there was nothing behind it worth protecting? He held the lantern in his teeth. Stones pressed against his back up the narrow shaft until there were no more rungs, and he pulled himself on to a cold floor. He felt the groove of the floorboards, unable to see anything outside the bubble of lantern light illuminating his hand. The space was tight at first, but the ceiling angled up, and he crawled further in until he had room to stand.

Dropping the handle from his teeth, he cracked his jaw and held the lantern up.

Jasper burst out a petrified cry. His head hit the roof as he stumbled back, arms fanned out to brace himself. To maneuver out, he'd have to turn his back, and that was unthinkable. He gaped at the thing under the echo of his own scream, heart pounding in his throat.

Pinpoint eyes flickered at him from the floor where its body lay in a contorted heap. The emaciated bones twisted over themselves, sheathed in slimy white sinew. It lurched— *clank*—and he saw the shackle around its neck fettering it to the wall. Its mouth opened, baring toothless gums as it croaked out some sound he didn't understand.

"What are you?" His voice came out a whisper. The creature lifted its head, pointing a sunken face at him. He held the lantern over the thing as best he could. Tattered fabric still hung to parts of its body, loose over the jumbled skeleton. The flesh—what little there was of it— looked diseased. Shriveled, colorless, riddled with pus or mold. The whole room reeked of wet dirt.

It looked at Jasper with a carnivore's glare before saying, "Help me."

The words came out rough, but Jasper understood them. It was a person, after all. His heart still pounded. He swallowed to reset himself. This was a human, a prisoner on the verge of death.

"You must free me. I need food."

"Who are you?"

It propped itself on its forearms, which appeared to take a lot of strength, and looked up at him.

"My name is Ans-e-helm." The speech was stilted and accented in a way Jasper couldn't place. "He chained me here to die."

"Who?"

"Are you the new keeper of the castle?"

"No," Jasper said, straining to understand him, "I work for the new owners. We got here a few hours ago. It's been empty."

"Empty," Ansehelm rasped as he breathed between sounds. "What is the date?"

"June sixth."

The hairless skull bobbed, taking it in. How long had he been here?

"Please." Ansehelm curled two knobby fingers, beckoning Jasper to come closer. "You must help me, I am starving. Please."

Jasper stepped forward, though he hated to. No doubt he could crush the frail man with his bare hands, but it was a frightening sight. He rubbed his arm, brushing raised hairs down.

Each step deliberate, he circled the body, one eye watching for any sudden movements. The chain connected from the wall to the iron band around Ansehelm's neck by fused seams. There were no locks. The best chance to free the prisoner would be to pull the hinge out of the stone. Jasper lifted the chain, surprised by how heavy it was. More than metal its size should be, it must have somehow been weighted. He gripped it with both hands and yanked as hard as he could, but it didn't budge. He tried again, with no luck. The chain was tiring, uncomfortable to hold for long.

"I can't get it loose." He stepped away from the bony mass.

"Then you must bring me food right away. Meat. It must be meat, and bloody." Ansehelm closed and opened his jaw. "And water."

Jasper gulped. "There might not be food." He didn't even know where to get water from.

"Mice, then. Worms. They do not crawl past me. It has been so hard to survive." He sniffed the air as he licked his gums. "Or leeches. Yes, leeches! I know they live in the water below. The blood will be like meat. I can eat them without teeth."

Jasper's stomach turned.

"I'll get you something to eat as soon as I can. But look, I'll get the others, and we can get you out of here—"

"*We.* No!" Ansehelm cried. "Do not tell anyone about me!"

"Why—?" Jasper was cut off by a voracious plea.

"Please, I am afraid! They who did this to me are still out there. If they discover you are helping me, I do not know what consequences will be suffered. When I heard someone coming, I thought it was one of them, but it is not. You alone have found me, and you alone can help me—only in secret!"

"Who did this to you?" Jasper asked. "The people I work for are powerful, they can—"

"No! You do not understand! I will not tell you who, because you will try to find them and in doing so bring torment down on me and all in this house!"

Jasper's brow furrowed. "What do you mean?"

"*He*—" The prisoner grimaced. "—and the others. *They* are vicious. Cruel. More than you may imagine. And powerful too. If you or your people attack them, they will attack you, and you will suffer as I do."

Balking, feeling a pinch up his spine, Jasper tried to parse what Ansehelm was saying. "I can't help you alone," he said.

"You can, and you must. These men wish me an excruciating death. If they learn I am rescued, they will find me and subject me to their torture again. They will torture my rescuers as well! But if I am fed and returned to health, then I may escape in secret."

"We'll keep your secret."

"No! The more who know of me, the more danger there is. Please, I beg of you not to risk my life, not to risk your life and the lives of all your people because you believe you know better. Please, please, you must do as I say, or I fear for what will happen!"

He wheezed, trembling from exertion. A response was almost out of Jasper's mouth before he stopped himself. The man was terrified and must have been delirious, having been trapped in total darkness and about to starve to death. The priority was to bring him something to eat. Once he had that, the man would be reasoned with.

"Okay. I promise I won't tell anybody about you. But you need a doctor," Jasper said, and the pinpoint eyes flashed at him. "I won't tell. I'll bring you food and water as soon as I can."

Ansehelm sighed and bowed his head.

"Thank you. I will be eternally grateful."

Jasper's mouth twisted into a nervous smile that caused one eye to squint. He backed towards the ladder.

"Would you like a quicker way?" Ansehelm pointed to a spot on the floor not far from where he was chained. Jasper crept towards it, unable to escape the dread of getting closer to the man than he had to. There was a rope handle, which lifted a square of the floor up on a hinge. Peeking under, he saw a white-walled bedroom not unlike Leo's tower room. There was the hatbox he'd carried in. The top of Elsie Lambert's head fluttered by. Instinctively, he dropped the handle. Ansehelm watched him with a toothless open smile.

"I can't go that way," Jasper whispered. Had she heard him scream? He scurried away from the trap door. As he climbed onto the ladder, lantern between his lips, Ansehelm called,

"The tunnels bring you everywhere in the castle!"

The voice resounded down the shaft. Jasper's hands were sweating, and he forced himself to go slow. The immediate fear of falling was the only thing that could take precedence in his mind over what had just happened. Now there were ghosts in every shadow. Fiends lurking in the tunnels to kill him. As for Ansehelm himself, Jasper shuddered.

He had to get food and water, but where? Jasper could bottle leeches up from the pond, blood like meat for the starving man. No, he couldn't do that to someone. There would be real food.

First, he had to find his way out. Straight back the way he came, except when he landed at the split, he couldn't tell where that was. It had been so obvious coming the other way, but now the tunnel mouths spilled into each other, askew from where he faced. There had been three ways, but now he counted four. A fifth too? Candle low, he couldn't see far. He had to pick soon, or he'd be in total darkness.

The mouth that was the widest must have lead to the main tunnel; Jasper turned down it. He was glad he held out the lantern first, because he was soon on the precipice of a pit—twelve feet wide and who knew how many feet down. The path continued narrowly around the drop, but it was hard to see the way clearly. The flame sputtered, and as he backed away, it went out for good. He couldn't see a thing now, fingers twitching for the matches in his pocket. Before he could light one, the whole pack slipped, and he lost them to the pitch. No vision, and the only sound came from himself, encased here apart from the rest of the world. He sucked in as much damp earth air as he could, because if he was breathing, he was still alive.

Pit behind him, he walked straight with one arm gripping the wall. That was how not to get lost. At some point, the dirt stopped, but he groped through the dark until finding it again. Must have been the split, but which way had he gone?

There could be another pit, or a prisoner, or someone who would chain him and starve him in the walls of the castle. He gouged his fingers into the dirt, an anchor as he went. An incline now, and the path narrowed, closing his arms in.

There was a line of light ahead, so faint it might have been an invention of his eyes. He followed it, going steadily upwards, and by the time the path ended, he had been squeezed into a half-crawl. The light was just above his head. Reaching up, he felt wood, a panel he could push, as a breeze came from underneath. Jasper would have collapsed in relief if the space allowed for it. He hoisted himself up through the ground and reached for the daylight.

CHAPTER FOUR

J ASPER EMERGED IN GRASS, scrambling out like a mouse from a hole. To his right, he could hear horses whinnying behind the wall of stable. No one appeared to have seen him. He rested his back along the castle wall, taking in deep breaths. It felt like days since he'd had fresh air. His pulse throbbed. Food, water. He needed some for himself too.

Rolling his neck, he walked past the stable but was stopped by voices. Two of the drivers had noticed him, the younger one petting a brown horse while the older one smoked on a hay bale.

"Hey, you! You're that new guy," the younger one called. "We found the wood stash. You been looking for it this whole time?"

"Huh? Yeah," Jasper said. He felt dazed. The older one made a face.

"You fall in the woods?" he asked. It took Jasper a second to realize how completely he was covered in dirt. He touched his brow and felt mud. The young driver gave him a pity-smile.

"I'm Ned," he said in a slight brogue. "That's Earl. This is Felicity." He scratched the horse behind the ear. Earl gave Jasper a nod.

"You really got lost, eh?" Ned grinned.

"Yeah, yeah, I…" He tried to think of an excuse, but the words didn't come. He should tell them everything, right now, and then tell the Lamberts. They could be in danger; a man might die.

But suppose what Ansehelm had said was true. There could be evil men hiding in the mountains, ready to kill everyone should their crime be exposed. It was odd no one was at the castle when they arrived, after all. He should keep the secret he had promised to, at least for now.

"What is it you do?" Ned asked.

"I'm Leo's valet."

"Oh." Ned seemed as if he didn't believe it. "Anyway, I can show you where to get cleaned up." He motioned for Jasper to follow, explaining that they had found the kitchens and servants' quarters. There was no sign that anyone had lived there recently—and there was no food in the kitchen. Not even a bag of flour. Proulx had rushed to the town, though the markets were likely closed by now. At least there was firewood and flowing water.

When Jasper looked back, he couldn't see the space he had crawled out of, spotting only the lantern laid in the grass. They passed the carriages and Leo's car, housed safely next to the horses. The smell of wood smoke eased him as they entered the kitchen.

It was a long room lined with boxy cabinets between stoves and wash bins. Double rows of counters ran down the middle. Across from where they had entered, a set of stairs led into the castle, and to the side was an empty room. Storage, he guessed. Nothing in it. A two-log fire had been started in the pit of a massive brick oven. One of the maids, Florence's, was warming her hands. Another was going down the aisles, systematically opening cabinets and emptying their contents onto the counters. Hinges creaked, followed by clattering bangs of wood and metal being dropped, then hinges again, more banging.

"Dottie, *why?*" the woman warming her hands snapped. Dottie huffed but did not waiver.

"We need to find everything. Open everything. Lord knows what could be in here." She dumped a pile of wobbling knives on the counter. Jasper saw one almost fall and stab her foot.

"Proulx will rip you a new one for it," the other woman said.

"There might be food we missed in here," said Dottie. Black hair flew from its pins to form a wild halo around her face, "What are *you* doing to help, Irene?"

At that, Irene noticed the men.

"Who are you?" her eyes shot to Jasper. Wooden spoons smacked down. Ned answered for him.

"This is Jasper, Leo's new man."

"I've seen you before," said Irene.

"Yeah, I did some work around the Madison Avenue house," Jasper said.

"And you're here now."

"Yeah."

"Those are—" Irene circled an index finger at him. "—travelling clothes?"

The uniform. He'd left it somewhere. He could feel the anxiety creeping onto his face. They were looking at him, the maids in their black dresses and white aprons. He winced as pots banged together.

Dottie turned to him. "You should quit. Quit while you're ahead. My mother used to say that, bless her soul. If you leave now, you won't need the Lamberts as a reference, and you can walk away like it never happened. I can't, I've been with them too long. I'm not ahead." She slammed a drawer open and shut.

Irene rolled her eyes. "Where did you work before?" she asked.

"Here and there. I had something steady for a while packing meat."

"I meant, as a valet. For which families?" Irene said.

"Oh. None." Jasper rubbed the back of his neck.

"Don't say meat," Dottie said. "I'm starving."

A copper bell rang next to the stairs leading into the castle. Dottie swore as she marched away to answer the call.

Jasper asked where he could get cleaned up, and Ned pointed him through the kitchen to a partially enclosed yard. There was a water pump, rusty, but it produced a fresh, cold stream. Wood stacked six feet high rested to the side. If, when he had stood at the castle entrance hours ago, he'd walked the other way, he would have found this in minutes.

But then, the man in the tower would certainly die. He still might, if Jasper couldn't get him food in time.

Would the Lamberts be upset to learn he had been poking around their new estate when he was supposed to be working? Almost definitely. Leo would defend him, surely, but drawing their attention now might have consequences he didn't want to incur. It strengthened his resolve to keep the prisoner's secret. He would figure out how to deal with the Lamberts once he'd brought the man some sustenance.

Opposite the kitchens, on the other side of the pump, an overhang led to rows of dormitories. The rooms, each a hall of its own lined with bare cots, stretched down one side of the wing. Down the other doors were closed, except one which swung open to reveal a cleaning closet. Nothing to eat, but there were brooms. Bags had been piled inside the first two dorms, and Jasper found his among them. He fished out a canteen, drank what was left, and filled it at the pump. His stomach rumbled. At least he wasn't as hungry as Ansehelm. What could he bring him? Leeches? The thought made him shiver. That would be cruel, though the man has asked for them. There certainly weren't any chunks of rare meat to be had.

Rifles were stacked near the wood, and he thought of going out and hunting. But no. He didn't know what he was doing. Killing street vermin and mopping slaughterhouse floors were not the same as tracking wild animals. He'd get sucked into the forest—and if he did make it back, it would garner too much attention.

He had to get the prisoner to tell him what had happened. When he was less hungry, when Jasper had earned his trust, he would talk.

Before there was time to wash, Ned appeared, saying that he was needed upstairs. Jasper opened his mouth to argue, but what could he say? He was in no position to decline. Ned grumbled as they went, the kitchen stairs bringing them directly into the great hall. Dottie looked at them apologetically next to Elsie, who waited with arms crossed over a candy-striped sports coat. The puff of the sleeves almost touched her ears. Without a word she motioned them into the apartment parlor. The doors to the bedrooms were shut tight, and Dottie held a finger to her lips, whispering that the other Lamberts were napping.

Elsie pointed to a red armchair and said, "Move that up to my room."

"In the tower?" Ned balked.

"Yes, in the tower, where else?"

"Miss, perhaps we should wait for Mrs. Lambert to wake. You know she is particular about furniture," Dottie said, earning a sneer from Elsie.

"No, Dorothy, we will not wait, because she will tell me not to move it, and I want it moved. There's nowhere to sit in that room." She looked expectantly at the men. With no recourse, they both lifted the chair. The legs were short, making it awkward to lift on top of its weight. Jasper walked backwards, head swiveling between watching where he was going and what he was holding. Already so tired, his arms weakened as they crossed the hall. Elsie's heels clipped beside them.

He backed onto the first stair. The entrance was narrow, and the chair wouldn't pass through easily. There was a thud as the top hit the doorframe, but they pushed it through. Elsie snapped at them to be careful. Jasper took another backwards step up, feeling with his foot to make sure he judged correctly. All he could see was red; the chair took up almost the whole width of the tower stairs. Ned grunted on the other side.

Jasper was jolted as the chair hit the wall. Elsie snapped again.

"It might not fit, ma'am," Ned said. Jasper couldn't see the part that was stuck, trying to follow the driver's lead as they maneuvered. His palms were sweating, arms and back strained to balance. Ned pushed forward, and Jasper took another step up. It was steeper; the chair got stuck again. The base jerked in his hand.

"You got it?" he called.

"Yep," Ned said. "Hold it higher on your end."

Jasper tried to lift, but it was stuck. His limbs ached. "I can't get it."

"It doesn't fit, ma'am," said Ned.

"*Make* it fit!"

"Hold on," Ned grunted, "let me…"

Jasper heard Ned's feet scrape as his voice trailed off. With a jolt, the chair shook loose, and in a split second, his hands slipped. The other side dropped, and the chair went tumbling down the steps on top of the driver.

A crash; wood splintered through the fabric. There were shouts as Dottie and Jasper jumped to Ned, pulling him from under it.

"What is *this*?" Cordelia Lambert shouted through the hall.

"Ned's been hurt, ma'am," said Dottie. The driver moaned. Blood was leaking into the hair on the back of his head.

"*Verna!*" Mrs. Lambert yelled behind her, then turned back. "What on Earth were you doing?"

"I need a comfortable place to sit," Elsie said. "There's only a small chair and the bed in that room, so I was taking this. But these clods dropped it."

"Is that one of our new armchairs?" her mother said. Dottie was padding Ned's hair with her apron. His pant leg was torn on one thigh. Jasper bent to examine it.

"Your leg hurt?"

Ned nodded. Jasper pressed on it gently. Something was wrong with the bone.

"I *need* a chair moved to my room," Elsie said to her mother.

"It might be fractured," said Jasper.

"You should have asked your father or I. Now the chair is broken, and driver has been injured!" Mrs. Lambert tossed a hand in the air.

The woman in the nurse's cap appeared. Her eyes went wide at Ned groaning on the floor. Jasper moved to let her in.

"It's not my fault they broke it," Elsie said. "They're *clods*."

Mrs. Lambert exhaled. "Perhaps. Elsie, you must be more discerning with to whom you give delicate or important tasks. See this one, neither of us know him, and he is dressed like he just came off the streets. You, who are you anyway?"

It took Jasper a moment to realize he was being addressed. "I'm Leo's—"

"Who else was I supposed to use?" Elsie asked. "No one's here! I need a nice place to sit."

"Now no one can sit in it, because it's broken. My new chair," her mother sighed. "This is a lesson for you, Elsie: you do not know how to deal with the help. Really, you don't." Elsie looked at the floor, arms folded, face pinched. Cordelia asked, "How serious is it, Verna?"

"I can't tell yet, ma'am," the nurse said.

Mrs. Lambert eyed Jasper, "You, get yourself cleaned up at once!" Her jewelry clinked as she shook her head. "We were supposed to bring only the *trusted* staff."

"Yes, ma'am," Jasper said. They needed to get Ned downstairs anyway. An arm around Jasper's shoulder and the other around Dottie's, they walked him on one leg. Verna cleared their way. Irene, still at the fire, shrieked when she saw. They brought him to one of the cots, and as soon as he was safely on the bed, Dottie snapped up furiously at Jasper.

"*Did you drop it on him?*"

Jasper held his hands up.

"Wasn't his fault, Dot," Ned coughed.

"Drop what?" Mr. Thorley demanded. He had appeared along with Earl and another maid called Maja.

"It was an accident," Ned said while Dottie launched into the tale. Verna was listing supplies to Irene, who wasn't sure she could find any of them but still whisked away to search. Earl handed Ned a flask.

"Alright, everyone," Thorley called. "Give Ned some space, and let Verna take care of him. Dorothy, Maja, come with me. We need to attend to Missus and Miss."

Unsure what to do, Jasper lingered while the others cleared out. Ned grinned at him.

"Serious, I'm not angry. Wasn't your fault."

"She's mad wanting to sleep in that tower," Verna muttered. She lowered her voice. "I don't want you thinking I've lost my wits, but I heard something in that room. There was a sound as if someone were being frightened to death."

Ned laughed. "Where?"

"In that tower! Not more than an hour ago." As soon as she said it, Verna clamped her lips shut.

Jasper swallowed and forced his mouth into a smile. "Feel better, Ned," he said and hurried away.

░

The lantern was where he had left it, shielded in grass. The day was dragging, and under the clouds it felt as if dusk were already there. He hurried to the garden, not pausing until he was inside its walls. Alone, he let himself exhale. Scents of peonies and mulch wafted over him. He bent, dragging his body like a puppet. Exhaustion was seeping over him, but there was still so much to do.

Spilled on the countertops, he had found a sack and a drawstring net. He left the net under the green water, swatting mosquitos away while he waited. Maybe he'd catch a fish. The leeches had to be feeding off something. Raw fish was more appetizing than parasites or frogs. If there were enough, he and the others might be eating that tonight themselves. He picked the ripest peach he saw, pale yellow with just a bead of pink, and rolled it in the sack with the canteen. There must be something else—blue- or blackberries—flourishing in the weeds. The pink berry bush he doubted was good to eat. Finding no more fruit, he hoisted the net out. Wriggling leeches and pond scum were the catch. *Leeches. Yes, leeches.* Perhaps when faced with eating them, it would yank Ansehelm from his state and he would act rationally.

Jasper dropped the net in the sack, slung it over his shoulder, and walked directly to the base of the third tower, able to avoid the other side entirely. For the first time, he hoped he would not run into Leo. His back was wet where the sack rested. Not heavy, but his arms still hurt from before. With each step, his aches strengthened. He nearly hoped that Proulx found no food, so there would be an excuse to go straight to bed once the sun set.

The door to the tower room was wide open, offering a perfect view of the secret tunnel. Resting patiently on the desk was the uniform, its folds still crisp. The thought that Leo had been up here flashed through his mind. He shook his head, trying not to indulge his imagination for once. He latched the door to the room shut so no Lamberts could find it before he was done. After, he would come this way and grab the uniform, so as not to risk dirtying it. Armed with backup candles and matches, he headed in. At the split before the tower he took a moment to orient himself. There were only three paths, but one to the right had been carved unevenly large, and there was a jumble of planks stuck into the corner where it and the main tunnel met. The remnants of an abandoned construction, perhaps, he could see how it had tricked his eye in bad light. That way must be where the pit was, and the path left must have been where he went out before. When he had energy back, he could explore.

Jasper was panting by the time he reached the prisoner's cell. Thinking of the nurse, he tried to keep quiet, forcing himself to take smaller breaths. White gums curled in a smile as Ansehelm pawed through the sack. Jasper was apologizing, but when Ansehelm felt the leeches, he slipped one in his mouth without hesitation. Red and green blood dripped over his lips.

"Thank you," he said as his bones chattered with satisfaction. Jasper tried to suppress a gag. His own hunger and exhaustion made the sight harder to take.

"I'll get you something real once I can," he said. Ansehelm crunched another.

"But this is perfect! Please, I know it is hard for you to stomach, but I prefer this. They are nutritious and—" He opened his mouth to show his lack of teeth. "—easy for me to eat!"

"Yeah," Jasper laughed a little. "Okay."

The chain rattled as Ansehelm stuck his face in the net. Jasper wiped his brow and bent over, hand on his knees. Eyes to the floor, he avoided watching the man eat. The gums smacked.

"You must bring me these at least once a day." Ansehelm looked at him. "Until I have my strength back."

He needed a doctor. Jasper bit his tongue.

"Look, I can't free you myself, but with the others—"

"No!" Ansehelm looked up in a frenzy.

Jasper scoffed. "You could die!"

"No!" Ansehelm swallowed, taking a moment to calm himself. "I *will* die if you tell another soul. The risk is too great. Since you cannot free me alone, I will wait here and gain my strength. But you must swear not to tell anyone. Do you swear?"

"But…" Jasper shook his head. "Why?"

"The men that did this to me are all around. They are dangerous. You are strangers here. You may answer to a powerful man, but he does not know what is at work on this mountain. Now, you could cut me loose and call a doctor, but word would spread quickly, and *they* would attack when I am vulnerable. Right now, as they believe me to be trapped and helpless, I am safe."

"Fine, then," Jasper said. "But tell me who they are."

"No. You are a young man, and if I tell, you will decide they are not so tough, and you will try to fight back. And you will lose. Then we will both be dead. You could find yourself chained here too, and I do not think you would like that."

"I'm not the reckless type."

"I do not believe you." Ansehelm smiled.

"You're telling me that there's a gang of murderers out there, but I can't know who, or even where, they are? Are they in this castle? Are we safe?"

"Yes, yes," the man said, almost dismissively. "They are not in these tunnels—not now—and they would be loath to risk exposure. They will not harm you or yours if they have no business with you. And if they do not know you have found me, they will have no business. Now, do you swear not to tell another soul and to bring me what I need to regain my strength?"

"Only if you swear everyone in this castle is safe," Jasper said. Ansehelm slid a hand under his chest, pinned between his heart and the floorboards. The other he held up, goo dripping down his fingers.

"I swear you all will be safe, as long as *you* tell no one about me." He spit out the words.

"Okay. I swear—"

"Hand on your heart," the man said. Jasper put a hand over his heart and raised the other as Ansehelm did.

"I swear I won't tell anyone about you, as long as we aren't in danger," Jasper said, watching the man's odd smile. It was somewhere between delight and disgust, he thought, but maybe that was the effect of his ghastly face. He wanted to press him on what had happened but thought it wise not to rile him up right then.

"There's a girl staying in the room below you," he said instead. "She's getting over an illness. There's a nurse with her a lot, and a maid, so be careful they don't hear you."

Ansehelm nodded and looked at him with a grin. "She is no friend of yours?"

Jasper cast him a puzzled look.

"I know these matters," the man said with a laugh. Blood spit out as he crunched on a leech.

"I work for her family," was all Jasper said. "I have to leave now. I'll be back, don't worry." He crouched and twisted himself onto the ladder.

"You have not told me your name, when I have told you mine."

"Jasper." He supposed he had not offered any information on who he was any more than the prisoner had. A servant dreaming of stealing treasure. Nothing he'd be eager to reveal to anyone.

"Thank you for your help, Jasper," Ansehelm said, the outline of his hand barely visible as he waved goodbye.

The tunnel mouths remained confounding, and Jasper resigned himself to pick one, hoping for the best while trying to push away the image of those gums. The candle was dwindling, and his stomach growled. All he'd eaten was a hard biscuit and coffee before dawn, back at his apartment. 47th Street felt so foreign, and he hadn't even been gone a day.

Should he keep his oath? He had sworn, but what did that mean except to appease a delirious, dying man? There could be truth in what Ansehelm said—it could all true, in fact. What did Jasper know? At least for today, with no food and the missing estate staff, he felt he should keep quiet. There would be time later to make an informed decision. Ansehelm was their target, whoever they were. They didn't want to risk exposure, that's what he'd said—they wouldn't bust in and announce themselves to a wealthy society businessman's family. If he told the Lamberts right now, they could get Ansehelm out and to a hospital, but then what? Ansehelm would be vulnerable there. The Lamberts might still be safe in the castle, protected by their laurels, but Jasper could be fair game. He wasn't even one of the trusted staff. Leo would miss him, but no one knew that. Odd man out. Yes, better to not say anything. He could help Ansehelm without risking an iron chain around his own neck.

Plank stairs—he cried in relief when he reached the stone wall at the top and slid back into the third tower.

CHAPTER FIVE

AT DUSK, PROULX RETURNED. Jasper could smell it from the servants' quarters— asparagus, raw beef, sweet onions, cheese curds. There wasn't much. They would need to get more first thing tomorrow, but it was enough to feed everyone tonight. They would eat immediately. Well, the family first.

Jasper milled to the side as the kitchen bustled, fidgeting with the wrist of his white gloves. The uniform was a tailcoated black suit, baggy in some places and tight in others, especially the neck with its starched, high collar. He couldn't get the creases to smooth out. It had come folded over a pair of glossy shoes which his feet slid around in. He had not walked far in them yet. Leo was with his family in the apartments when news of dinner came, so there had been no need to fetch him. Since that afternoon, he'd only caught Leo in fragments, chatting with his family in a trail of smoke. Uncanny to picture him ever meeting the grotesque prisoner.

Monsieur Proulx shouted orders as he scrambled to manage the old ovens. The sous-chef, whose name was Frankie, found equipment from the counter piles Dottie had made while she picked out serving trays. They *were* silver. Savory air warmed the kitchen. The maids and Mr. Thorley gossiped while they prepared, able to work smoothly despite everything. They understood without saying it what to do, and Jasper couldn't find a way to help. He kept his eye on them, watching for cues. If he asked too many questions, he would seem unqualified, and if he seemed unqualified, they would suspect. He would be anxious until he was alone with Leo, when he wouldn't have to pretend to know anything.

The family took their meal in the great hall. They had dressed for dinner, a bubble of gowns and tailcoats glittering faintly at one end of the long table. Leo was handsome in his suit, leaning back in his chair to give Jasper a quick smile when his plate was served. The meal had started, and the servants waited to the side to be needed. Jasper stared at Pieter Van Hoensbroeck's portrait from his place along the wall. There weren't quite enough candles to keep the hall bright, and the painting had an austere expression under the shadows.

They ate furiously except Elsie, whose pout grew until her lip touched her nose. Little was said. Mrs. Lambert forced a laugh now and again, which came out too loud and lasted too long through the empty space. From the head of the table, Mr. Lambert surveyed his family. With none of them smiling, he held up his fork and said,

"It's not the best cut of meat, but Proulx worked it well."

"It's barely edible." Elsie pushed her plate away. Florence put her fork down too.

"We should not have had to starve all day only to be served this dreck," she said.

Her mother turned with a tilt of her head. "Certainly dear. But we must make do despite our unfortunate circumstances. Everything will be sorted out soon. Elsie, the doctors said you must eat."

The youngest Lambert sulked as she chewed on gristly beef.

"Father, I'd give a piece of my mind to whoever sold you this place," said Florence.

"Now, now," said Mr. Lambert. "Let us not disparage Mr. Calvin. He and his people at Irving Trust have always acted with the utmost professional caliber. He said there was a groundskeeper and an estate staff would be assembled; I trust that was so. The problem must be elsewhere. Tomorrow I'll go into the town and sort this out."

"Perhaps you can *telephone* Mr. Calvin," Mrs. Lambert said, looking at her children far too excitedly as she did.

"I don't think they have those up here," said Leo.

"No gas either," said Elsie.

"True, but—" Mrs. Lambert covered her mouth to cough then continued. "We'll get by with fires and candles, as they used to in your great-grandmother's day. Won't that be a lark?"

"No," Elsie said.

"Father, I may join you in town tomorrow," Florence said.

"It will be all business, dear, nothing for you to bore yourself over," William said.

"We need to go furniture shopping as well," Florence insisted. "We are down a chair."

"And a driver," Leo added. Mr. Lambert frowned. Cordelia explained what had happened while Elsie clenched her fists under the table. But William did not seem distraught.

"Darling, if you need a chair in that room, we will find you something," he said. "Your health is why we are here."

Florence tipped her head back to finish her wine, then held the glass out. Irene was quick to refill it.

"What does Kasteel Verlossen mean?" Mrs. Lambert asked her husband.

"Well, dear, Kasteel means castle. And Verlossen means..." He trailed off.

"It means redemption," Elsie said.

"How do *you* know *that*?" snapped Florence.

"I read it in a *book*." Elsie stuck her tongue out.

Mr. Lambert turned to Leo.

"My boy, what would you guess is the square footage of just this room?"

"Ah." Leo looked around at the dark corners and motionless tapestries. "One...hundred...thousand..."

"A hundred thousand? That's daft," Florence said.

"Leopold, you need to be able to estimate square footage quickly," Mr. Lambert said. "A man selling you a property may exaggerate, even lie to you. You must bring a keen eye to negotiations."

"You didn't see this place before you bought it," Leo said. Florence wiped her mouth to hide her smile, while Mr. Lambert stared daggers.

"The situation is completely different. I have every reason to trust Mr. Calvin." He shook his head. "You're smart but not wise, Leo. That's always been your problem. I've said it from the start, haven't I, Cordelia?"

"Yes. Darling, it's true." She gave her son a chiding glance.

Leo's glower moved from his father to Jasper. One elbow on the table, he shook his glass side to side. Suddenly realizing what he was supposed to do, Jasper hurried over to pour.

"My, what a big glass," Florence said. Leo seemed shocked at first when he saw his wine filled almost to the brim, but he morphed into laughter.

"He knows I hate to wait on alcohol," Leo said.

"Leo Lambert," his mother reproached. Florence laughed with her brother.

Flat-faced, Elsie said, "Yes, you're a drunk."

"Elsie Lambert!" Cordelia scolded. Jasper slunk back to the wall. Mr. Thorley looked at him with a curl of his lip.

"Leo, who is that? What happened to Charlie?" Mr. Lambert asked.

"Oh, I hated him." Leo waved a hand.

"Did you dismiss Charlie?" his mother asked.

"No. He left with the circus after it came through last week."

"Really?" Elsie asked. Florence batted her eyes in bemusement.

"Quite so. He juggles torches while walking the tightrope now." Leo scooped onions into his mouth.

"Well, you get what you get on short notice." Mrs. Lambert glanced over Jasper before changing the subject. He bit the inside of his lip. Back in the townhouse, he had heard Leo give a man named Charlie orders through the bedroom door, asking for drinks while he stayed out of site under the canopy.

As the meal finished, Leo lit a cigarette. His father recounted the contents of the book he was reading, detailing naval strategies deployed by the Union during 1812. That ended the evening. The younger children went to their tower rooms while Florence retired with her parents to the apartments. Before he left the hall, Leo grabbed Jasper by the elbow and told him to bring up a scotch in half an hour. The touch felt cold, but it was an act, of course. Sill, Jasper felt uneasy as he cleared the table.

╫╫

In the kitchen, the rest of the staff clustered on stools around a counter where their meal was just being laid out. Earl and the third driver, Horace, helped Ned, who greeted them like heroes. Only Verna was missing, attending to her charge. Dottie and Maja darted ravenously to the food.

"You did bring wine for us?" Irene asked the cooks.

"Of course!" Frankie was uncorking the bottle as she spoke.

"Let Jasper pour it," Dottie said. Thorley and the maids laughed, but it was genial, and Jasper relaxed as he sat. The dinner was the same as the Lamberts', if not as pretty and with even tougher meat. For a few minutes, it was quiet aside from utensils scraping and teeth chewing. The silence was broken piece by piece as they ate their fill.

"Thank you, Proulx and Frankie," Irene said, starting a chorus of thanks. She was clear-eyed, a wool shawl draped elegantly over her uniform. Mr. Thorley sighed, hands folded under his nose.

"Here we are," he said. "Like servants to the kings of old."

"And Mrs. Greeley wanted to come," Dottie remarked. Irene smirked.

"She's probably at the townhouse sleeping in their beds."

"She and that Elmer," Maja spoke in a Polish accent. "I don't like him. He gives me the—" She wobbled her hand, searching for the expression.

"Let's all be glad Elmer isn't here." Thorley sounded genuinely relieved. Jasper wondered who that was, licking a piece of curd stuck on his teeth.

"Yeah, we just have ghosts," Ned said, to jeers from the maids.

"No, no don't say that. I am serious, it is not funny," Maja said. Dottie crossed herself in vehement agreement.

Jasper checked his watch and asked, "Is there scotch?" Proulx laughed at him.

"Is that what yours wants?" Irene said.

Thorley leaned forward. "Did he really fire Charlie?"

Jasper shrugged. "I don't know."

Collectively, they shook their heads.

"My mistress is right about that." Dottie held her pinky out and tipped her thumb to her lips. "*Drunk.*"

"Oh, yes," Irene cackled. "He hides it now, but it will get worse with age, let me assure you. By the time he's an old man, he'll be pawning his wife's jewelry off for gin."

"Miss O'Hannigan." Thorley clucked his tongue.

"How is he to you?" Dottie looked at Jasper. "Charlie hated him."

"He's…" Jasper cleared his throat. "…fine. He's alright."

"See how he is after you can't bring him his whiskey," Irene said. Jasper opened his mouth as if he were laughing along with them.

"I agree with Neddie," Frankie said. "Place like this has to have ghosts. Can you imagine how many people lived and died here?"

Dottie snorted. "Do not invoke the devil."

"It's not invoking, Dot," Ned said. "It's making a logical assumption."

Proulx left the table, shaking his head.

"Logical," Earl said with a snort.

"Definitely. The older a place is, the more death it has seen, and ghosts come from the dead." Ned and Frankie grinned together.

"They come from the devil," Maja said.

"Please. It's almost a new century." Irene rubbed her temples.

Ned leaned on his elbow, resting his chin on the back of his hand. "Ghosts don't care about the year."

The conversation was pierced by a clamor from above. Jasper recognized Elsie's shriek. All of them rushed up, fanning into the great hall at the same time her parents and sister emerged from the apartments. She sprinted towards her family, blathering that someone was in her room. The Lamberts' faces went white as they hugged her. Verna trailed behind, winded by the time she caught up.

Elsie had seen someone or something, she claimed, in the ceiling. A ghoulish face had sneered at her. She blinked and there it was, like a ghost.

"Did you see this?" William Lambert asked the nurse. An oval cigar hung out of his mouth. Verna bit her lip.

"No," she admitted, "but I heard something, earlier today, up there. I don't think it's rats, Mr. Lambert."

Mrs. Lambert threw a hand to her mouth to stifle a cry. From the crowd of servants, Proulx stepped forward, shoulders up and ready for a fight. He exchanged a grim look with William. Florence, hair down and in her nightgown, squeezed her sister's shoulder.

"Are you sure you saw someone?" Florence kept her voice soft and even. Elsie nodded, in tears. "Verna, what did you hear?"

"It sounded like a cry. Or scuffling."

Florence squinted her eyes. "Scuffling like rats?"

"*I saw someone,*" Elsie sobbed into her mother's arms.

Mr. Lambert frowned. "Someone in the ceiling?" he asked, skepticism creeping in. He stepped around to consult with Thorley and Proulx.

Jasper sunk behind Earl, hoping that if he were noticed, he would look just as concerned as anyone. Perhaps he should tell them. But what if it was true that Ansehelm, and themselves, could become targets if the secret leaked? Why wouldn't it be? There were dangerous people up here; what had been done to the prisoner was not an accident. And if he told them now, with Elsie crying, they'd be furious at him. They'd just see a sneak and a crook; powerful people were always the least understanding. Mr. Lambert could have Jasper arrested if he felt like it.

William Lambert announced that Proulx would investigate with the young men, that was, Horace, Frankie, and Jasper. Horace gulped, pursing his lips in apprehension, an expression Jasper tried to mimic.

Frankie could barely hide his smirk. "Best get the rifles," he said. Proulx sincerely agreed, sending him to fetch them.

"*Invoked*," Dottie whispered, slapping Frankie's arm as he walked by. She went to console Elsie with the others. He returned minutes later, handing out the rifles with an eye roll. Jasper clenched his hand around the cold wood. Armed, they gathered behind Proulx and headed for the tower.

Sudden stomping footsteps made them all jump, even Frankie. But it was only Leo, appearing from out of the castle depths, clutching his watch in hand. He saw Jasper first.

"Where the devil is my sco—what's all this?" His demeanor shifted as he realized what was happening, withering under his family's glares.

"Your sister has had a horrid fright," Mrs. Lambert said.

"She may be in grave danger," said Mr. Lambert.

"Oh." Leo turned a little red.

"The *men* are about to investigate," Florence said. Leo looked them over, grimacing at the rifles.

"Let's go." Proulx marched up the steps, forcing the others to follow. No one objected to Leo staying behind. Flanked by her mother and nurse, Elsie watched them almost gratefully.

She had clearly taken a good chunk of their candles, because the tower room was brightly lit. They were spread everywhere, along with open suitcases, clothes, books, trinkets. A shawl draped down an armless chair, the one that had not been good enough. The party looked up but could see no face in the ceiling. Jasper tried to spot the trap door but couldn't, to his relief. If the cell was discovered, maybe Ansehelm would have enough sense not to mention him.

Proulx stood on the chair, peering up through the beams. Horace pulled the dresses in an armoire to the side and snapped back, like he thought something was going to jump out. Frankie looked under the bed. To make himself seem useful, Jasper knocked on walls. Proulx got down, moved the chair, and checked another spot.

Above the bed—that's what Jasper had seen when he had looked through the trap door. His heart pumped faster as Proulx got nearer to the spot. The chef lingered over a patch of ceiling, pressing up, and Jasper was certain he'd lift the trap. But no. Proulx moved on. Not long after that he announced that the ceiling was solid.

"She made it up," Frankie said.

"There's no sign of anyone else being here," Horace said. "Jasper?"

"I didn't see anything unusual," Jasper said, sighing as if he had given it careful consideration.

Proulx told Frankie to cut the ghost talk out as he led them downstairs. The others were waiting exactly as they had left them. The chef announced they had found nothing, to everyone's relief but Elsie's.

"I did see someone—something—"

"Some*thing*?" Florence chided. Leo had found himself a glass of wine, which he sipped after anyone spoke.

"There is nothing up there, darling," Mr. Lambert said. "It was a trick of the light, combined with your imagination and weariness."

"Yes. You ought to go to bed," Cordelia said.

"Not in there, I won't!" Elsie shook her head.

"You picked the room," her brother laughed.

"Oh, Leo, not *now*," Mrs. Lambert sighed. "Elsie there's a spare room in the apartments; you can stay in there."

"There's nothing wrong with the room. It's perfectly safe." Mr. Lambert cocked an eyebrow at his daughter.

"William, she's frightened," Mrs. Lambert said.

"There's nothing to be frightened of here. What could be up there that they didn't see? Now darling, you do not *have* to, but if you sleep there tonight, you'll see that there's nothing wrong."

Elsie looked at him with wet eyes, shaking her head.

"I have an idea!" said her mother. "Perhaps one the men will stay up there, just for tonight. If anything is the matter in that room, they will surely encounter it."

Elsie nodded, while Mr. Lambert mulled over the plan.

"I'm not sure we should indulge these fantasies, Cordelia."

"It's simply a precaution. For peace of mind." Mrs. Lambert smoothed her skirt.

"Yes, just for tonight. In the morning, you'll see there was nothing to worry about." William smiled as he came around to it. "Now who…"

He surveyed the staff. Horace and even Frankie had slunk back; Proulx folded his arms. Mr. Thorley reminded him that the drivers and chefs needed to go into town first thing in the morning. Better for everyone to get a good's night rest.

"The room is not haunted, Mr. Thorley, nor is there someone in the walls," Mr. Lambert said. "So they *will* get a good night's rest."

"I'll do it," Jasper said. For the first time, Mr. and Mrs. Lambert looked pleased with him.

"Anyone else?" Mr. Lambert asked. No one spoke up.

"I don't mind doing it alone," said Jasper.

"Brave boy." Mr. Lambert clapped him on the back. "Not that there is any danger."

Jasper glanced at Leo, whose face was pinched behind his glass.

"Yes, thank you very much." Mrs. Lambert reached her hand out to him then pulled it back as if she had spotted something dirty. "You will sleep on the floor, of course? It would not do to have you in the bed my daughter sleeps in. You understand."

He said that he did.

Leo sulked off just as his father declared the matter settled. Frankie told Jasper to keep the rifle.

"Not that you need it, 'cause we didn't find anything," he added.

"No, 'course not," Jasper said. After the family dispersed, Mr. Thorley took him aside.

"Thank you for humoring them," the butler said, his nostrils flaring in a skittish tic. "Do be careful, though. Mr. and Mrs. Lambert dislike unpleasantries and are not prone to paranoia, but we don't know how long this enormous, isolated *place* has sat here unguarded. I'm not saying there is an intruder but, well, at least be mindful of rats."

Jasper promised he would.

He rinsed himself clean again before sealing in the tower room for the night. Dirt would give him away. Irene had found him blankets, which he arranged on the floor, then settled into the bed. The mattress hissed as he sunk in. More comfortable than the one in Leo's. He turned over, facing the desk. It looked like the one in the third tower, absent a sorcerer's tome, wide with locked cabinets and clawed feet. The wood looked redder in the candlelight. On top, close to the bed, was a diary stacked on a Dutch-English dictionary. There were some other books still bricked in a suitcase, and he half-considered looking through them. Even thinking about reading made him tired. He reached to snuff the candle but paused when he heard a creak from the ceiling.

The skeletal face leered from behind the beams like a fever dream. Jasper understood why it had made her so afraid.

He stood on the chair, as Proulx had done, and was greeted by Ansehelm's smiling gums.

"What are you doing, opening this?" Jasper whispered. Not that there was anyone around to listen.

"I heard you, Jasper, through the cracks," Ansehelm said, miming putting his ear to the floor.

"Here," Jasper handed him a pack with what food scraps he had been able scrounge. "How are you feeling?"

The hand lunged out and snatched it like a viper on a mouse.

"I am better. Thank you. I believe I can recover with your help." His speech flowed more evenly, but there was still a crude rasp to it.

"You know she saw you. Why did you open it the first time?" Jasper asked.

"It has been so long since I have seen anything outside of this tomb," Ansehelm said. "I hoped to glimpse the new masters of the house. That was the daughter?"

"One of them."

"How many?"

"Two. And a son."

"And what are you to these people?"

"I'm a valet," he said. "You know I'm only up here because they need to prove to their daughter there isn't anyone living in the ceiling."

A halting laugh came up from Ansehelm's throat. "They made you the bait." He stretched an arm out, pointing a finger at the clawfoot desk. "Behind the headboard is a compartment. In there is a key."

Jasper glanced at the eyes flashing, eager for him to follow. He climbed from the chair and felt around the back of the desk until his fingers slipped under a latch. When he had produced the key, Ansehelm said, "In the left drawer will be a paper wrapped in red ribbon. That is a map of all the tunnels in the castle."

It took him a minute to jiggle the key in, as if the lock had calcified. Finally, it snapped open, revealing a compartment stuffed with parchments and leather-bound journals. They seemed old, though not as arcane as those in the third tower. He picked over them until he caught a glint of red. When he unrolled the waxy parchment, it was as Ansehelm said: an ink-drawn diagram of the castle with the tunnels overlaid on top. Circles marked the secret entrances. He saw one in the third tower, by the stables, the trap door above, and more. There could be one in every room. The labels were difficult to read, scratchy writing with some oddly drawn letters. Focusing, he realized it wasn't in English either.

"Ke-u-ken," he sounded out. He flipped open Elsie's dictionary, and there it was. Keuken—kitchen.

"You are literate?" Ansehelm said. Jasper gave him a long look.

"Yeah," he said. He wasn't educated, but he'd gone to school as a boy. Perhaps where Ansehelm came from that was unusual.

"How did you find this?" Jasper asked.

"I have lived in this castle a long time."

"There's supposed to be a groundskeeper, but he hasn't appeared since we got here," Jasper said, studying the man's face for a tell. Hard to decipher something so like an apparition. "Did he do that to you, or are you him?"

"Do not ask!" The trap door slammed shut. Jasper groaned. He had prodded too much. Back on the chair, he called through the ceiling, "Sorry!"

With a creak, Ansehelm appeared again.

"You ask dangerous questions. If the men who tortured me even think you suspect them, they will not hesitate to kill you, torture you, to say nothing of what they will do to me. Again."

Why? was on the tip of his tongue, but he stopped himself. Clearly, he would get no answers. And perhaps he should be more cautious, poking around these secrets. But Ansehelm had to give him something. For now, he would try a different tactic.

"Then you should be careful that nobody else sees you," he said.

"Yes, you are right." Ansehelm licked his lips. "And I am sorry to have frightened the young lady."

"She'll live," Jasper muttered.

"Why is it you do not like her?" he asked. Jasper didn't answer. It was true, he just hadn't thought about it plainly. And he was thrown by how easily he had been read.

"I understand how painful it is to be surrounded by people who are so indulged." Ansehelm practically spat after he said it. Jasper cracked a smile. He didn't like seeing young girls terrified, but after the chair…

"She had a scare coming," he said.

Ansehelm matched his grin. Jasper shivered, and picked one of the blankets from the floor. They wouldn't notice it was gone. He balled it up to hand to the prisoner.

"Thank you. Goodnight." The chain rattled as Ansehelm closed the trap.

Rolling the map up, Jasper caught the light of his own eyes in the mirror. He tied the ribbon back around and hid it under the valet's jacket, snuffing the candle out. In the dark, he looked out at stars in a purple sky and the silhouettes of mountains threaded in the gloom.

The next morning, the family was happy to hear that his night was uneventful. Certainly, there was no one hiding in the walls.

CHAPTER SIX

LEO WAS MOODY WHEN he was brought his breakfast. From the bed, which he sat on in just his robe, he dismissed Jasper curtly. The breakfast inspired complaints too—only sausage and dry oats. What did he expect? It was the last of what the chefs had been able to pick up yesterday.

The tower stairs were chilly as Jasper descended. He caught flashes of grounds drenched under rain through thin windows. The other Lamberts had been happy to see him, relatively, after his night in Elsie's haunted room. He didn't know what was upsetting Leo, but in all the time Jasper had known him, he was always upbeat, so the mood couldn't last long. He tried not to dwell on it.

The walk from the kitchen to Leo's had been a pain. From downstairs, he had to go through the great hall and pick one of two corridors which connected to the rest of the castle. Winding hallways and barren rooms branched off from the main stretches, turns leading in towards the courtyard or out to the sides. The paths led into the armory and back towers eventually, but Jasper had gotten turned around a few times. The sausage was probably cold by the time he delivered it. The big, empty spaces, focusing on balancing the tray with nothing but the sound of his own feet, felt more isolating than the tunnels. At least the journey took him away from the others' notice.

He recalled his idea of learning the grounds well enough to become the new caretaker. He probably could, having found a secret entrance on his first day, but maybe it was a job he didn't want. Vicious murderers knew about those secrets too. The *why* nagged at him as he meandered back through the armory. He should be patient. Eventually, Ansehelm would talk. Perhaps when he got off of bugs and back onto real food. There was likely truth to what Ansehelm said, but Jasper was sure the villains could be stopped if he got the Lamberts involved. They had influence, they were wealthy. Mr. Lambert knew the mayor. He may dislike unpleasantries, but he would pull strings to protect his new property. It all would have to be handled carefully. But, Jasper figured, when the time was right, he would convince Ansehelm it was the best course of action, then he'd talk to Leo. Best to leave out some details, like how he had let Elsie be scared out of her mind and how he'd kept the tunnels a secret. He could skirt around those. Leo would understand, and they'd talk to his father, who would talk to his friends. Once everything was sorted and safe, Jasper would be in their good graces. So maybe he would get the castle after all.

Wanting to familiarize himself, he picked a different route back from Leo's. The path took him past a library with huge half-empty shelves and books stacked in towers from the floor. He wondered who had made those piles and how long ago. The dust agitated him, so he left them alone.

Continuing along, he popped his head into new rooms. Their doors were unlocked. Some led to whole other apartments, chipping gilded paint a remnant from when they housed monarchs. A wall was occasionally garnished with a portrait. Here and there sat a piece of furniture that seemed to have been in place for centuries. Lone holdouts, like the single sword hanging on the armory wall. He meandered towards the center, where two-story stacks of anterooms bordered a courtyard. They had the same half-emptiness but with lower ceilings. He knew there were places here to get into the tunnels, but wherever they were, they eluded him. He had buried the map in his bag to keep it safe.

A covered path lined the courtyard, but he avoided it altogether on account of the horrendous rain. He felt bad for the crew that had gone into town: Proulx, Frankie, Earl, Horace. Less bad for Mr. Lambert, who would find an office to sit in and argue with a clerk while someone brought him hot tea.

Jasper considered whether he was being unfair. The Lamberts were no better or worse than any other wealthy family. That was just how things were, and it wouldn't help to be spiteful. Plus, he had Leo. When the weather cleared and the full staff came, there would be nothing to do but be with Leo.

If he wasn't still angry. Jasper hunched, remembering all the sullen looks he had gotten since dinner. It had started when he overpoured the wine and grew worse when he had volunteered to stay in Elsie's room. Is that what Leo was mad about? Jasper didn't know. Before last night, Leo had always been excited to see him. Whenever he showed up for a job at the townhouse, Leo would find a way to be near him, to linger. Covered in grime and sweating, Jasper would hear a whisper telling him when to sneak up. The way Leo's window was positioned, it was easy to scale, camouflaged behind ivy vines. Once in the bedroom, he'd be treated like a guest.

It would be that way again, only the situation was new and tense with everything going on. He had always been treated well. Leo was generous when they were alone together, and attentive in his way. Always giving Jasper something. And Jasper liked seeing him happy, being proud of whatever fancy thing he was sharing or joking through a story. They cared for each other. He knew Leo would show it more if they didn't have to hide. That his family put him under stress. It was different than it was with Jasper's family. Lamberts didn't just move out when they got tired of each other.

That only went to show that how he was treated in private was how Leo really felt. Jasper was lucky. Before Leo, it had only ever been old, drunk men. Hiding in basements and alleys for privacy. It was such happenstance—almost pure luck—that Leo had found him. He doubted it would happen again.

Jasper had hurt him, even if he didn't understand why, and he'd have to right it some way. He had no orders at the moment; he could go back to Leo right now and start. But maybe he should give him more time alone. That worked with his mother, when her moods got bad, to leave and trace the streets for a while. Last February, he'd done that despite the snow coming down, and when he got back to the apartment, she had apologized. What had it all been about? He couldn't remember, but the act of the apology, he did. So he left Leo alone for now.

Ansehelm would need more water and more to eat. Leeches again. He had seemed happy with them, and Jasper wanted to appease him. If he were trusted, the man would talk. He took the time to change out of the uniform.

Outside the servants' quarters, someone had left the bolt cutter, and he picked it up on his way to collect Ansehelm's meal. Once the prisoner was free, he would have to take him to a hospital, and the Lamberts would know. He dreaded the thought; he needed to start formulating his excuses now. Maybe Ansehelm could stay hidden for the next few months. No. He pushed that thought out. He couldn't leave a person to rot just because it was convenient for him.

Knowing he had dry clothes waiting, the rain was tolerable, the summer storm not too bitter. He let the rain fill a bottle as he pulled the writhing net out of the pond.

⧻

Ansehelm's garbled body lay in motionless sleep. Though he knew what to expect, Jasper still jumped when he saw it, a gasp escaping his lips. The man's eyes popped open like a machine turning on. They fixed on the bolt cutter.

"Fantastic. Did you sleep well last night?" he asked, holding his hands out to take the net.

"I did," Jasper whispered. Ansehelm chomped the leeches, unconcerned with volume. Cutter in hand, Jasper tackled the middle part of the chain, trying not to choke the prisoner. "I don't think I can get the collar off, but you won't be—" He stopped talking as his muscles strained. The cutters scratched the metal but barely made an indent. He pressed as hard he could, one foot securing it down for a good grip. After a few arduous minutes, he looked down apologetically.

"It won't break," he said. Ansehelm did not seem distressed, but instead looked him up and down with a scheming glint.

"Can I trust you with another secret, Jasper?"

"Yeah," he promised, feeling Ansehelm's eyes pierce him.

"You have already found the laboratory, correct?"

He shrugged. "I found a room with a cauldron?"

"Yes," Ansehelm said. "Fetch me a book from there. I am sure it is still on the shelf—"

"Laboratory?" Jasper repeated.

Ansehelm wheezed, "That is what it was called in the old days. This book—"

"You gonna do some reading?" Jasper was getting frustrated and his comment came out snide. He felt a little bad, adding, "Because I can bring you candles."

"You misunderstand," said Ansehelm. "We will open this book together. I imagine it is difficult for you to tolerate my secrets, but you have been so very kind to me, and trustworthy. Now, listen to me with great care. There are hidden knowledges in this world that, due their natural power, require they only be shared with a select few. Certainly, the rest of the people you have come with should not be privy to them. It vexes me that they are free down there and may stumble upon what they should not. But *you*, I will give you a taste. I promise you it will astound, if you will accept."

Jasper thought of the strange runes in the book. A little spike of fear sent his blood rushing. What did Ansehelm have in mind, summoning the devil? But what would it *really* be? Jasper wasn't superstitious, but with that kind of talk, he at least wanted to find out what Ansehelm thought was so special. It seemed that it was the man's way of saying thank you too, and Jasper should accept. He nodded yes.

"Very well," Ansehelm said. "The book is titled *Libro luminare minus nota naturae et efficacius occultus artificiosae tractationes.*"

"Come again?"

Ansehelm repeated the words slower, adding that the cover was brown. Jasper made out *luminare* and *tractationes*, committing them to memory as best he could. He hurried, knowing he would soon have to rejoin the Lamberts' world. Combing the shelves, he found two that he thought matched the title, both bound in oily leather with roughhewn pages. Back in the central tower, Ansehelm held his bony hands out for them.

"Ah, yes, this one," he said, picking the scrawnier volume and pushing the other to the side. Jasper held the lantern light up as Ansehelm scanned blotted Latin.

"Here!" He pointed. "Bring me water, salt, paper, black ink to write with, and a bone."

"A bone?"

"Any bone. From any animal."

Jasper had expected to be told a secret, not given another chore.

"What is all that supposed to do?" he asked, checking the time. He had to bring Leo lunch at noon and was cutting it close.

"You will see when you have brought it to me." There was the toothless smile again.

"I can't right away. I have to work."

Ansehelm bowed his head. "Yes. Of course."

Would Leo still be upset from this morning? Jasper's mind was on that, and what's more, the butler who would let him hear it if he were late. It shook him out of his stupor. Ansehelm was talking nonsense. Still, he promised he would be back, repeating the list of ingredients over in his mind. There was no harm in entertaining a frail, suffering old man. At least with this, Ansehelm had promised him an answer. And just maybe it really would be worth something—more special than a car, or castle, or real estate, or scotch.

⊞

Before lunch, Jasper headed back to the kitchen only to learn there wouldn't be any. The party had not yet returned, and they were out of food again. Irene invited him to help clean tapestries. It wasn't something he could refuse.

In the great hall, he held the heavy fabric out as the maid beat it with a racket. Dust clouds swelled up. He ignored his hunger pangs. At the table, Elsie consulted between her dictionary and another book, occasionally jotting something in a diary. She looked rather happy, engrossed in her work with no trace of fear or whininess.

"How are my tapestries coming along?" Mrs. Lambert called, strutting out the apartments. Mr. Thorley followed a few paces behind her.

"Quite well, ma'am," said Irene.

Elsie, pulled from her books, turned petulant as her mother passed. "There's no *lunch*," she said.

"I know, darling."

"Well…" Elsie bit her bottom lip, eyes flaring. "Well, I *hate* that."

"Do not talk that way, dear. It sounds inelegant." Cordelia wagged her finger. "Say 'that pains me grievously' instead."

"But Mother, this is terrible! I'm starving. We came up her for my health, and now there is no food, and there was a horrid man in my room—"

"Please, no more of that talk. You were in that room just an hour ago, so it cannot have been that frightening, could it have?"

Elsie folded her arms. "I can't believe this is happening to *me*."

The butler caught up with Mrs. Lambert, who turned to him with politely clasped hands.

"Pardon me, ma'am. I was hoping you would speak to me on a matter," he said. "If it is not too much trouble, the rest of the staff, and I, could use the afternoon off. Since there is nothing to prepare—"

"Afternoon off?" she squeaked. "Certainly not! We are in a crisis, or hadn't you noticed, Mr. Thorley?"

He cleared his throat. "Yes, ma'am. It's only, we have also gone without food and have had little rest—"

One of Mrs. Lambert's shoulders slumped as if a weight had been dropped on it. "*Please*, Mr. Thorley, if you are bored, find something to clean. This place is gigantic and filthy, but it's ours now, and I will not have it covered in dirt."

He gave her a *yes, ma'am* and dropped it, throwing a tight-lipped frown to Irene.

Florence emerged from the far end of the hall, announcing, "Mother, today is *dreadfully* dull."

"Alright," Cordelia sighed. "Why don't we take a walk through the castle and see what's here?"

"I told Father I wanted to go into town, and he left without me!" Florence huffed. "He didn't take Leo instead, did he?"

Jasper almost answered, but it wasn't his place to talk, was it?

"No," Mrs. Lambert said, "and don't start, Florence. Between you girls and all this, I *just...*" She sighed with a slender hand cupping her chin.

"I already walked around the castle," Florence said. "Now I've finished, and I'm bored. I wish we could go outside."

"Then why not sit and tell us what you saw?" Cordelia Lambert forced herself into a gentle smile. "Mr. Thorley, bring us some tea. We don't have tea? No? Very well, hot water, then."

They sat near Elsie, who barely looked up from her books, while Florence recounted her morning. For a moment, Jasper worried she would have found the tower room, or worse, the tunnels. He knew he had closed everything up, but he didn't have a way to lock the tower door from the outside, and there was no reason she couldn't find the false wall as he had. Even if none of them ever found the tunnels, he didn't want them to know about any of it, not the cauldron or old books. The laboratory, Ansehelm had called it. Couldn't it be just his?

But Florence Lambert hadn't explored that deeply. She had seen the sparse armory and library with its strange piles, going in and out of rooms as Jasper had. There was a room by the courtyard with an elaborate chair that could only be described as a throne, which she thought was quite charming. And near the front of the castle, opposite the great hall, was a chapel.

"It's completely dilapidated," she said. Mrs. Lambert shook her head.

"We oughtn't have the chapel dirty," she said, glancing at the servants. When the tapestries were acceptably beaten, she had them scrub the apartments. Maja joined them with a mixture of unslaked lime she'd found, which made the furniture smell like too-ripe fruit. Jasper was crinkling his nose when William Lambert appeared, soaked even with his umbrella. The trip to town was a success, he declared to his wife. The rest of the food and supplies were in, and a proper estate staff was being assembled as they spoke. The new people would be here as soon as they could, only the roads were bad on account of the weather. There had been a misunderstanding with Mr. Calvin's arrangements, an innocent mistake, and Mr. Lambert was in good spirits about the whole thing.

Thorley told Jasper to help the others unload, suggesting that he change clothes first. Down in the dorm, Ned lay close to the entrance, eating from a pouch of roasted nuts. The crunch of his teeth sent Jasper's stomach growling. He must have been staring, because Ned said,

"Brought these from the city. Give you some if you promise never to help me move anything again."

Jasper matched Ned's wide smile and sat on the cot next to him. His leg was propped up on a crate with a pillow stuck under. Gauze squeezed his head, exaggerating his brow. He dropped a clump of pecans into Jasper's palm.

"This place is kind of scary, isn't it?" Ned said. Jasper slid a nut into the corner of his mouth and talked out one side.

"Yeah. Kind of," he said. The image a squirming leech flashed in his brain. He almost gagged but pushed it down, focusing on the familiarity of the pecan.

"Of course, it's rather dark down here. I hated the dark when I was a boy. One of *those* children, I was. Crying to my parents every night." Ned laughed. "I knew it couldn't hurt me, but I didn't care, I just didn't like."

Jasper laughed with him. "I was scared of my mother. But you know how moms are. Seems scary, but she loves us."

Ned glanced to the side, looking bemused for a moment, but he was soon back grinning at Jasper.

"Dottie assures me there will be dinner?"

"Yeah, they just got back. Matter of fact, I've gotta change and help."

"Ah. Won't keep you, then."

Jasper thanked him, chewing as he found the bed he had claimed yesterday. Picked one all the way at the back. It *was* dark in here: windows towards the ceilings, far from their eyes, and blank walls to absorb shadows. He wondered what else Ned had been afraid of in his life. He pulled his old clothes out of his bag.

The first time Leo spoke to Jasper had been frightening in its way. He hadn't understood why he was being talked to by this man, leaning against the wall in a silk shirt and shining black hair. Jasper had been sure he had somehow imposed himself. Done something wrong. Why else would the son of the house acknowledge him? But in the end, there had been no reason to be scared. Jasper had found himself in a beautiful room with a beautiful man, as if he had been plucked for a reward. That's how it felt every time Leo invited him in, like he had been to chosen to enjoy a brief capsule of luxury.

That's what this trip was supposed to be. Now, he shuffled into the rain to haul crates through the mud. It wouldn't be like this forever, he told himself. It might end tomorrow. The sun would be up, the kitchen full, with Leo holding him through the heat of a summer day.

Leo's noon meal had been missed by hours. He didn't storm down this time. As soon as Jasper was able, he made tea, freshly unpacked, and carried it with dry crackers up to the room. He hoped Leo wasn't still upset, and his unrest made the walk excruciatingly long. His toes kept jamming in the uniform shoes. When he opened the bedroom door, it was to Leo still undressed and still frowning. With an apologetic smile, he explained how lunch had been missed, but that since they had just got tea, he thought Leo would like some. Yes, he would, he nodded. Jasper closed the door and set the tray on the table to pour.

"Don't embarrass me again." Leo took the tea.

"The wine?"

"No." Leo blew the steam away. "Yes. No."

Jasper's heel kicked a candle stump. Dozens of them lined the floor and furniture, as in Elsie's room. The maids had brought them up last night, some even placed in the fireplace next to fresh wood. Jasper felt a guilty pit in his chest, suddenly sure that Leo would be mad at him forever. But when the blue eyes turned to him, they had the tender spark he recognized.

"Did you drop a chair on Ned?" Leo asked, sounding more like his jovial self.

"No," Jasper said. Now, they were both grinning.

"That outfit makes you look domesticated. You're usually…" Leo waved his hand. "Rougher."

Jasper cleared his throat. Leo said,

"Take that off."

The fear from a moment ago vanished in smoke. Jasper was more than glad to be back with him, and it was clear Leo felt the same way. As they lay laughing together, Jasper toyed with telling him about Ansehelm, or asking if he really had fired Charlie, whoever that was. Leo didn't mention anything else about the night before. Instead, they both complained of hunger and the rain.

CHAPTER SEVEN

FTER LEAVING LEO, the idea of scuttling around the tunnels seemed dreary. Jasper wanted more time together, wishing for nice, bright days. He didn't want to change outfits again. But he had promised Ansehelm he would return, and there was time now before he would be missed again. He was excited enough about the book, if only to see what Ansehelm thought would happen. And he figured anything the prisoner revealed about himself would help explain the mystery, even if indirectly.

Downstairs, Ned napped, and the others were absorbed with work. Avoiding Thorley, Jasper pinched salt and a bone from last night's waste, gathering them with the other ingredients in a pack he hid under his jacket. His real clothes were getting disgusting. Damp made them stick to his skin.

As he entered the attic cell, he dreamed of a green hill, he and Leo digging their nails into clovers.

The book lay open near the prisoner, who smiled wide as he combed through the pack. Jasper sat on the floor, trying to keep the boards from creaking, while Ansehelm brewed a concoction. He dipped the bone into the ink before stirring it in the water along with the salt. In the corner of the paper, he drew a rune of some kind, tearing it off to join the mixture. With a shake of the bottle, the liquid turned bubbly black.

"Now, pour this over the chain. Careful not to let it touch you or myself," Ansehelm said. Jasper cocked his head.

"Are you serious?"

"Yes, I am *serious!*" he spat. "Gentle with it. Only pour a small amount. Do not let it splash."

"Sure," Jasper laughed, crouching between Ansehelm and the wall. The lantern light showed the vain scratches the bolt cutter had made. Acid fumes irritated his nose as the liquid dripped down. With a hiss, the iron melted. Jasper's eyes went wide.

Scared to hold the bottle, he set it on the floor, terrified to spill a drop. Ansehelm's bones creaked as he pulled himself forward, and the chain split.

"How did you do that?" Jasper backed away.

"It is all here." Ansehelm tapped the book. "Of course, it appears simpler to you than it is."

"But that's amazing! How? And could you—" His words shriveled as the scene pulsed in his mind. Ansehelm drew some symbol, and now salt water could melt iron. The man's talk was not cheap: Jasper was astounded. He shook his head, trying to prioritize his reeling thoughts.

"I need to get you out of here," Jasper said.

"No!" Ansehelm protested. "Not *yet*." He was still on the floor, only an inch from the spot he had been confined to all this time. Jasper threw his hands up. The man seemed fine with dying in the walls, so be it. He had to admit the idea of Ansehelm crawling around freely put his nerves on edge. But that felt so ungenerous, he scolded himself for it. This was still a sickly man. If he did try to hurt anyone, Jasper could snap him in half.

Ansehelm's brow crumpled in annoyance. "I promised to give you a taste of these secrets, and you have. Now listen to me. I am too vulnerable to leave this castle yet."

"Look, I swore I wouldn't tell anyone about you, but it will take a long time for you to get better if you stay in here eating bugs. You need medicine. The people I work for are powerful, they can help you." Jasper didn't look at Ansehelm; he was fixed on the acid potion by the wall.

Ansehelm glared. "As long as no one but yourself knows about me, I will be safe in these walls."

"If you tell me who your enemies are, we can protect you."

"Doubtful," he scoffed. "You are not dealing with what you understand. You have just seen something you would have thought impossible, yes? You must believe what I tell you. Please, as long as I can eat, I will heal." He said it matter-of-fact, as if a little rest could cure him.

"Alright," Jasper said, the word coming out weak. If even now Ansehelm didn't want to leave, he must be truly afraid. Maybe he was acting more rationally than Jasper gave him credit for.

Jasper straightened his shoulders and glared into the beady eyes. "You have to do your part and not get caught by the Lamberts or any of the others. *And*—" Jasper lurched forward with his finger pointed, and thought he saw

Ansehelm flinch. "—remember you swore none of us would get hurt. This stuff is dangerous."

"Yes! That is what I have been saying," Ansehelm laughed.

"You swore none of us would get hurt."

"You have not and will not. At least not your masters or the others. *You* ought to be careful, I would say. But all you must do is to keep my secrets as I have been telling you."

Ansehelm resumed flipping through the book. Jasper left the lantern on the floor and stepped back into the dark of the cell. It felt safer to be hidden just then, free to grimace. What he had seen was stomach-churning and invigorating all at once. How could it possibly have worked? It was extraordinary enough to draw the attention of evil men. Ones who wanted power, or who feared Ansehelm for his knowledge. It was devil work, wasn't it? Something a witch-hunting mob would kill over. Perhaps a veneer of ignorance was the best defense.

"See," Ansehelm said as he turned the pages, "here is something else you can bring me: three leaves of wild mint, six green acorns, moss from the top of a rock. It must grow at least a foot from the ground. Now, if you keep my secrets and respect my wishes, then I will teach you something of what is in this book."

"Really?" Jasper's mind raced. The idea seemed too monumental, so he just demurred, "I don't know if I can get all that."

"It is all in the forest," said Ansehelm.

"What is that potion supposed to do?"

He rested his hands on the open pages, mouth curled up like the smile on a painted skull. "I will show you once we have made it. That is the best way to learn."

"Will it—" Jasper tried to articulate his thoughts. "I mean, there are natural ways to make acid like what you did before. But are there ones that—"

"You will find a spell for every wish a sorcerer has ever had," Ansehelm said. "Strength, wealth, binding lovers, invisibility, healthy crops, banishing rodents and insects and weeds, harm to enemies, protection—"

Jasper's ears perked up. "Protection from what?"

"From whatever the creator of the spell wanted protection from!"

"Well, shouldn't we—you—we do one of those?" Jasper asked. He couldn't imagine how it would work, but there must be one that fit their predicament. Protect secrets, their bodies, the house.

Ansehelm said, "There is," and pointed a nail at the recipe. "Mint, acorns, moss."

Jasper twisted the hair on the back of his head. "How does it protect us?"

Head nearly resting on the book, Ansehelm's eyes were only slivers, their flash hidden, but Jasper could feel them on him. Still assessing whether he was worthy, perhaps. The man didn't like questions, he knew, but was it enough to cause Ansehelm to detract the offer? His heart twisted at the thought of the miracle he had just seen being kept away from him.

"You'll teach me about this stuff?"

"Very much so. As a reward for your help and because you have proven yourself trustworthy. Secret keeping is important where these matters are concerned. You *must* trust what I tell you."

When he lifted his head, the bones in his neck protruded through his skin. There must be spells for healing too. That's why he wouldn't risk a hospital or the Lamberts' help. That must be it, but Jasper kept his thoughts to himself.

Ansehelm wanted to show him. And once they were safe, then what? Wild feelings rushed over him. Beyond wealth or strength was something intangible. He had no words for it and could not hold on to the feeling long. Like glimpsing a blue sky behind clouds, like knowing something was going to happen the moment before it did.

Jasper swallowed. "Deal."

Back in the tunnels, jitters creeped over him. Away from the attic cell, he began to doubt his memory even though he recalled everything about the potion and Ansehelm's promise with crystal clarity. Before putting the servant's uniform on again, he drenched himself in the rain, trying to clear his strange feelings out.

Jasper was on time to fetch Leo for dinner, but the pair arrived back at the great hall late. They almost didn't make it, the way they kissed, and Leo cracked jokes while Jasper helped him dress. They chatted down the tower steps and through the armory, until the threat of the others was too great. In the hall, Jasper broke away wordlessly to begin serving.

Over dinner, Mr. Lambert discussed the day's excursion. The town was little more than a valley hovel, though he had found a realtor there who struck him as a responsible gentleman. That man had answered all questions, to the best of his ability, and had shown him where he could send a telegram. It was the realtor who promised to assemble a new staff, having connections with those who managed large estates. He was surprised to hear the castle was deserted. As far as he knew, the groundskeeper, a one Robert Morlen, was still gainfully employed there. Despite that mystery, or perhaps because of it, Mr. Lambert was sure all this had been the result of a massive misunderstanding. He reminded his family, dressed in different gowns and tailcoats from last night, that these kinds of things were easily resolved.

Florence asked if he had noticed any place to sport, which turned the conversation to summer activities. Leo suggested setting a net up across the courtyard. His sister agreed and declared that some of the grounds should be dedicated to croquet, as she had a new set she'd brought up with her. She would suggest where the course should be, only she hadn't been outside yet.

Elsie leaned up from her chair and told all of them to be quiet. "Shhh, shhh, Leo, everyone." She glanced at each of them and the servants, pressing her splayed hands down. "*Listen.*"

Silence descended over the hall. Jasper felt like he was at the bottom of a funnel, Pieter Van Hoensbroeck looking down at him from the mouth. They could hear wicks burning and the whoosh of air breathing over the walls. Faintly, Jasper made out an unplaceable scratching sound.

"Did you hear that?" Elsie whispered.

"No," Mr. Lambert said. The others, at least some of them, relaxed at his proclamation. Jasper noticed Mr. Thorley twitch.

"That thumping." Elsie leaned over the table. "It was the sound I heard in my room. Like someone in the walls."

"By someone, do you mean mice?" Florence said.

"No. Didn't you hear? It went one, two. Like a man crawling."

Mr. Lambert stuck his fork all the way through a potato, and the prongs hit the plate with a ring.

"*Etiquette,*" Mrs. Lambert said to her daughter, and Elsie sat.

As the meal continued, Jasper found himself watching the portrait. What had he needed redemption for?

To appease the children, Mrs. Lambert brought up croquet again. They spoke about it less eagerly. Elsie frowned until she could be dismissed from the table. Even Leo seemed uncomfortable, his eyes darting every so often over the walls as if something there had caught his attention.

When the castle was full with the new staff, they would all be less jumpy, Mr. Lambert declared.

CHAPTER EIGHT

THE STORM CONTINUED the next day, and no one came. The mountain roads were untraversable. At least the kitchen was full, and the prospect of three full meals tempered moods. Jasper snuck a fresh baked roll for Ansehelm. Water dripped on them as he held it out, the warm yeast smelling strong over the damp. Ansehelm's nose crinkled.

"See how thick the crust is?" He pressed it with a finger. "I cannot eat this, nor could I eat your peach. The leeches, they—"

"Brought 'em." Jasper flopped the net down, avoiding looking too long at the rippling parasites.

"I had a full set of teeth not long ago," Ansehelm said. "*He* pulled them out. Pulled out my teeth!" He leaned his open jaw back and pointed to a just-visible hole in his gums.

Who? Jasper stopped himself from asking it just yet. The man scooped a handful of leeches into his mouth, not bothering to wipe off the blood that splattered over his face.

"Did you bring the rest of what I asked for?" he asked, not finished swallowing yet.

"Storm's too heavy." Jasper shook his head. He was disappointed himself. After fishing out the leeches, he'd dried off under the empty armory hooks, hoping no one would be around to ask him why he'd gone outside. His thoughts had lingered on what the new potion would do. Yesterday's was out of sight.

Clutching the roll like a ball, he asked if Ansehelm knew Robert Morlen.

"Yes. I have met him."

"Look, I gotta ask." Jasper careened on his heels. "Is he one of the men who did this to you?"

"He is untrustworthy. Why do you not eat with me, Jasper?" Ansehelm said. Hesitating for just a moment, Jasper sat. The iron collar had turned so the chain hung down Ansehelm's chest, the split edge scraping the floorboards. He winced whenever he moved but didn't pause, not seeming to care if he hurt himself or not.

"Have you been crawling around the tunnels?" Jasper asked.

"Yes!" he said heartily. "It is good to work my muscles again."

"You know they can hear you crawling through the walls." He pointed below. "The daughter is getting obsessed with it."

Ansehelm waved his arm dismissively. "They hear sounds, but they do not hear *me*. Do you understand the distinction?"

"Yeah," Jasper said. "Just cautioning you. You still don't want to leave the castle?"

"Not yet. Too dangerous." He popped a leech in his mouth as Jasper broke the roll open.

"But…" Jasper racked his brain. "You must be in pain."

"I am. But not as much pain as I could be in," he said. "Although I am exceedingly weak. Your help is very much needed."

Jasper curled dough over this tongue, swallowed, and said, "Don't get mad, but I'll remind you they have morphine at the hospital."

Ansehelm looked confused. "Do not speak of hospitals. I told you, I wish to stay hidden. And since I am *here*, I can begin to teach you *this*." He patted the book stacked to the side and looked at Jasper, who gave him a nod in affirmation. Satisfied once he had gotten that, Ansehelm asked if he was from the nearby town.

"No, the city. We're all from there." Jasper laughed a little. "To be honest, I've never been to the mountains before. Or even the woods."

"You have never been to a forest?" Ansehelm sounded incredulous.

"I mean, I've…seen…trees…" He took a bite to cut himself off. "Where are you from?"

"Saxony."

"Where is that?"

"It is the duchy between the Elbe and Saale rivers."

"Yeah. Sure," Jasper said as if those words meant anything to him. He asked how long he had lived in the castle, wondering if he had anywhere to go besides it.

"Oh, *years*."

"How many?"

"Thirty."

"You came here in 1869?"

Ansehelm's lip twitched up, blood and goo dripping from it. "If the year is 1899, then, yes. I am guessing it is before *you* were born."

Jasper nodded, chewing. Ansehelm seemed agitated talking about time. He should change the subject before the man shut down again.

"What needed redeeming?" Jasper asked. "I mean, the guy who built this, Van Hoensbroeck, why did he name it redemption?"

Ansehelm's head swiveled like an owl's, facing him directly with eyes as wide as the sunken skull allowed.

"Do you know?" Jasper prodded.

"No," Ansehelm said, "but I know that he was an alchemist and a necromancer."

"A what?"

"A manipulator of the dead."

That caused an unchewed piece of crust to slide down Jasper's throat. He coughed through it as Ansehelm continued, "I have read something of the rituals he carried out, and I believe Pieter would have plenty to be sorry about."

Manipulating the dead. Experiments. Jasper brushed the crumbs off his hands. Is that what had been carried out over that cauldron? Devil work, he thought.

"The laboratory. Were there dead bodies in there?"

"Yes," said Ansehelm. "Why do you look so startled like that? It was a long time ago. There are no ghosts, if that is what concerns you."

"But you're using his books for your..." It was bizarre to say. "...spells?"

"Do not be concerned. I do not dabble in that unsavory magic," he said. His tone made Jasper think he had taken some offense. The vision of a mob circled Jasper's brain.

"Some people think all magic's unsavory," Jasper said, adding quickly, "Not me. But. Y'know, if some people were after you because of that…" He trailed off.

Ansehelm hesitated but looked Jasper over and said, "I will give you some more answers now, so consider yourself lucky. Your Robert Morlen became obsessed with Pieter Van Hoensbroeck's doings, though fortunately he was not a very talented magician."

Jasper's eyes went wide. "So he did do this to you—"

"*No*," Ansehelm said.

"But he's alive."

"I do not know."

"Look, if there's some danger we could be in…"

"You, and the other newcomers to this castle, will only be in danger if any of you decide to battle my tormentors." He shot a beady look right at Jasper. "And then, in the end, it is I who will suffer the most. They must not think for a moment that I have an ally, or worse, that I have escaped these walls. I keep trying to make you understand this, and you keep asking your questions."

For the moment, they were both silent, the sound of rain clear above their heads.

"Yesterday, you asked for a way to protect yourself. Now, there is such a thing, and I have already given you the ingredients. But you did not bring them, so. I have told you a little, and you continue to pester me, so." He slurped a leech, lower lip jutted out as he sucked it under.

Jasper ran a hand over his face. "Necromancy. First you said it happened a long time ago, but now you're telling me Morlen was involved. That must have happened recently. There aren't remnants still in the castle? Of their rituals?"

He shuddered, imagining bodies and blood and strange curses.

"Well, see how many answers you are getting out of me today! Of Pieter's? No, I never encountered one. And if you are asking if he ever raised the dead, no, he did not. I know, because he would have written about it, the braggart. Of Morlen's? I suppose there may be a dissected cat stuck somewhere. Already, I believe I mentioned he was not very good. He did also like to boast. A, how do you say it, *pushy* person." He cackled and spat out some slime. "That is very like the men of today. They think they are entitled to the secrets of the world, that they can stick their hand into the fire and remain unburned. No respect for mastering a craft."

A piece of crust had fallen and lodged between the floorboard cracks, which Jasper picked at while avoiding Ansehelm's eye.

"*You*, I believe, could truly learn," Ansehelm said. "You are less *pushy*. Certainly less addlebrained than the rest of them, with their ridiculous chatter. I hear it, you know, on my crawls." He waved his bony hand towards the trap door and Elsie's bedroom. "Does it not grate on you too?"

"I don't have much of a choice," Jasper said.

"I understand your concern," Ansehelm said. "You wish to protect them, and they are fools, which makes that all the more difficult."

"Guess so," Jasper said. He flicked a finger towards Ansehelm's neck and the melted edge of chain just scraping the floorboard. "Isn't it hard to drag that thing around?"

Ansehelm smiled. "I suppose you will tell me I need to be quieter."

"It's fine," he said with a sigh. "Most of them think it's mice."

"But some do not. Does it frighten them?"

"Yeah." He shrugged.

"You enjoy that everyone is afraid but you!" Ansehelm cackled triumphantly. Jasper protested, but the man was sure of himself. A kernel in the back of Jasper's mind told him it was true.

When he left, he promised he wouldn't bother Ansehelm with fruit or bread anymore. He was glad to have gotten the man talking, not that much had been answered. All this strange business, and Ansehelm had managed to say precious little about himself. Who had he been? What had he worked in the castle as? But then, that was an assumption. He could have owned this place. Maybe it was his armchair Elsie had wanted so badly; maybe she was in his bedroom. Maybe he had built the tunnels. Or maybe he had worked with Morlen, and they had discovered its secrets together.

Mr. Lambert must have had records of past owners and employees, something with Ansehelm's name on it. Jasper wished he could ask. For now, all he could do was eavesdrop. Anything to fill in the gaps between the man's stories.

What he could be certain of was the potion. He had seen it—even if he had doubted it later, it was real. The prisoner had trusted him enough to show it to him, whatever that was worth. He imagined people from the town, whispering rumors of a necromancer until they showed up at the gate with torches. It was as much an assumption as any, but Jasper couldn't shake it.

He would investigate himself, as much as he could, in case Ansehelm was lying. And he would tell no one, in case Ansehelm was telling the truth.

Down the ladder, Jasper dropped the lantern from his teeth. He massaged his jaw before unfurling the map. The paper was just large enough to be unwieldy, the lantern and his knee holding down opposite corners. There was the central tower, the tunnel he stood in marked by two thin lines drawn under a rectangle. There was the path out to the stables and back to the third tower. But he would take a different route this morning.

Split mouths muddled the way. According to the map, there were only three ways: left, right, and forward. Jasper turned as sharp left as he could, to the point of hugging the wall, as if the wrong mouth might suck him in if he got too close. Safely down the correct tunnel, he swung the light side to side, counting the turns that branched off. Ten, eleven, twelve. On the right side. He slipped down the offshoot, narrow and low, a maze of smaller tunnels branching from it in turn. He kept straight. Three, four. There was just enough room for him to face forward, grainy earth brushing the hairs on his arms. Planks jutted out in a makeshift ladder. He didn't climb nearly as far as in the towers, soon finding himself inside a wall. Wood beams nailed in a zigzag up all the way. Someone could climb higher, if they wanted to. The trap door was easy to spot from the inside, with a small rope handle right above the ladder. He cracked it open and, seeing no one, emerged into a high-ceilinged room.

Damask curtains ran the height of the walls, which he pulled back to pounding rain. In the corner was an armoire with edges carved into floral patterns. There was still some color on them, though most of the paint had flecked off. Red and white. The only piece of furniture left. Scratches and dents marked the wood floor. Had it been a bedroom? Maybe a study, or one of those rooms in big houses dedicated for some specific purpose—card room, drawing room. Laboratory. Jasper laughed to himself. He tried the armoire door but it wouldn't budge.

"What are you doing here?"

He jumped when he saw Leo.

"Exploring. I walk this way, sometimes," Jasper said. He glanced at the wall, relieved he had closed the trap door.

"Not dallying too much, I hope. I missed you after breakfast." Leo embraced him only to let go a second later with a snap.

"What's wrong?"

"You have some dirt on you, Jasper," Leo said, wiping his vest. "I suppose you wouldn't be able to help it."

Jasper wiped his shirt too, not that it made a dent. He hoped Leo wouldn't comment that he was out of his uniform, though it was surely noticed. He said something vague about doing handiwork and hoped there would be no follow up questions.

Leo rolled his sleeves up and held Jasper's face with his palms, kissing him as the rain beat down.

"Is it hard being up here, with only me?" Leo asked.

Unsure what that meant, Jasper shrugged.

"I'm sure you have plenty of others in the city," said Leo. "I hope it's not too boring for it to only be me."

"No, um," Jasper said. What did this man imagine his life was like? But Leo's hands felt cool against his flushed face, and he let himself be pushed against the damask. Fingers hooked him under the jaw to pull him in for another kiss.

Leo let go with a shake. "I wish…" he trailed off, gulping down what he had started to say. "There's lunch today, isn't there?"

"Yeah. I don't see why not." They had food, didn't they?

"Fantastic. Tell them I'd like cucumber and chicken on toast. With mustard. And fennel potatoes. With lemon scones for tea. Listen: that's important. Flo always wants currants or figs or something awful like that, but if you get to Proulx before her maid does and tell him to make lemon, that's what he'll do."

"Got it. Lemon scones. Chicken, cucumber, toast, mustard, fennel potatoes." Jasper rubbed his neck. "What were you going to say you wished for?"

Leo blinked, back arched as he decided whether to answer. "Only sometimes, I think I'd like to live a life more like yours. Free to do as you wish."

Jasper said nothing, letting him walk away while listening to the scrape of his own clenched teeth.

╬

On his way back, the saint-lined wall of the chapel caught Jasper's eye. The statues were carved in bland triptychs over walls blotched with mildew stains. A second look and he saw grime had set in everywhere. Some of the pews were even broken, pieces scattered, as if there had been some disaster a long time ago no one had bothered to clean up.

Alone, Dottie wiped an intact pew, trying to summon the shine forth from the wood. She noticed him and said, "Enjoying your time off?"

"Huh?" Jasper stepped into the chapel. Her bonnet bounced as she turned her head.

"Didn't you hear? She gave us the hour off."

"Mrs. Lambert?"

"Yes. You didn't know?"

"No," said Jasper, "when did that start?"

Dottie shrugged. "After breakfast, she said we could have an hour off before lunch." She reached into her apron to check her watch. "So, that's thirty, well, really twenty-five minutes more. Twenty-seven, precisely."

"Oh." Jasper considered if that was enough time to nap. "Wait, then why are you cleaning?"

"Dunno," she said. She moved the rag over the same spot like she was petting a dog. As he walked inside, his footfalls and her scrubbing produced the same soft echo.

Water splattered on a stained glass window of red, green, and purple. Below was the cross, and an organ missing keys.

He wandered to the broken pews, one nearly cut in half, and ran his finger along a spike of splintered wood.

"Terrible," Dottie said.

"Wonder what happened," Jasper said. She paused her petting.

"It looks like someone fired a canon." She shook her head. "Who would do something like that? In a *church*?"

"Must have been an accident of some kind."

"You know, people owned this before the Lamberts. Rich people. And the bank was paying for its upkeep—that's what Mr. Lambert said—yet no one fixed this. They let it stay like this, destroyed. It's the *church*. There must have been a priest here at one point—" She really scrubbed now. "—and what will *we* do on Sunday? It's Thursday; that's only four days!"

"You always go to service?"

"Do you not?"

Jasper shook his head. He braced himself for some lecture from her, but she was muttering at the dust.

"This is absurd!" Dottie whipped the rag in the air.

"The chapel?"

"The whole thing!" She held her hands out like claws by her head. "Miss Elsie was bed-sick for a month, and the doctors said she could recover by taking frequent walks in nature. They meant the park. I waited on her hand and foot with Verna, bringing her everything while she coughed and sneezed and griped, and now I'm here, doing the same with less food and having to run up and down those horrible stairs. Did you know that only last month a brand new hotel opened along Central Park? Do you know what it has?"

"What?"

"Elevators."

Jasper laughed. She cracked into a smile and let her elbows rest on the pew.

"Honestly, how did you get roped into this Jasper?" she asked. He rolled his tongue in his cheeks.

"Leo and I are friends—"

Dottie's expression flattened into smirking disbelief.

"I mean," he said, "he was friendly to me a few times when we met, after I'd done some jobs at the house."

"Well, he can be charming when he wants to be," Dottie said. "Do you like him? So far, at least?"

"Yeah," was all he said.

"Miss Elsie doesn't like him. He is mean to her; I've seen it. She can be a brat, but she's sensitive, not like the other two." Dottie sighed. "None of them like each other. I suppose I take Miss Elsie's side, because I work for her. It's hard not to care about someone you've doted on, whether you get paid for it or not."

"Suppose so," Jasper said.

"That's not the only reason; I'm a youngest daughter too," Dottie mused. "The youngest Cartwright of four, born to George and Helena."

"I'm in the middle, so maybe that's why I get along with Leo," he said.

"Where in the middle?"

"Sixth," he answered. Or was it seventh? He squirmed, realizing he didn't remember. Infant's faces bubbled up in his mind. He didn't want to talk about it anymore.

"I'm sure you can go to the church in town. On Sunday." He walked towards the pulpit.

"But what if they don't let us go? Or if it's still downpouring?"

Jasper lingered on the raised stage. He spotted a bible, and Dottie joined him as he put it on the stand. It was as dusty as the books in the laboratory, with the same oily feel to its pages.

"How old do you think that is?" She butted him out of the way, peeling it open. A date was inscribed inside.

"1692," he read. The rest was in Latin, in an elaborate script with gilded borders on each page. Enamored, Dottie flipped them one by one, reading an occasional passage out loud.

"Vivent mortui tui interfecti mei resurgent expergiscimini—" She ran her finger over the line. "—et laudate qui habitatis in pulvere quia ros lucis ros tuus et terram gigantum detrahes in ruinam."

"Am I the only one who doesn't speak Latin?" Jasper said.

"Hm?" Dottie blushed. "I can't speak it, I'm just sounding out the words. I mean, I don't know what it says, exactly, but I *know*. In my heart."

Jasper stepped back, realizing how risky his comment could be. Dottie's knee bent.

"What was that?" she asked.

"What was what?"

"Something pushed my foot up just now."

Jasper recreated his step, and they watched as a row of floorboards bent up in tandem. They looked down, noticing the crease between those and the rest of the pulpit. She fit her fingers under them.

"It comes up!" she said. "Like a secret door." She grinned at Jasper, who worried he didn't look surprised enough.

"Maybe we shouldn't open it," he said.

"Are you kidding?" She pulled it up with a heave and screamed.

It wasn't an entrance to the tunnels, but a space just big enough for the coffin that sat in it. Dottie clasped her apron to her mouth.

"It's under where the priest stands," she whispered. Jasper swallowed and bent to open the coffin.

"No!" Her hand pinched his shoulder.

"We have to check," Jasper said. "If it's—it could be—"

"Murder," Dottie whimpered into the apron. He lifted the knotted pine lid.

Nothing. It was empty except for velvet lining. They relaxed, only a little.

"Alright. Nobody's dead," Jasper said. Dottie still clenched her knuckles.

"But why did someone put that there?" she asked. Jasper didn't know. He thought of the necromancer whose portrait hung in the hall.

"Should we tell them? The Lamberts?" he asked.

"Of course," said Dottie. She was shaking, so he held her shoulder as they backed out of the chapel.

CHAPTER NINE

ELSIE LAMBERT THREW her arms in the air. "Oh, that is, *disgusting!*" she cried. Dottie served her a plate of pork and summer squash. Cordelia and the children sat around the circular table in the apartment dining room.

"Really, a coffin," Florence jeered.

"Who was in it?"

Florence opened her mouth, but her mother cut her off.

"None of this talk at the table."

Leo held up a mushy squash on his fork. "Well, it's not what I would have liked." He shot his eyes at everyone but Jasper.

"I love it!" Florence said. She turned pointedly to Jasper. "You there, another helping of the squash."

"Don't order my man around," Leo said, as Jasper dashed towards the serving bowl. Florence cracked a smile. Elsie laughed too and fixed her gaze on him.

"You there, I've dropped my napkin." She pinched it between two fingers and let it fall to the floor. Jasper stifled a groan.

"Well! Come on, now!" Elsie said. "Pick it up and then fetch me a fresh one."

He had the napkin in hand when Leo said, "Jasper, I order you to not listen to her." His mouth was in a tight frown.

"He already *is* listening to me. So *there*." Elsie stuck her tongue out. "Fetch me another one!" Jasper stood still with the napkin, eyes darting between her and Leo.

"Mother!" Elsie said. "Order Leo to fire that man for not following my orders!"

Mrs. Lambert simply shook her head. Jasper was still in place, not sure what to do with the cloth he was holding. Leo folded his arms. The others ignored them, until Elsie's fiendish expression fell into a little frown.

"At least give it back," she said quietly. He dropped the napkin on her lap.

They retired to the parlor for tea, where Mr. Lambert joined them. Leo sneered when the scones were served. Vanilla, not lemon. Jasper took in their musky-sweet scent.

Elsie cleared her books from the table and onto the couch with her, consulting them whenever she wasn't directly addressed. Dottie melted into the corner, emerging only to refill her mistress's tea. She had asked to lie down after the incident with the coffin but was told she'd already received time off. Jasper thought to step in and help her, but he didn't want to upset Leo or garner any of their attention again.

Mr. Lambert said he was glad to have been able to work with no interruptions and pontificated on the importance of peace and quiet. He was well into the speech when Elsie held her book aloft, arm curved to the ceiling.

Only once everyone had noticed her did she proclaim, "I have completed my translation!"

Her siblings glared. Mrs. Lambert touched her wrist.

"Darling, there's a scratch on your arm," she said and asked Maja to fetch the nurse.

"Mother, please. This is a serious scholarly announcement. I found this journal in the old desk in my *chamber*," Elsie said. Neither Leo's eye rolls nor Florence's frowns daunted her. "It is in Dutch, and it is dated 1693. I have translated key passages using this." She lifted the dictionary. "Which I thought to acquire prior to our journey, given my nature as one always in pursuit of knowledge."

"Are you, dear?" Mr. Lambert asked sincerely.

"You did not translate that whole thing from Dutch into English," Florence said.

Leo shut his lips around a cigarette as Mrs. Lambert examined the journal.

"It really is from 1693. William!" She showed him.

"If I may, I have begun my translation thusly." Elsie cleared her throat, reading from her diary, "First entry, March the twelfth, in the year 1693. I starteth the day on the sun shine but dreary it is. For what reason? Remaineth my uncle, horrid. The German devil hath cometh to stealeth mine money!"

"Stop saying 'eth'," said Leo.

"It's a linguist's trick," Elsie said, matter of fact. "To invoke the time period in which it was written, I wrote my translation in Shakespeare's English rather than the modern."

"That was not Shakespeare's English, dear," her mother said.

"I don't care for Germans either," was Mr. Lambert's contribution.

"Second entry," Elsie said.

"*Good god.*" Florence looked like she was going to faint. Verna, having just entered, paused as if she didn't know which sister to attend to.

Together, Leo and Florence successfully vetoed any more reading of the translation. Elsie pouted as the nurse dabbed iodine over her arm. They all seemed a bit sick of each other, to Jasper's relief, as it meant tea was over. The plates had just been cleared when Mrs. Lambert called over Thorley, Jasper, and the maids.

She stood with her chin up and elbows out, saying, "I know we are waiting on this new staff, but they aren't coming today and may not come tomorrow. I need you to spend any time you have between serving us cleaning the rest of the castle. I cannot stand how filthy it is."

The five exchanged glances. Maja asked where she wanted them to start.

"The hall. The tower. The rooms around the courtyard, so we may use them. I suppose they will be pleasant when the weather improves. Wherever my son is staying as well. You've been there." She flicked her eye at Jasper. "Tell me, is it horribly *filthy*?"

"Um…" He could tell there was an answer she wanted, but he didn't know what. "No. Not horribly." Mrs. Lambert breathed a martyr's sigh and asked them to get to it.

Mr. Thorley led them, picking the great hall as their start. Jasper glimpsed Horace and Frankie carrying the empty coffin outside.

They found a ladder tall enough so Jasper could brush the cobwebs near the top of the tapestries. It was a strange thrill to look down at the floor every so often, his hand gripping the rung so tight he knew he couldn't truly fall. When the weather cleared, he would find a cliff and see the forest from up there. He'd suggest it to Leo. They'd go out in the woods and look down at the castle together. Though Leo's demeanor at lunch, his comment earlier, wriggled around Jasper's mind. He tried to be positive. There would be plenty of time with Leo in his usual, cheery mood, together in private and with Jasper not really working, as promised.

It took two *You!'s* for him to realize Mrs. Lambert was summoning him. She was with her eldest and Irene, who stood winded behind them.

"Come," said Mrs. Lambert, giving him the barest of glances. Climbing down, he followed them out of the hall and past the chapel. Florence complained about wanting to set the croquet set up. It had been a Christmas gift, ivory balls and oak mallets, and she hadn't gotten to use it all. They stopped in a room whose lone piece of furniture was a long bookcase.

"Move that." Mrs. Lambert snapped her finger from Jasper to the case. "Irene, help him if you need to."

The maid rubbed her upper arm as she watched Jasper push in vain. The bookcase wouldn't budge. Eventually, she joined him, pressing as he shoved his weight against it. Florence put her foot out near its base.

"There *is* a draft here," she said.

"So much to fix," her mother mumbled. "Resting already?"

Leaning against the wall, Jasper said, "It's solid wood, and I don't think it's been moved in a long time."

"I'm quite certain of *that*," Mrs. Lambert said. "In the future, a 'yes, ma'am' will suffice."

"Yes, ma'am."

"Aren't you the one who couldn't hold on to a chair?" Florence asked with a wry smile. Mrs. Lambert, arms folded and crest of dark hair sitting high on her head, looked like a figurine being turned as she faced him.

"Who are your references? Or did my son not ask that before he hired you?" she asked.

"Well, ma'am…" Jasper mentioned the job in meatpacking and reminded her that he'd cleaned out her Madison Avenue gutters that past March. She and Florence raised eyebrows.

"So, he dismisses Charlie and picks you out of the gutters." Mrs. Lambert shook her head. Florence took in her mother's displeasure gleefully. Jasper stared at the wall, arms straight at his sides, looking rather inane. Fine. He wanted them to ignore him.

They were ordered to follow into another room, smaller but fuller, with a hope chest and vanity. Above that hung a large mirror, gold carved into intricate patterns along its border and topped with the image of a roaring lion.

"Exquisite." Mrs. Lambert clasped her hands. "That will hang in my bedroom. Irene, please."

Irene reeled back to catch herself as she took it off the wall. "It's heavy, ma'am."

"Heavy? It must be real gold." Cordelia's eyes lit up. Jasper stepped forward to help, stopped by her snapping, "If you drop my mirror, you'll pay for it."

The threat made him almost leave Irene to it alone, but he couldn't.

"How much do you think it's worth?" Florence asked idly, pawing through the chest.

Mrs. Lambert threw out a number that made Jasper's eye twitch.

"We ought to ask father what the gold prices are right now," Florence said. "Isn't this cute?" She had fished out an infant's gown. Irene and Jasper each held a side of the mirror and walked it into the apartments.

Leo was still there, eviscerating a cigarette while his father talked. They set the mirror in the Lamberts' master bedroom and returned to the parlor. While William took a breath, Mrs. Lambert said,

"Leo, if you're going to get your servants off the street, you should at least pick stronger ones."

Leo pointed his head at her, forcing a sneer off his face.

"Your mother is quite right," Mr. Lambert said. "I'm not certain what this 'off the street' business refers to, but the worth of the unrefined classes is in their physical strength. This does not apply only to domestics! For example, I had a foreman once who put too much intellectual work in the hands of his laborers to disastrous results. The whole project was delayed by months."

"How awful," Leo muttered. Jasper hoped to at least catch his eye but was ignored, and he returned to the cobwebs.

╫

Dinner was braised lamb au jus with stuffed mushrooms, and as Leo reached for the last cheese-filled puff, a ball rolled across the floor. It came out of the apartments, an orange-striped ivory croquet ball, rattling softly over the stones. One by one they noticed until they all were transfixed. It stopped a few feet from the table.

Florence looked pale, her fork halfway to her mouth holding a rapidly cooling cut of lamb.

"Where did that come from?" Elsie asked. The door to the apartments was open a crack; Cordelia swore she had closed it.

"I say," Mr. Lambert called, taking stock of the servants present before guessing, "Proulx?"

"Why would he be in there?" Leo asked.

"Why would he roll a ball on the floor?" said Elsie.

"Why would anyone?" Mrs. Lambert asked. Florence stood with a huff.

"That's mine," she said, hesitating before picking it up as if she expected it to bite. She marched to the door and pushed it wide open. Of course, the parlor was empty.

"Darling put that away, we're in the middle of dinner," Mrs. Lambert said.

"It *was* put away," Florence said.

"You must have missed it," Leo said. His sister stood frozen before her bedroom door.

"Florence?" Mr. Lambert said.

"Irene, did you take this out? Did any of you?" she demanded. None of the servants had. "Elsie were you playing with them? Leo?"

"Don't get your feathers ruffled, Flo," Leo said.

"It didn't unpack itself! It didn't roll itself across the floor! There might be...someone..." She backed up as the thought came over her. Mrs. Lambert squeaked in fright.

"That's not possible," Mr. Lambert said.

"William, it could be," his wife whispered.

"Women," he muttered, then told Thorley and Jasper to check it out. They walked past Florence, Mr. Thorley looking a little nervous. He seemed grateful when Jasper went first, opening Florence's bedroom door to a croquet set on the floor, bag unbuttoned. The rest of the balls rested compliantly inside. The butler latched the door to the apartments closed when they left.

"No intruder. Shocking," Leo said.

"I believe Flo." Elsie crossed her arms as her sister sat, glowering, back at the table. Jasper bit his lip so as not to show his smile. He looked away from Florence's peeved expression.

"What could have caused such a thing?" asked Mrs. Lambert.

"Maybe it was the wind," Leo said. "Did the maid leave the window open?"

Florence, raising her hand as if to slap him, said, "The wind did not unpack the bag!"

"Oh, perhaps we do have an intruder," Cordelia whimpered. Her husband shook his head.

"Now, see here!" he yelled, not quite to anyone in particular, though he commanded everyone's attention. "There is no intruder. I cannot manage with you all feeding into these silly ideas. Even if some villain were foolish enough to break in here, he would soon find that we are not to be trifled with. Therefore, there is nothing for you all to worry about."

"Elsie, you will not stay in that room any longer," Mrs. Lambert said to Dottie's visible relief. "You too, Leo; I don't want you off on the other side of the castle."

"Mother, no," he protested. "There's only one free room in your apartments anyway, and there have been no hauntings where I'm staying."

"Hauntings? Why did you say that?" Elsie said.

"It's either ghosts or the wind." He smirked at her.

"Or a man," said Florence.

"I agree with Father that there is no intruder," said Leo. "And that even if there was, he would do well to leave us be."

Mr. Lambert nodded, face contorted like he was trying to push through a stomach knot.

"We have *already* been through this. There is no one here or up there." He pointed from the apartments to the tower, indignation brimming to the surface. "I purchased this place for us all to relax and enjoy, and I will not have anything drive us out. Now, it is an old building. There may be something structurally unsound which causes balls to roll and the like. Nothing that can't be explained or even fixed. Soon, the business with the help will be sorted, and we will get to repairing it. I know we're in the country, but this is still civilization. There's nothing to harm us." He nodded to signal the matter closed. Florence crossed her arms.

A crash from the apartments sent them shrieking. Proulx bolted from the kitchen with Frankie in tow.

"Well, what caused *that*?" Florence said, teetering between vindication and fear.

"Leo can go investigate," Elsie said.

"Shh!" Mrs. Lambert hissed at her.

"Children, please." Mr. Lambert banged his glass, turned to the servants, and said, "One of you see what that was."

Proulx met his eye.

"It is not an intruder! We went over this. Just, one of you see what it was and clean it up!" Mr. Lambert wiped his forehead. "I assume something needs to be cleaned up."

Thorley and Proulx were the first to converge at the entrance. The thought that Ansehelm had hurt himself, that he was trapped in there, came to Jasper's mind. He made it to the front of the crew, dreading to hear one of them scream, to shout that there really was a man. If Ansehelm was discovered now, he didn't think his own involvement could be explained away. They checked Florence's bedroom again, the dining area, and the master bedroom. Thorley jumped back with a gasp but soon regained his composure, wearily shaking his head.

"It's the mirror." He rubbed his temples. Gold gleamed from the floor, on top a spray of shattered glass.

When they informed her, Mrs. Lambert looked positively devastated.

CHAPTER TEN

A FTER DINNER, LEO announced he was heading to his tower, but would the valet follow him with a Cognac? Mr. Lambert said, "You know, you children never thanked me for giving you this place," as Jasper slipped into the kitchen. Heat still wafted from the brick oven, and the whole place smelled of garlic. The chefs stood with their arms folded, Frankie brandishing a spoon, while the maids filled them in on the events at dinner.

"They were scared 'cause a ball rolled on the floor?" Frankie arched an eyebrow.

"It was odd," said Maja.

"Very odd," said Dottie. Proulx snorted, displeased, though Jasper couldn't tell by what.

"Drafts do all kinds of strange things," Irene said. "I grew up in an old house, and items would always fall or end up in strange places."

"I grew up in a new building that was built bad, had the same thing," Frankie said.

Dottie scrunched her shoulders up to her chin. "It's all too much. The coffin—!"

Maja crossed herself.

"There wasn't anybody in it," Jasper reminded them.

"I don't like it. It's blasphemous," said Dottie.

"How?" Frankie asked.

"It just *is.*"

Proulx grunted, unclear as to whether he agreed or not. Watching Jasper from the corner of his eye, Frankie told him he was not using a proper brandy snifter and handed him a different glass. A slightly different kind of round, stout cup. Jasper tried to remember if the castle had come with such precise drinkware or not. He wouldn't put it past the Lamberts to have brought some from Manhattan.

"And she's *staying* in the damn tower!" Dottie cried. Jasper gave her a sympathetic smile as he carried the drink up. Liquor sloshed, he had to keep steady so it wouldn't spill. As he passed the apartments he heard a commotion, and Mr. Thorley whipped out looking vexed as ever.

"Mr. Lambert has misplaced his cigars!" the butler threw his hands up. Jasper frowned in commiseration, not breaking stride.

Leo was the only one left in the great hall, lingering by one of the arched doors with his back against purple cloth, leg crossed over the other. Except for the medieval tapestry behind him, he looked how he had the first time Jasper had met him: draped in a doorframe, relaxed, ready to have a good time. Jasper could go for that too, and he shrugged out his agitation from earlier. So what if Leo could be a little petulant? That was to be expected from a rich; it was inevitable that he'd stomp his foot now and again. And the last few days had been odd for everyone. Jasper was sure his own behavior had been abrasive at some point.

Fresh candle in his fist, Leo pivoted down the corridor. Jasper kept a few paces behind. Neither spoke. When the glow from the hall was gone, Leo stopped to light the wick. It shone out as Jasper caught up to him, drink tray extended. Leo took a gulp and offered him a sip. Sweet, hot flavor saturated his tongue. Maybe it did taste better out of this glass. He stuffed the white gloves in his pockets, Leo kissed him, and the light cast down over the doors to the chapel.

"Can you believe that?" Leo said.

"The coffin?"

"No. Well, yes. But no."

"The ball?" Jasper looped a cautious arm around Leo's waist.

"And the mirror."

"It's not weird for a mirror to fall," Jasper said.

"Didn't you install it?" Leo pulled away to show his smirk. "I'm jealous. *You* got to go exploring around here."

Jasper laughed. "What did you do all day?"

With a half-shrug, Leo twisted inside the chapel. "Well, I *explored*, but I didn't find anything *interesting*. Like you and Dorothy did."

The peaks and valleys of the splintered pews were one solid form in the dark. To Jasper it looked like a knight on a horse brandishing his spear. An illustration from somewhere in childhood filled out the silhouette. Silver armor, a white horse. Black horse? A green, blue, red flag. Maybe yellow.

"I keep thinking about knights," Jasper said.

"Me too. Everyone else asleep, and no one waiting on either of us." Leo swooped over and kissed him. Lips tingled from the brandy. There was a pop as Leo pulled away and said, "Where's this coffin; I *do* want to see it. Oh, they got rid of it already, didn't they?"

"Yeah," Jasper said, licking his lips. At the pulpit they peered down at the empty space where the coffin had rested.

"Wonder if the intruder slept here," Leo said, lantern dangling over the spot.

Jasper turned his whole head to look at him. "You don't think there's anything to all that, like your sisters do?"

"There is certainly *not* a man sneaking around the castle." Leo turned too, studying Jasper. "*You* don't think that?"

"No."

"Right. You're the one who declared it was all clear, when you had your little investigation the other night," Leo said. "Besides, why would an intruder roll a croquet ball over the floor? He would steal it."

Jasper stepped back, watching Leo bent over the hole with a hand on his chin like he was in a detective serial. Some of the earlier agitation crawled in.

"I—" Jasper hadn't thought through what to say, but Leo was looking at him. "I don't know what to do when your sister talks to me like that."

Leo cocked his head.

"Today. At your tea time," Jasper said.

Standing up straight with a frown, Leo said, "I *did* tell you she was awful. You certainly will not be fired, so that's nothing to be worried about. You could have handled it more gracefully, which normally isn't a problem for me, but perhaps here it's a trait worth cultivating. Ask Clarence, I suppose."

"Who's Clarence?"

"Oh. Mr. Thorley." Leo snorted. "He should answer all your questions; that's his job. Anyway, don't worry about Elsie. She's a brat, and it's worse now since the scarlet fever. Expects to be doted on as if she's still at death's door.

Anyway, I did my best to defend you, but of course I had to stay within reason."

Jasper slumped a shoulder. Maybe Leo didn't usually defend his servants; if he started now, it would reveal too much. That was unkind, Jasper chided himself. He didn't want to be angry.

"It'll be easier when the full staff is here," he said. Leo beamed, face lit from below.

They left with their arms around each other. Leo shared his drink, Jasper pointing at shadows as they meandered the corridor. Wet air made them press closer together. They poked their heads into chasmic rooms, gaped, joked about ghosts. At a corner, Leo stopped to revel in a suit of armor.

"I love this!" he said, lifting an arm plate. Jasper grinned. The suit was almost complete, not that rusted either. "He stands guard here, all this time. What a fellow!" Leo flashed a smile and clipped forward. He did have a handsome smile and an airy way when he was happy. Much kinder than the other Lamberts.

A part of Jasper felt guilty keeping the secret from Leo. He didn't seem afraid, but falling mirrors, sounds from the walls, and intruders had to rile up something in him. No harm, though. He was probably happier not knowing about it, not having to deal with it. Could Jasper imagine Leo Lambert fishing out live leeches from a dirty, cold pond? No, even if he hadn't sworn to keep the secret, Leo wouldn't like knowing this one anyway.

When they grew bored of exploring, they hurried up to the tower, both working their matchbooks until the room was warm with white and yellow candlelight. Freshly lit, the flames cast a bright, inviting glow while the rain pattered outside. Jasper took his jacket off, looking up to soft glances. Leo watched him undress, then pushed him on the bed.

"Can you do that thing for me?" Leo bit his ear lobe as he spoke. It was something Jasper had learned from a naval officer; Leo thought it was fantastic. Afterwards, he took a sip of the brandy to wash his mouth out. They rested together, tangled in the old comforter. Leo squeezed him like a pillow, and he let the warmth ripple over him. On the floor, wax pooled over the candle holders. Leo's breath settled into a low rhythm.

"You must not sleep here," he said, petting Jasper's hair.

"I know." Jasper forced himself up, scraping his clothes back on. The rest of the brandy mulled in the snifter on its tray. He snuffed the candles while Leo's fingers dangled in his. Finally, he broke from him, taking the last light out of the room.

Back on the tower steps, the air was clammy. Pressure behind Jasper's eyes grew as if his brain were trying to pop them out of his head. He massaged his temples. The pressure dissipated, or he just grew used to it. Running his fingers down, he felt the bridge of his nose, with its bump and broad slope. When he and Irene had moved the mirror, the glass had faced upright, and he had been constantly catching his reflection in it. He was glad the thing broke. He jabbed his ring finger under his cheekbone and relished how uncomfortable it was. The stairs ended. He put his hand in his pocket and breathed in the dry armory air.

Without the glass to balance, he walked quickly, jostling the candle flame and casting wild shadows over the stones. Leo's suit of armor seemed to wave, and he found himself smiling hello at it. Just as he passed it by, something dropped on his head. He rubbed his skull, looking down to see an oval cigar wrapped in a red-gold band. He looked up and around but saw no one.

"Ansehelm!" he whispered, listening for thumps in the ceiling. Nothing. He remained alone. He ran the cigar under his nose, smelling acrid tobacco.

If he returned it to Mr. Lambert, he would have to explain how he found it. He sniffed it again, aromas wafting out of the waxy wrapper. It was missing the harsh chemical reek cigars usually had, at least the ones he was used to. He wondered how much of his month's pay it cost. It felt less depressing to guess once he had decided to smoke it. Getting caught would be disastrous, so he'd slip into the tunnels.

He entered through the third tower. Safely in the familiar stretch of tunnel, he started the cigar. Rich smoke filled his lungs. He was still in the uniform, but oh, well. It had seemed important before not to dirty it, but he wanted to enjoy this more. At any rate, the gloves were off, safe in his pockets. The map was stashed in his bag, but he recalled there was a path that went up the other tower. Leo's. He held the candle holder up and, spotting a wide tunnel breaking off on the right-hand side, decided to try it. Sure enough, he reached another slope up, more gradual like the one to the laboratory than the ladder to Ansehelm's. There wasn't any secret prisoner at the top either, but a small enclave. Big enough to sit in. He blew the candle out and let himself settle there, hidden. Embers from burning tobacco glowed at every inhale. Feeling along the side he felt the handle of the trap door and, as slowly and quietly as possible, slid it open.

The enclave was flush with the floor. Candle holders full of dried wax lined the border between it and the room. He saw Leo's knees and profile, head bent down, sitting on the bed. A few re-lit candles burned on the desk, enough that Jasper could see he was still naked. He held the snifter in one hand, lifting it mechanically to drink.

His nostrils flared and Jasper snuffed the cigar. He knew he should leave, but Leo's stock-stillness was captivating. Vulgar to admit it, but what had he come here for if not to spy? He stayed crouched in the enclave like a goblin. Leo sat and sat.

In a blur, Leo sprung to his feet and lobbed the glass at the wall, shouting as it shattered. *"It's not fair!"*

Jasper shrunk back, as if were possible to hide more in the shallow enclave. Over again Leo shouted, repeating, *"It's not fair,"* in a whine of raw pain that Jasper would never expect could come from Leo Lambert. Part of him wanted to leap out, comfort him. Or maybe instead, he would shout just as loud. Throw a flaming candle with boiling wax at the wall. Puff smoke in his face.

As abruptly as it had started, it stopped. Leo sat back on the bed, head bent and still. Nose sniffing, his face turned towards the wall. Jasper didn't want to see anymore, wanted to snap the trap shut, but the sound would be too loud. He could already hear his own harsh breathing like thunder. The smell of the cigar loitered. Leo stood; Jasper could see his feet walk closer. The wall rumbled above Jasper's head as Leo banged a fist against it. He must not see the opening yet. Jasper was sliding the trap closed, forced to go slow. Another bang, Leo was moving down. His knees bent. At any moment he could notice the sliding wall, but if Jasper made a sound, it would be guaranteed. Slow. Another bang, right above the enclave. Finally, the trap shut. It shuddered as Leo hit it and hit it again. Could he hear that it was hollow? Jasper held it closed—even if Leo got his fingers in the seams, he would not let him open it.

The bangs stopped, and Jasper scurried down from the tower as fast as he could. He felt gross. He went straight to the water pump and washed himself in the dark. Naked, but who could see? No one else would come this way at night.

The rain helped. He wrung the uniform out, hoping to squeeze out every scent and speck of dirt. Dripping wet, he snuck back to his bed. The others were asleep already— Thorley, Horace, Ned, Earl, Proulx, Frankie. He was as a quiet as he could be, though he thought he saw Ned wake and look at him.

What would someone see if they were to spy on him? Not *that*, but of course, he had never slept in private.

Before dawn, when there was just enough light to see by, Jasper headed outside. He wanted to bring Ansehelm his meal before the Lamberts sucked away all his time, and he wanted to find that new batch of ingredients. Even though he had to go into the woods. For now, the rain had stopped, and he had only to contend with mud and morning dew. He mused on what kind of potion acorns and mint would make as he passed the garden to the overgrowth. In the dawn, the thicket was all blue.

He met the stone wall sooner than he imagined. The borders of the castle were not so wide after all. A plain gate opened with a pull of the latch. No one had cared to lock the back.

Beyond it, woods twisted over the hills, slowly turning emerald at the eastern points. As he crossed into it, he felt an electric tick up his spine. It would be easy to get lost in here. Lost, and never see Leo or anyone else again. But the idea of turning back was unpalatable now that he had smelled the raw air.

There were natural paths he tried to keep on, ferns and thorns whipping his legs as his head dodged low branches. For a few minutes he wandered, acclimating to the forest that enveloped him. But he had a mission. Acorns. He studied the branches until he found them between lobed, oval leaves. They were green, still-growing, and he had to twist each off. One fell, and after retrieving it, he pawed over the ground, testing this new realm. The soil was thick with sprouts, damp and cakey. Slippery earthworms snaked around his fingers. Moss. He saw it growing everywhere now, eyes close to the ground with the sun rising. From a rock at least a foot high, he scraped the spongy plant.

Wild mint. Where was that? All the leaves melded together. The sound of shattering glass bumped over his memory. He swiveled, checking that he could still see the gate. Barely. Fear of the woods crept up again. He curled his shoulders to shake it out.

Some putrid smell hit his nose. He couldn't tell where it came from, but it made him almost wretch. He couldn't stay out here much longer anyway. Mint would have to wait. Back inside the walls, he spotted the chopped remnants of the coffin, thrown in the brush.

The pond water was cold as he pulled the leeches out, and the sack he carried them in froze his skin.

Ansehelm was sleeping again, laid out like a board under the bolt he had been tethered to for so long. He woke when the sack dropped next to him. As he dug into breakfast, Jasper asked,

"Were you in the walls last night?"

"I am always in the walls!" he laughed with bloody lips. "I know what you are asking. The answer is yes." He crawled to the side and hoisted himself up, digging his fingers into the grooves of the wood. Though it looked painful, he could half-stand, using his arms to pull himself and ignoring how his bones cracked in their joints.

"See? I am already getting stronger, able to exercise my limbs!" he said before collapsing back to the floor. The nub of his clavicle poked out from under his skin, kept inside the body seemingly only by webbing. It looked dislocated, but he paid no mind, slithering over to resume his meal.

"The ball? The mirror?"

Ansehelm nodded. "I hope I did not upset *you*, Jasper."

"No," he said. He smiled thinking of the absolutely horrified look Florence had given a croquet ball. He bet the stone floor had scratched its ivory. "Honestly, it was kinda funny. But I don't want you to jeopardize your safety."

"I will not. I can tell the character of that family, and I knew they would not catch me. Too much bickering over disbelief. Not clever enough to see the cracks in their walls." Ansehelm was popping the worms into his mouth one by one, spindly fingers working over the net without hesitation.

"Why bother doing it at all?" Jasper asked.

"Would you like another cigar?"

Jasper took it, lighting it up then and there. It was more comfortable here, watching a skeleton's bones pop out than it was seeing Leo's fit last night. That cigar he had tossed— barely smoked—in the tunnel, and he welcomed another chance at the taste. He offered to start one for Ansehelm too.

"No, I do not smoke them."

"Then why'd you take 'em?" Smoke curled over his tongue.

"I dislike that new master of the house," he said.

"So do I," said Jasper, giving him an eye. "You're not some kind of thief who stole from the wrong people, are you?"

Ansehelm spat out some chitlin as he laughed.

"Dislike, is that why you did that stuff? Breaking the mirror and all?" Jasper asked.

"More or less," Ansehelm said. "I do appreciate you bringing me my meals, Jasper, when you must also work for those people."

"Yeah. Of course," he said, embarrassed all of the sudden. Ansehelm's sincere smile bore into him. He held out the other pack. "I have moss and acorns for you. Couldn't find mint."

"Try again. I am sure it grows out there."

Fermented tobacco mingled in Jasper's lungs with the mountain air. He told the story of the coffin he and Dottie had found.

"A coffin under the pulpit? What do you think of that?" Ansehelm asked, arching his neck from side to side.

Jasper didn't have a quick answer. He tried to parse surprise or recognition from Ansehelm's ghoulish face, but the man showed nothing. "It's strange," he said. "I don't know why anyone would go through the trouble to build all that. There wasn't a body in it."

"Perhaps it was for the priest."

"You mean someone trying to kill him?"

"Or mock him."

Leeches swarmed to escape the net as Ansehelm plunged his hand in, but he scooped them up before they made it out, arms bending like tree branches.

"When did they last have a priest here?" asked Jasper.

"I do not remember," said Ansehelm.

"You know, you're so convinced that if anyone finds out about you, you'll die," Jasper said, "but you'll sneak around where the family lives?"

The man cocked his head as if he hadn't considered that, or at least expected Jasper not to. His eyes scanned again, followed by a nod to himself, as if he had just come to a decision.

"It is hard to be idle when people like that are in my house," Ansehelm said.

"*Your* house?"

"Yes!" He hissed it. Jasper held his hands up, cigar dangling from his lips.

"I do not wish them to get comfortable. I want them to leave. I dislike them, but I like you, Jasper." Ansehelm's voice softened.

"Thanks." Jasper inhaled. How could Ansehelm be so afraid and yet so reckless? He remembered himself last night, spying on Leo like a fiend while burning his father's cigar under his nose. An absolutely foolish risk, when Jasper thought about it. Maybe he should be more understanding. "Look, I'm not trying to tell you what to do, but if you keep breaking mirrors and all that, they'll figure you out. Or if they leave, I'll leave too. So what's your plan?"

"I need more time," he said with a defensiveness Jasper was coming to recognize. "If all goes well, you will not have to leave. I will have everything back, and you can work for me."

Jasper took the cigar out of his mouth.

"Do not look so incredulous," Ansehelm said. "It is possible, even if you cannot see how. You must not ask me to do anything before I am ready."

He had a strange friendly glint in his eye. Jasper looked down, shuffling his feet. Water dropping down his eyebrow made him wince. He placed an empty bottle, one he'd brought yesterday, on the floor to catch the leak.

"That should be fine. It's not too heavy." Jasper held his hand out to measure the drip. "Is it dry over you?"

Ansehelm said nothing, forcing Jasper to look back and meet the pinpoint eyes.

"It is not raining on me. Thank you."

"Anything I can do to help you—food, of course, but to protect you too—"

"Then please do as I ask and do not take matters into your own hands." Ansehelm jutted his chin towards Jasper. "Otherwise, I will have to ask you to leave as well. Because it *is* something you would like, to work for me and live here?"

"Yeah." He gave a weak nod. Something about the eyes, the leak, the leeches, made Jasper feel numb. Too much at once. He pointed in the corner, barely catching the outline of the potion. "You'll teach me—"

"Yes."

"Here." Jasper handed him the unfinished cigar. "I have to go. I know you don't smoke, but these are good. Expensive. I wouldn't let it go to waste."

Ansehelm's smile followed him out of the cell. Alone, squeezing down the ladder, the offer settled in his brain. Live in the castle. Space enough for everything, and if someone wanted to impose on him, they would have to scale a mountain first. What a relief to really live like that. And to learn about—what to even call it? Most people could never conceive of it. He barely did himself. A rune. Leather bound books. Sky behind the clouds. By the time he was down the ladder, he was shivering with excitement at the prospect. How would Ansehelm get the castle from the Lamberts? Jasper didn't care.

All that was clear was ink and bone being stirred into bubbles, and the sting in his nose as the potion ate through chain. There would be more like that, and new ones truly beyond belief. Secrets reserved for a select few.

Outside the tunnels, he felt conspicuous, as if the others could tell there was something different about him now. It took a while to tamp his excitement down, forcing himself to be neutral as he changed and began his serving duties.

The breakfast tray held toast topped with scallion eggs. He opened the tower bedroom door to broken glass, and Leo said, with a self-deprecating laugh, that he had dropped it on accident, and would Jasper mind sweeping it up?

CHAPTER ELEVEN

J ASPER SCRATCHED AT something behind his ear the whole walk back from breakfast. Leo's room really was the farthest distance from where his parents were, slicing diagonal from his tower to the corner where the apartments and kitchens clustered off from the great hall.

Downstairs, he dumped the glass shards in a bin next to the woodshed. The mud was thick, and the rain picking up again. The door to the servants' quarters swayed in the wind. Through it he saw Ned waving, beckoning him in.

"Jasper, thank God," he said with a cough. His leg still rested on the crate, wrapped in a thin cast. He stretched his arms towards the end of the bed.

"You okay?" Jasper asked.

"Hardly. I'm thirsty and bored and the door won't stay shut. Do me a favor and hand me my satchel. Everything I need is in there."

The bag had ended up in the aisle, out of his reach. He moaned in relief as Jasper handed it over.

"Thanks, you're a lifesaver. Is Verna with Miss Elsie?"

"Think so."

"Ah, well. Send her down to me if you can." Ned patted his leg. "It feels worse today."

The bag was wide open on his lap, contents brimming over its flaps. He took a swig from a flask, then pulled out a book.

"I'll look for her. I'm sure it'll heal up fine," Jasper said. Water splashed down on the page Ned was reading. They both looked up. A second later, another drip came down from the ceiling.

Ned closed the book. "Aren't I having a lucky week."

"Let's put you on a different bed," Jasper said. He positioned himself to hoist Ned up, but the man barely shifted his hips before crying out in pain.

"God, I don't think I can move," he said, rubbing the wet spot where the leak was soaking his shirt. There was room enough between the cots to slide the bed over, and Jasper heaved one side at a time, absorbing the grate of the bed against the floor. It took a few good pushes, but he was able to get him below dry ceiling.

"Well, thank you." Ned gave him a sad smile. "You know, this is shaping up to be my second luckiest week ever. My *luckiest*, that was about eight years ago. I'd just gotten married. My wife brought food over to my mother's on account of her being ill and, swear to God, they both fell dead from the same sickness a few days later. I went broke burying them both, and no woman's looked at me since. It really happened that way, on my honor." Ned held his palm up.

"No week can top that," Jasper said.

"Exactly!" Ned said. "So there's nothing to worry about now."

Jasper spent the rest of the morning fixing the leak, finishing just in time to eat quickly before he would need to serve lunch. There was soup today. Frankie's creation. Creamed artichoke and chicken. The sous-chef poured him a cup unprompted.

"What do you think?" Frankie asked.

"Delicious," Jasper said as Frankie beamed. Maja walked by, and he offered her some too.

"It's the family's meal, don't give it all away," Proulx said to him.

"You like it Maja?" Frankie asked as she slurped.

Jasper began pouring the soup into a deep silver bowl. He didn't relish carrying lunch up, feeling a soreness in his arms. Of course he was tired, between everything this morning. The rain didn't help. His father had always complained when it was wet out, that this or that hurt. Jasper guessed it would happen to him. All his strength dwindling into aches.

Then what would he be worth? He heard the thought in Mr. Lambert's voice. The ladle slipped out of his hand, clanging to the floor. Proulx frowned. He tried to clear his mind as he wiped it off. He couldn't dwell on every little thing they said and did. It wouldn't change anything, just make him more miserable.

Besides, what did it matter when he knew of something they didn't have the brains to even imagine?

That afternoon, on his way to wring out a mop, Jasper almost walked straight into William Lambert. He had been lost in thought. Mrs. Lambert glared, though her husband appeared not to notice he was there at all. Mr. Thorley was with them and took the opportunity to give Jasper another task.

"Go ask the drivers if the roads are clear."

Feeding their horses, Earl and Horace laughed at his question.

"Who wants to know?" Horace asked.

"Mr. Thorley."

Earl grimaced. "The boss isn't trying to go into town, is he?" Rain flew under the roof of the stables, splashing water and mud up their ankles. Jasper found Thorley in the great hall still with the Lamberts, who sank into frowns when he told them the answer.

"We've driven in rain harder than this," Mr. Lambert said.

"In the city, yes," the butler said, tone gentle. "But to get down the mountain…"

"Spare me, Mr. Thorley," he said. "Certainly a horse can get through, if not a carriage? I simply must send for new cigars, and I have more than one letter for the bank."

"Oh, William, where is the help we were promised?" Cordelia put her hands on her cheeks.

"That's what I would like to know, dear."

"My word, at this point it's simply unacceptable!" she said.

"Highly unacceptable!" he agreed. He pointed a finger at the ceiling, elbow bent at a perfect angle. That was another reason to get to town: the matter of the help needed to be sorted at once. Thorley sent Jasper back down to ask if a horse could get through.

"Tell 'im *no*," Horace said. Earl backed him up with a grunt. Felicity whinnied.

The Lamberts stood waiting for the response.

"They said no, sir," Jasper said.

Mr. Lambert's eyes bulged.

"Well!" he blustered. "Go back down there and tell them *yes*." Thunder rolled outside. "Why aren't you moving, boy?"

Jasper dreaded having to ask again. When he appeared in the stables, Earl clutched his pipe by his shoulder as if he were going to throw it at him. Horace said,

"In all the years I've worked for them, I've never refused to drive them anywhere until now. Because if we go out on that road, we will get either buried alive in mud or lost forever in the woods. There's not a third option. Why don't you explain *that* to them?"

Jasper relayed to the Lamberts a more cordial version, but he still had to tell them no, and their eyes lit up in flames.

"Why, this is downright *insubordinate*!" Mr. Lambert said. "And *you*. Your uniform is filthy."

"It's muddy in the stables," Jasper said. "Sir."

"You could walk more carefully," said Mrs. Lambert. Jasper avoided her gaze.

Thorley, who had been biting a knuckle, stepped forward with a paternal smile.

"Sir, if I may, one driver has already been injured. And should there be an accident, which is likely, your mail would be lost."

Mr. Lambert gave him a slow nod, unconvinced.

"The letters would end up in the woods. To be found by God knows who, and if you had any sensitive information in there…"

Mr. Lambert was nodding faster.

"…people up here may be liable to try to take advantage of you. I loathe to suggest it, but it is a possibility. And even if that were not the case, it would still be awfully inconvenient to compose those letters again."

"Yes, yes." Mr. Lambert waved a hand. "Alright. Such horrid luck. I am beginning to think this property may not have been an ideal purchase."

"Oh, William, no!" His wife grasped his arm. "I'm certain it will all work out. You were only thinking of our dear daughter, and I am sure it is a good investment as well. Isn't that what Mr. Calvin said?"

"Yes, it is," he said.

"I know you're a smart man, and a wise man. It's not possible for you to make a very poor decision."

He sighed, saying, "Darling, I've made poor decisions."

"But not *very* poor."

Mr. Lambert smiled at that.

Jasper stole time away before dinner to nap. He fell asleep to lightning in the windows and visions of magic spells.

Over her roast duck dinner, Elsie was macabre. She complained of horrid nightmares and that she felt weak. Leo teased her that it was the ghost.

"Please do not start that again," Cordelia sighed.

"Better we discuss ghosts than intruders," Leo said as Jasper refilled his wine. He gave too little now.

"You believed it last night, Mother," Florence said.

Mrs. Lambert glanced at her husband before saying, "There is no intruder, and I insist that you children do not bring up the topic again. We have quite enough real trouble, with a short staff and all the repairs this building needs. No need to scare ourselves over imaginary trespassers. Really, that sort of thing doesn't happen."

"It happens to some people," said Elsie.

"Not to *us*," Mrs. Lambert argued.

"Why not?" Elsie asked.

Mr. Lambert looked pouty as he spoke up.

"My daughter, I dine regularly with the mayor. I have sold property to the governor. I once met the president. The federal army itself would come at my behest. No deranged man is going to meddle in my affairs."

"What if he got to us before the army came?" Elsie asked.

"He would not, *because*..." William thought about it. "...the fiend would hear me—if there was one—and know he had picked the wrong man to burgle."

Elsie considered the logic, eventually giving him a little nod of acquiescence. Already, Jasper had to pour Leo more wine.

⧻

How many minutes of restless sleep? When he'd sunk into the cot that evening, he'd barely been able to keep his eyes open, but as the others blew out their candles one by one, and the dorm went quiet, Jasper started tossing. Kept up by mind chatter, his body filled with energy, and the cot became monstrously uncomfortable. No choice but to give in and stand. He'd been thinking about the third tower.

Feet livened by the stillness of the night, he walked into the castle wilds. He'd brought plenty of lights but found he didn't want them. It was refreshing to shift over the corridors hidden, blending into the dark, able to be no one. He couldn't tell where he'd move more than a second ahead, but he walked in a flow without stumbles or bumps. Space seemed to bend with him, a step one way and there a hall popped into existence. He flexed his arms to the side, tempting an obstruction. Nothing but air. The castle veered around him in a welcome, letting him know walls did not have to be solid here. The way behind was smudged into nothingness.

Not until the door of the third tower was shut behind him did he strike a match. The candles fit poorly in the wall holders but baked the room in bright yellow all the same. It was the clearest light he'd seen the laboratory in. Glass bottles and metal contraptions reflected the flames, the cauldron shone black, book spines glowed. He wondered if one day, he'd know every item in this room intimately. Perhaps to the point they would even become dull. A funny thought. In that future, if he were bored, he would find another spell to do.

Jasper drummed his fingers on the cauldron's edge. Magic could give you money, strength. What else had Ansehelm listed? Anything and everything, wasn't it?

It had been uneasy with Leo that evening, after everything Jasper had seen, but he wanted to push through and not let his own spying ruin anything. There must be a spell to control thoughts.

Scanning the books, he spotted a few in sort-of English. *Secrets of Alchymy, Celestial Medicines, Daemonologie In Forme of a Dialogue.* He opened the squat *Secrets of Alchymy* with its pages bordered by fleurs-de-lis. It had been printed cleanly, and despite the occasional odd letter, he had no trouble deciphering the words. That turned out to not make much difference. It was old, circuitous writing punctured with cluttered talismans and concepts he couldn't make heads or tails of. Planets being derived from colors; whatever philosopher's mercury was.

Another book was more practical, listing cures to preserve sight, fight diseases of the head, gout, leprosy. How to give a horse a long life. A spell for curing cramps. That recipe went: melt gold, copper, and iron; forge into a ring engraved with a magical script and wear at the hour of Saturn.

Jasper wasn't going to be doing that.

For a spell to turn invisible, you had to wear nothing but purple robes while fasting for three nights in a cave, then sacrifice a boar with a silver sword that had been forged on a full hunter's moon.

Still curious, he read on, but it was becoming clear that even if he understood what to do, he wouldn't be able to. Maybe if he became a blacksmith. Or, somehow, a maker of fine jewelry, or better yet simply rich, because these alchemists had enough solid gold lying around to spend it on a cramp.

Ansehelm's spells were simple. There would be magic Jasper could do, he just had to be taught. He put the book down, eyes lingering on a bottle which cast a mint-green glint. The hue wasn't from the glass itself but what was inside, a cut of ivy suspended in gel. His lip twitched. The thing gave him the shivers.

At a hospital when he was young, he'd been scared out of his mind by some bulbous pink thing, preserved in a jar of formaldehyde, which he'd slowly recognized as a tongue. He'd seen it while wandering off, and it sent him running back to his father, who said that's what doctors did to the tongues of children who misbehaved.

An ivy vine wasn't a human tongue. And remembering it now, the tongue must not have been human either, cow or pig instead. Funny how he'd believed that until just this moment. The green jar still felt menacing.

On a shelf close to the desk, he picked through a stack of papers. Some were loose, others still with envelopes. A wax seal flaked off one and fell to the floor. He made out Van Hoensbroeck's name on several letters, and one addressed to him was, on second glance, in English. The same difficult English as the books, and the script was blotchier, but the first words stood out:

Here is the solution fore your probleme.

The fading paper threatened to rip at its creases as Jasper laid it on the desk.

Fore protection against enymies, devills & spirits malefices prepare <u>exactly as indicated</u>. The results of the heretofore rituall maye be placed vpon a person or, if don in enough quantity, a dwelling maye be filld. Thereupon the rituall will drive evil out with equall strength as it does prevent evil to enter in!

Into a dyshe of copper laye crushd lead, the crushd heades of Peonie flouers, the petals of whiche haue beforehand ben pluckd & discard'd. Set the dyshe as you would the Alembic & poure 2 parts water to 3 parts oil. On a peece of parchment drawe in Lead & place on top of the mixture this:

Inked in the middle of the page was an X, dotted with small circles on half of its stems, enclosed in a diamond.

Only in the darke of nite ought you set the fire underneath, & do not let it out vntill all moisture has ben burnd awaye.

If you haue followd these instructions, you will find vpon the dishe a Sphere of garnet whiche maye serve as an Amulet for the warding off of all evills.

My friend, I feare you will suspect a ruse given the symple nature of the foresaid rituall, but please let me assure you of its veracity. I myself performed this on behalfe of a much afflicted young woman known to my wife. She wore it the garnet sphere, vpon her person for some daies & all her torments vanished. It is my sincere hope & beliefe that you will find it the same.

  – E. Ashmole, London, 1685

Jasper rubbed the back of his neck wondering what problem of Van Hoensbroeck's this was meant to solve. And what kind of person Van Hoensbroeck was that he would find those instructions simple.

But then, it was, wasn't it? Nothing more than mixing ingredients in a bowl and letting it boil. No engraving gold or fasting while wearing purple cloaks. Unlike wild mint, he knew where to find peonies. Write in lead? With a pencil. The letter showed exactly what to draw. What was an alembic?

Along a shelf, he ran his fingers over an empty bottle sitting in a metal tray, bulbous glass suspended on four brass legs. Behind it was an oil lamp which fit underneath; when lit it would heat the glass or whatever else was on top. He popped the bottle off and twirled the tray. Back further were more knickknacks: metal caps, glass stoppers, a red-brown dish. Copper. It seemed real as far as Jasper could tell, and why wouldn't it be? The letter was Van Hoensbroeck's; of course he would have tried the spell. Everything it needed must have been here.

Jasper cleared the desk. The copper hummed as it settled on the tray. The mound-shaped lamp still had a good wick on it. A shake by his ear told him there was liquid inside. The tray and dish were sturdy. The lamp was ready to burn. He was smiling wide. The spell *was* simple, so much so that he could do it tonight. It had worked for E. Ashmole's wife's friend, it had probably worked for Pieter Van Hoensbroeck, and if Jasper didn't get it right, then Ansehelm could. Protection was something they needed. They could make as many garnet spheres as they wanted.

What else did he need? Combing the shelves again, he found blank parchment, a long bottle which was—he forced the stopper open—yes, oil. Enough for the lamp and the spell. He didn't know if the type of oil mattered, but anything in this room must work for magic. A box with seven compartments, carved with seven different symbols, rested towards the back of a top shelf. Teasing it forward with his fingers, it occurred to him that even oil must congeal after a few hundred years, and both that bottle and the lamp must be more recent than Van Hoensbroeck. Ansehelm's? Or Robert Morlen's? The box slid into his palms.

He unlatched the first compartment, bearing a circle with a dot in the center. Empty. The second one was carved with a crescent moon. Empty. So were the next two, but in the compartment after that he found marble-sized spheres of metal. Steel or iron. The next, fuller, looked like silver at first, but when he picked a ball up, its glint was dull and yellowy. The seventh compartment held a single dull chunk that laced his fingers with lead dust. Perfect. Better than trying to squeeze it from a pencil.

All that was left were peonies and water. He dipped his head out the window. Damp, not raining, and under the clouds, it looked as dull and dense as the lead.

Outside, the night air crawled over him, sweat pooling under his clothes even as he shivered. The forest murmured beyond the walls. At the pond, he caught the shimmer of fish darting away from the lantern light. So, there were some. None ever went into his net. He dipped the canteen into the freezing pond. A pinch on his finger, and he nearly spilled all the water he'd collected pulling the leech off. He hadn't put his hand in that deep, but maybe it recognized him. Decided to attack the giant that came daily to carry its friends off to their doom. He ripped a handful of peonies from the ground on his way out.

Away from the garden, a pierce of cackles stopped him in place. Coyotes. Out in the woods somewhere; still, he checked his surroundings. Weeds, grass, fog. He looked twice to his left. Between the netted branches was a head, shoulders. His eyes froze on it. The lantern only shone so far. A shadow, it looked like of a person.

If it was there, it was high up, standing near the top of the wall. Impossible to tell on which side. The overgrowth obscured it as much as the dark did.

"Hey!" Jasper called, shaking the lantern. He could still see the figure; it might have moved. Might have not. Slowly he laid the flowers and canteen down and shifted his hand around his pocket knife.

"Hey, look, this is private property; you can't be here." He tried not to sound frightened, like he was in his building, brothers and the guys all around. Like he had never heard of necromancy or found a man chained in a tower. "I don't think you have any business with Mr. Lambert at this time of night, so get lost."

No movement. The coyote cackles billowed up again, and he jumped. When he looked again, there were only the branches curling at the top of the overgrowth. Whipping back inside, he told himself no one had been there in the first place. Seeing things.

The warm red-gold of the copper greeted him in the laboratory. Even if someone was out there, he'd be more than protected soon enough.

Sigil in the copper. Water, oil, crushed peony heads, lead. He refilled the lamp, licked his fingers to straighten the wick, and lit it under the brew. It was the dead of night. He left with the lamp's glow in his peripheral. Once the moisture evaporated, it would be complete. A garnet sphere to ward off all evils.

Carrying the amulet in his pocket, walking down 10th Avenue, he'd watch the pickpockets and cops careen out of his way, repelled by a force they couldn't comprehend. Or perhaps it would work differently—instead of a repellent, people would see him and, for no reason they could understand, take a liking to him. The last person in the world anyone would want to hurt. Nobody's enemy.

He realized that since seeing the shadow by the wall, he'd been running his tongue over the thirty-two teeth that were, thankfully, still in his mouth.

CHAPTER TWELVE

U P BEFORE DAWN, Jasper was putting his boots on when the servant bells rattled. The others shook awake, poor Ned covering his ears with his pillow. Mr. Thorley noticed Jasper already dressed.

"You're up; go see what the trouble is. I'll be there," he yawned, "as soon as possible."

Biting down his annoyance, Jasper headed upstairs. The apartment parlor was dark, but he heard William and Cordelia moaning behind their door. He knocked and was met with them both in wet, stained dressing gowns, water dripping from their jowls.

"It's you," Mrs. Lambert hissed, wringing her shawl out in his direction.

"Everyone's coming—"

"This ceiling must be fixed at once!" Mr. Lambert bellowed.

"What—"

"We were woken up by this cold, disgusting rain water in the middle of the night!" he said, pointing at the ceiling and the soaked bedsheets below it.

"A leak?" Jasper was glad he was in his old clothes. "I can take a look, no problem."

"You certainly will," said Mr. Lambert with a harrumph.

"Be careful! Don't dirty the sheets any more than they already are," Cordelia snapped as Jasper pushed the bed to the side.

"Yes, ma'am," he said. The ceiling was low, painted wood, which he could see clearly enough when he held a candle up. There wasn't any visible water damage, nothing leaking now, and no obvious hole. He glanced back at the Lamberts, who were soaked like a bucket had been dropped on them. There was no way that much water had come from this ceiling.

"Oh, yeah, I see the problem," he said. "Pretty bad leak, but I can fix it. Might take all morning, though. I won't be able to do it and my serving duties."

"*Fine*," Mr. Lambert said. The butler appeared with Maja, who took them away to get cleaned up. Jasper grabbed a ladder and tools as the Lamberts dressed; they didn't need to know he wouldn't use them. They him left alone in the room to work. Before closing the doors of the bedroom, he asked Mr. Thorley to drop him off some coffee and breakfast.

He got the fire roaring and twirled a scraper in his hand. There was a patterned rug under his feet. He laid down, running his fingers over tight chords of fabric. He wondered how his mother was doing. And how the boarders were, alone with her, without him as a buffer between them. Mrs. Cappelli might murder her. Thinking that pinged some guilt—his mother was hard to get along with, but she wasn't a monster. No better or worse than any person who had been through what she had.

There was a knock. Dottie had brought him a pot of coffee and plate of eggs. They gossiped about what had happened, Jasper playing up the seriousness of the leak. He tried to fill the door frame in order to block her view, in case she had more guile than the Lamberts. She didn't appear to suspect. There was more to complain about besides the leaky ceiling, she reported, as a letter from the town realtor had arrived, informing them of unexpected delays regarding the new staff. Something vague about contract mix-ups, full of excuses if you were to ask Mr. Lambert. The realtor also kept mentioning the issue of the vanished groundskeeper, which William found irksome, as it should not affect the hiring process. For Dottie, the new people couldn't get here fast enough. Jasper agreed, and when she was gone, he ate by the fire.

He would have to keep the lie going with Leo too. Another one. Not something he relished, but he didn't feel bad—he wanted a break, and they wouldn't give it to him for free.

It wasn't like he told Leo everything, otherwise. Even before the castle, he rarely shared, not for any real reason but because he wouldn't bother talking about himself. It never felt there was room to. In the Madison Avenue house, when he was laying on satin pillows and being offered some leathery liquor in a crystal glass, he didn't want to bring up his life in the 47th Street apartment. And Leo didn't ask. So

Jasper was telling a few direct lies on top of the omissions. Nothing he couldn't keep up.

On the far wall, a panel slid open against the floor, half covered by the bed. Jasper crouched near so he could face it as best he could. Two eyes glowed from within.

"Ansehelm?"

"Jasper."

He apologized for not visiting that morning.

"It is my own fault," Ansehelm said, sinister glee in his voice.

"What'd you do?" Jasper laughed. "Dump water on them?"

"Yes."

Jasper could not see his face, but he was sure Ansehelm's lips were curled in that skull smirk.

"What for?" Jasper asked.

Ansehelm grunted. "The bottle you had so kindly put out for the rain in my tower was full. I thought of pouring it on the girl. But the parents irritate me more so, particularly that new master of the house."

Jasper shook his head, grinning despite himself. "Why do that to somebody at all?"

"To allow myself some pleasure."

He said it almost innocently. Jasper bit the inside of his cheek to stop himself from laughing. Ansehelm got his kicks like a child would. He remembered a younger sister who used to bite legs whenever she was unhappy.

"You're not worried about getting caught?" Jasper said.

There was a pause before Ansehelm asked, "Did your masters say they suspect a man?"

"They think it's a leak."

"See? That is so foolish, it proves that they deserved it." The pitch in Ansehelm's voice rose. "They do not even understand the roof over their heads."

"Well, I got a morning off."

"All the better."

"You want some coffee?" Jasper figured Ansehelm should reap the rewards of the prank too and brought the tray over. "There's plenty left. Eggs? You don't have to chew." He pushed some onto a saucer and held it out. After some hesitation the bony fingers sucked it into the dark.

"Thank you," Ansehelm said.

"Oh, and I didn't tell you—I'm trying out this protection spell." At first he felt silly saying it out loud, but when out of the dark the pinpoint eyes fastened on him, Jasper couldn't help a twist of pride.

"How did that come to be?" Ansehelm leaned forward, face half visible now.

"In Van Hoensbroeck's old papers there was one, supposed to make an amulet you can use to protect yourself. It was in English. I started it already, it's easy to do—"

"Easy. Now you think it is all easy."

"I mean, the steps weren't hard. You need a copper plate, but there was one, and if it works, it might really help you—"

"Oh." Ansehelm's mouth hung open, skin sagging like it would snap. "The copper plate. Spheres of garnet, yes?"

Jasper nodded.

"No, it will not work."

Jasper's heart sank. "I already started it," he said in protest. Ansehelm retreated back into the dark.

"What I mean is that it will not protect me. The spell is sound, but the letter mentions devils and spirits, does it not? It is for protection against the otherworldly opponent. But we deal with men, so it is useless. Bring me wild mint, and we will make a spell that will help your peace of mind."

"You mean, it drives out ghosts? Or demons?" Jasper asked.

"'Yes' is the simple answer I will give to *you*, who has no knowledge these matters." Ansehelm snorted. "I will show you a spell that prevents bodily harm if you bring me the ingredients I ask for."

"But the spell I started does work," Jasper said. "It'll make an amulet."

"Yes," Ansehelm said slowly. "It could be done by a skilled practitioner. There is more one must do than follow material instructions. Still, I wish you luck on your first attempt. If you fail, as is likely, please do not moan about it to me. It is burning somewhere hidden from prying eyes, yes?"

Jasper gulped down a nervous grunt. He told Ansehelm yes. None of the others had been in the third tower yet; he hadn't thought of it as a problem. Too swept up in excitement, but he was sure it would be fine.

"You doing okay crawling around with that thing on?" Jasper clutched his own neck.

"I am," he said. "It has been so long, I am used to the weight. Although I must move so very slowly. That is painful in itself."

"You don't think you should rest?" Jasper asked. He couldn't see, but the scoff from the dark made him imagine Ansehelm's expression twisting in disgust.

"I do rest. I have been forced to be immobile for so long, you do not understand the joy I feel even to see the tunnels. If you had not come along when you did, Jasper, I might have forgotten how to speak. Isolated from everyone and thing. Left to decay into living rot. No distraction, no sustenance, no relief. Only time that must be endured..." He dwindled into silence long enough to make Jasper twitch. "Have you ever starved?"

"Yeah," Jasper said. Sun-bright yolk bled over his fork. He remembered the hunger pangs, the family begging and crying and shouting. But never the way Ansehelm had; never to the point of death. Chewing on a strand of fried egg white, he said, "So you just felt like dumping dirty water on them?"

Ansehelm's tongue smacked against his gums. "I hear them, those people in my house, and sometimes I become so bothered by their foolishness that I cannot abide it. That is a failing of mine. Yet still, it is good to remind people—especially young ones—that the world does not bend to their will."

"The Lamberts would disagree with you on that," Jasper said.

"It does not matter what they agree to!" Ansehelm hissed. "People today always *arguing*. They think that if they do not want something to be, then it will not. That if the law or the church agrees with them, reality will change. Anyone can vindicate anything with words. I have seen it all—it is worth nothing but kindling. I could *argue* that it was immoral for my enemies to lock me in this tower, but that would not stop it from happening, would it?"

Jasper shook his head.

"Or from starving me! Or from torturing me! It happened whether I wanted it to or not, whether I believe I *deserved* it or if it was *justified*. Your masters have a paper that say they own the castle, but their servant boy already knows it better than they. What do these walls care for them? Yet they assume they are not vulnerable, because they believe they ought not be, because of their paper. The senselessness confounds me."

The speech rolled around Jasper's brain. "Senseless" wasn't the word that came to mind, not exactly, when he thought of the Lamberts. They only cared about what they cared about. What was the word for that?

From the dark, he heard fingers against the plate.

"I can try to get you more of those. Better than leeches," Jasper laughed. "Things will get easier soon. Besides, you can't plan to eat worms for the rest of your life?"

"No, that I do not intend," he said, giving a quick goodbye before the panel closed.

Jasper held the coffee mug in the fire to warm it up. He wondered how long it had taken Ansehelm to do all that, crawling down to the apartment bedroom with a bottle of rain water. Was that his plan, to irritate the Lamberts away? It could work. Of all the things in the world to hate, what the Lamberts loathed most appeared to be inconvenience.

Leo swung the bedroom door open to find Jasper on the rug.

"You're not working?" he asked.

"I *just* finished," Jasper said.

"Excellent. Do change and bring me lunch." Leo slapped the wall before darting away, and Jasper accepted his sojourn was over.

Cordelia and her daughters sat slumped in the great hall as Jasper passed through, pearl strings clicking on the table wood. The storm was up again, it was dark even at noon, and they were running out of candles, but, of course, no one could get down the mountain. They needed gas installed, but how could they plan that when it was taking this long just to get a staff up here?

"I am sick of holding my tongue about this ghastly place," Florence opined. "A ridiculous purchase, no modern amenities, no one running it, everything in the hands of incompetent country rubes. Unacceptable that our arrival wasn't prepared for, and incomprehensible that it still is not rectified. If the mail was able to come, staff could come too, but I suppose no one wants to work!"

Elsie licked her lips. "We'll have to chop down trees for warmth and hunt rabbits in the woods. Can you imagine killing a rabbit?"

Dropping into the kitchen, Jasper felt himself being looked at. Dottie, Irene, and Frankie had on gleeful smiles.

"Mister and Missus really picked the worst room in the place, huh?" Frankie grinned as the spoon he was holding dripped broth.

"Yeah," Jasper laughed. Irene bit her knuckle to hold her laughter.

"They deserve it for dragging us up here," said Frankie, sending the maids into scandalous cackles.

Without looking up from the stove, Proulx said, "Careful who hears you."

The four smirked silently with each other. Jasper said, "Oh, I need lunch for—"

"I'll fix it for you while you change," Frankie said. Jasper patted the coarse wool of his slacks as he walked to the dorm. Dottie said under her breath, "*Right on their heads.*"

CHAPTER THIRTEEN

FEET IN THE STIFF shoes, Jasper carried lunch the length of the castle, feeling dull until Leo greeted him with a hug and chipper smile. No broken glass. Lunch waited, Leo eager and tender, and afterwards Jasper wallowed on the bed as Leo moved on from him to the food. Chard, cheese, walnut salad, bacon, toast, and some kind of pastry with glassy orange frosting.

"I'm not surprised it took you all morning to patch that leak. Mother and Father were *drenched.*" Leo's toes brushed Jasper's thigh. "How big was the hole?"

"Pshh," Jasper said. "It must have been, I mean this, no, this big?" He stretched his arms awkwardly while lying on his side.

Leo shook his head. "Ridiculous. Absurd. I'm sure Father never had it inspected, but he has the nerve to lecture me on business. Preposterous. Speaking of, how's Billy's mood doing this afternoon?"

"I didn't see him."

"I had to have breakfast with them; it was unbearable. Mother too. You wouldn't believe how much two old people can complain. Elsie gets it from them, by the way. And Florence is a complainer too, come to think of it. I absolutely cannot stand it sometimes," Leo said. The stem of a chard leaf stuck out his mouth as Jasper patted his leg in sympathy. Brushing the rough hairs felt tantalizing.

"After this, let's go exploring." Leo scraped his fork over the plate. "I have my sight on the last tower. No one's been there yet; there has to be something interesting stowed away. Oh, and I hate these, do you want it?"

Jasper was glad Leo held up the orange pastry, because it gave him something to react to. He wasn't sure what kind of face he made, but he regarded the crumbling cake deliberately as he took it.

"Probably just another bedroom," he tried to say like it was the most boring thing imaginable.

The spell was burning in there. They'd know something was wrong, think it was a stranger in the house. And they'd be right, however accidentally, which would get out to the town, and whoever Ansehelm's villains were would come back. A bite into the pastry and his tongue felt swollen from sugar, teeth stuck with bits of dry dough.

"Awful, aren't they?" Leo said, already dressing.

The false door was shut. He was sure of it. Almost sure. There wasn't anything that could incriminate him personally, which was a selfish thought. Brushing his tongue over his molars, he considered confessing to Leo about the spell. He could say he found it and was playing around. No need to include tunnels or prisoners in the equation. Leo would still be upset, but it might be the safest option, to trust him with a small secret rather than risk the full truth. But best if he never saw it at all.

Naked on the bed, Jasper pulled him into a kiss. Leo's hand cupped his head. Why explore when they could spend their time doing this? But Leo broke away, hopping on one foot as he put a sock on.

"Come on, I can't stay in bed all day."

Leo marched down and headed straight for the third tower. Across the battlements, Jasper pointed out the crossbow and every other stray weapon he saw below, hoping to sway the other's attention. When that didn't work, he backtracked down the stairs and into the armory, leaving a peeved Leo on the ledge above.

A sword hung just within reach. Jasper's fingers brushed the underside of the hilt enough to glide it off its hook, catching it before it fell. He staggered back, adjusting to its weight. The blade was larger up close, flat and long, with braided olive rope on its hilt. It sliced through the air with clear *whoosh*.

Now Leo had joined him, unable to resist. Jasper asked how old he thought it was as he showed the sword off.

"Certainly looks medieval." Leo took it, holding it out with his arm bent. "You know, I'm on the fencing squad at Columbia."

"So you know how to use that?"

Leo demonstrated a few lunges, legs quick, but his arm dragged by the heaviness of the blade.

"It's not a fencing sword," Jasper offered as a condolence.

"I'm not *very* good either," Leo laughed. "I only joined because—" He shut his lips abruptly and sliced the air.

Another set of footsteps. Both men looked up with a spike of fear. But they weren't touching; were dressed appropriately. Jasper cleared his throat and folded his hands behind his back, something that felt proper. Sword pointed down, Leo leaned on it like a cane.

"Oh, Mr. Lambert," Maja said. "I came looking for you. Your mother wishes to see you."

He sighed. "Now?"

"Yes, sir."

With a forlorn glance towards the third tower, Leo asked, "Can't you tell her I'm busy?"

"Ah…" Maja squinted. Cordelia Lambert knew none of her children had anything to be busy with up here.

"*Fine*," Leo sighed. He strutted past her towards the front of the castle. A relief that the alchemist's laboratory was still Jasper's own. Still disappointing that their time together had been cut short. It was a long walk with Maja between them.

In the apartments they learned that all Mrs. Lambert wanted was her son's company, and Leo tried not to visibly sulk as Thorley conscripted Jasper away. They needed to inspect for water damage around the castle. Couldn't have more leaks.

"We'll start with Miss Elsie's room." Thorley marched across the hall with Jasper in tow. "You didn't happen to notice anything when you stayed there?"

"No. No leaks, I don't think. No men in the walls!" He cracked a smile. Thorley didn't return it.

"We ought to check anyway. How many days ago was that?" he sighed, casting a glance at the tower base. "Is the blood still visible?"

There were some brown-gray spots where Ned had landed. Thorley shuddered as they climbed, declaring that they would have to clean it again.

Elsie wasn't there, her books and clothes strewn over the room. The butler was careful to step around everything, not even picking a pencil off the floor.

"Tell me if there's anything that needs to be fixed before Miss Elsie gets rained on too," Thorley said. If they wanted to check the ceiling, Jasper reminded him, he needed something to stand on. With a huff, Thorley cleared off a chair.

Jasper stepped up and stared at white plaster. He didn't really know what to look for beyond the obvious; Thorley could probably do just as well at this as he would. His faking this morning might have given them the wrong impression. "I'm not an expert," he said.

"I'm certain you are not," the butler said. "Just go do it."

Jasper scanned for cracks and discolorations, lingering over the bed where he knew the trap door to be. Difficult to make out even when looking for it, which was a good sign. Thorley asked if he could see well enough between the roof beams. He said yes, though he could not. The room seemed fine, the attic cell a buffer between it and the roof. He announced he didn't see any serious damage.

"Good. Good." Mr. Thorley wiped the chair off. "You know, Jasper, I believe I last saw you in March. You were at the townhouse almost a week, and when I gave you your wages, I remember we had a small conversation. You never mentioned you had met Mr. Lambert."

Jasper turned to face him with an open mouth. "I didn't."

"No?" Thorley balked. "He knew you enough to hire you here."

Leo. The other Mr. Lambert. "Oh, oh! Mr. Lambert…junior." Jasper breathed deep and put his hands on his sides in a display of casualness. "Yeah, yeah, we got to talking."

"And?"

Arms crossed now, Jasper cut his nails into his palm.

"When did he offer you a job as his valet?" Thorley stretched the words as he basked in the absurdity of the situation. "Because the day before we left, Charlie Briscoe was set to accompany Mr. Lambert to the castle, but then there *you* were instead, and I learn second-hand that apparently he's been fired. So how and when did you enter into all this?"

To stall, Jasper cleared his throat. He thought of bluffing his way out of giving an answer altogether. Did the butler need an explanation? They were all employed by the Lambert family, whose members were allowed to change staff as they pleased. Leo must have a usual method of choosing who worked for him; hadn't he done that? Apparently not, and now Jasper needed a lie.

"Well…" He coughed. "What happened was…" He coughed again. Did it sound fake? "I didn't say before, because I was nervous. What happened was that the night before you all were leaving for here, Mr. Lambert saw me on the street. He said he'd just fired his valet. I don't know why, I never met Charlie, and Mr. Lambert never explained. He said he needed someone, and he recognized me. Maybe he thought I already worked full time for you. I was doing a job for another family on the block, that's why I was around there. And, he said he was going to a castle and, I don't know, it sounded fun." Jasper ended it with a big shrug, and a grin. His ears felt on fire.

Mr. Thorley peeled back, eyes narrowed. It wasn't too bad a lie, was it? The details all matched. Leo didn't come across well, but Thorley didn't seem to like him much anyway. And he had all but admitted to firing Charlie.

"So," Mr. Thorley said at last, "you have no experience as a valet, or *any*thing, besides as a handyman?"

Jasper shook his head. "See, that's the only reason I didn't tell you before, because it's embarrass—"

Thorley put a hand up. "And then when an… *idiot*…offered you a job you were grossly unqualified for, you agreed because a castle sounded like fun?" He'd hissed *idiot* under his breath, a catharsis he made sure to say quietly.

"Guess so." Jasper curled in.

Mr. Thorley turned away with his fingers on his temples, muttering, "*The both of them.*" A clamor up the stairs drew their attention, as Elsie and Florence blew into the room shouting at each other.

Elsie stuck her tongue out when she saw them. "What are you doing in here? This is my bedroom!"

"Checking for water damage, Miss Elsie," the butler said. "Don't want what happened to your parents to happen to you."

"Just get out, get out!" She threw her arms in the air, face red. "You too, Flo!"

"Elsie, you spoiled rotten child, I demand you apologize—"

Jasper and Thorley weren't there long enough to learn what it was about, slipping out the door as Florence berated her sister. The butler hunched lower as they descended, and by the bottom of the tower, he was entirely bent over. He shot Jasper a weary look.

"You are fit to fix leaks," he said, part question, part statement of reassurance.

Jasper nodded. For a moment Thorley hung there, looking at him with a resigned shrug. Grudging acceptance—that was fine enough. He had to remember to tell Leo the story so they could keep it straight.

Forcing himself up and smoothing down his sleeves, the butler led them into the apartments. Mr. and Mrs. Lambert were having tea in the parlor, and since they were so concerned about the ceilings, they tolerated Jasper and Thorley milling around. Jasper followed the butler's lead, skirting the bubble of space where the Lamberts sat. Maja clinked a gilded white pot as the pair chatted.

Cordelia could simply not forgive the incompetence of that realtor. William worried he was not spending enough time with his son, who was at an age where coaching in business and matters of life were crucial. Cordelia agreed that Leo was unfocused but believed he shared his father's raw acumen. He could—*would*—be a great success but perhaps needed more masculine influences in his life. As for the girls, Florence leaned too far into being a New Woman, but she had a good head on her shoulders, unlike her sister. At least Elsie had her health back. When the true summer weather rolled in, she would make a complete recovery.

Regarding the castle, William was, overall, entirely satisfied. All their problems thus far were unfortunate, leak be damned, but nothing that could not be overcome in order to realize his plans for the property. He had not become the man of business he was by shirking from complications. His wife applauded him, in the same breath pointing out that the clock in the parlor corner had stopped. Another thing to be fixed. And Mr. Lambert's watch wasn't working either. Perhaps it got rained on, Cordelia muttered. William asked Maja to fetch the other one, his grandfather's good watch.

From a stool, Jasper inspected seams up the chimney. A bulge under the plaster caught his attention, and he titled over the mantle for a closer look. Maja didn't know where the other watch had gone. Mr. Lambert huffed that it should be in its box where it always was—he did not store his grandfather's silver-plated Lagisse pocket watch just anywhere. Jasper pointed the bulge out to Thorley, discerning how serious it might be. The chimney had stayed dry, so the crown must be intact, but there could be damage elsewhere allowing water to seep between the walls. The voices behind him were growing sharper. The butler kept turning his head.

"Mr. Lambert, Mrs. Lambert, is something the matter?" Thorley asked. William grumbled that the maid could not find the watch.

Cordelia Lambert's head cocked, eyes narrowing as they switched from her husband to the servants. "Perhaps there is a reason she cannot find it." She locked on to Jasper.

How wet or dry the plaster felt preoccupied him until he noticed the background speech had stopped, and he pivoted to four pairs of eyes staring him down. He stepped off the stool.

"You were in our bedroom unsupervised all morning," Mrs. Lambert said. "Turn out your pockets."

Palms up, Jasper stammered, "I didn't take anything."

Her fingers were interlocked over her lap, borders of her skirt disappearing under the furniture, shoulders back. She could be posing for a picture if not for her face dripping with disgust. William's expression morphed to match his wife's as the idea of a thief took hold.

"You were ordered to turn your pockets out, boy," Mr. Lambert said. Jasper glanced at Thorley and Maja, poised in place. Bristling, he complied. Flimsy fabric splayed out of his pants and tailcoat. Matches, knife, his own watch. When she saw the round shape, Cordelia lit up, but it was only a moment. No one could mistake any of his things for her husband's.

Jasper swallowed. "I would never—"

Gliding towards the mantle, Mrs. Lambert eyed his hands as if a diamond might fall from them. "You were in here hours ago, and not in uniform. You could have already hidden away what you stole."

"No, really—" The words died, constricted by a hot nervousness that had overtaken him.

"We must search his belongings," William said to Mr. Thorley.

"Of course. This is a serious matter, which we will investigate at once." The butler gave Jasper a pitying half-glance and stepped behind him. A pseudo-arrest. Maja frowned over the teapot. Mr. Lambert asked Cordelia if she wouldn't stay here rather than endure the men's dormitory, but she was adamant about seeing the evidence for herself.

"I—" Jasper looked to Thorley in a last plea. "I'm not a thief."

Mr. Thorley sucked in a breath. "Then there will be nothing to find." He clapped Jasper's shoulder and pushed.

They marched him out, Thorley on top of him, Mr. and Mrs. Lambert drawn behind. For all the excuses they'd bought, *now* he was a liar. Well, they wouldn't find any expensive pocket watches stowed away in his bag.

They would find the map.

Jasper stopped dead in his tracks. Thorley nudged him; he had to keep walking. His chest hurt. What could he possibly say to explain it? Had to think rationally. He didn't have to tell them about Ansehelm or the tunnels. He needed to act like the map wasn't important. Say he found it on a floor in some empty room, covered in dirt, and just thought it was neat. He was going to show it to somebody but forgot, what with everything going on. Yes—he'd say he found it last night, after everyone had gone to sleep. What with the leak and all, it had simply slipped his mind. If pressed, he'd pretend he didn't know what it was at all, not being in English, the diagrams a bit too technical for his understanding. Playing ignorant could work. They thought low enough of him to begin with.

On the other hand, they wanted any excuse to call him a thief. Cordelia Lambert had been more angry than relieved when a priceless watch hadn't spilled out from his jacket.

Frankie gaped open-mouthed as the party descended into the kitchen. Must be serious if the Lamberts were down here. Jasper's pockets were still turned out. He'd just left them that way, and now everyone could tell what had happened. Kitchen steam felt cool on his neck.

Ned startled as they stomped, grim-faced, into the dormitory. Jasper's cot was all the way down, clothes laid over the headboard, amorphous cloth bag by the foot. Mrs. Lambert's lip curled as she stood with her husband over the cot. He was frozen against the wall as Thorley picked through the pockets of his old clothes.

Jasper saw Ned looking but couldn't read his expression from so far down. Some of the others had coagulated around dorm's entrance, poking half-faces in, ready to flee should the Lamberts look their way. Frankie, Horace, Verna, Dottie. Nothing in his other pockets. Thorley moved on to his luggage.

Oh, that. Something I found on the floor. I was gonna show it to somebody but forgot and, anyway, it's just an old piece of paper.

Maybe he'd get away with having the map, but what if they used it to find the tunnels?

The Lamberts watched unblinking as Mr. Thorley rifled through the bag. A razor, comb, more matches, toothbrush, a small and cracked mirror, a money clip. Thorley counted the bills and coins in a pouch to check it wasn't too high for Jasper's grade. It wasn't. Keys to his and his mother's apartment. Nail file. Another clip of calling cards and addresses. A mottled dime novel, pencil nubs, work gloves. No map.

He didn't know how that could have happened, but for the moment, he reveled in his luck.

Everything emptied out, Thorley held the bag open wide to Cordelia and William.

"Nothing that could have been taken," the butler said. He turned over Jasper's boots, just to be sure.

Mrs. Lambert glowered at the bag as if it had betrayed her.

"Take off those shoes," she barked and pointed at Jasper's feet. Biting down bile, he did, knocking them against the bedframe so the lint shook out.

It was maybe a minute that he watched the Lamberts' faces twist.

"We have not checked under the bed," William pointed out.

"Mr. Lambert!" Maja scrambled in carrying a dark, square box. The lid opened to an antique silver pocket watch.

William Lambert put his hand on his heart. The box must have gotten knocked out of sight when she cleaned, Maja explained. Mrs. Lambert looked back at the cot and said, "Check."

Mr. Thorley looked under the bed and in the sheets. Even lifted the mattress. Cordelia's glare lingered on empty space as William delighted in the box.

"All is well, then," he said and lifted his grandfather's watch from its blue satin lining, "My word, look at the time. Darling, let's do resume tea. I cannot drink it any later than this or I'll never sleep!"

"Yes. Let's." Mrs. Lambert forced her scowl off. The crowd at the entrance scattered as they left.

Jasper flopped, bent on the bed, scrunching his socks against the floor. Mr. Thorley had stayed to repack his bag.

"Told you I'm not a thief."

"Yes. Well." Thorley gave him an apologetic smile. "Try not to get on their nerves. You are the unfamiliar face around here. Why don't you take a moment to collect yourself? Not too much time."

The butler clipped out the dormitory, and Ned called, "Alright down there?"

"Yeah, I'm fine," Jasper laugh-groaned, shuffling over to the driver. "I mean, they misplace a watch for five minutes, and suddenly I'm about to be arrested."

Ned frowned lopsided while pushing bandages away from his eye.

"How's your head?" Jasper asked.

"Better. Leg, on the other hand…" He shrugged. "Verna says the break was worse than she initially thought. I don't know what can be done except wait and hope it isn't infected. But the head injury is less serious, and I would hate for it to be the other way around."

"I hope you get better soon."

"Same here, same here." He rubbed his temples. "This room is starting to get to me. Right before you all came down, I swear I saw…"

Ned looked away and back with a shudder.

"What?" Jasper asked.

The driver pursed his lips. "Now, understand that these are the visions of an injured man who has been confined to a bed for five days. I'm rational enough to know I'm seeing things. It was as if there was something moving along the floor." He pointed down the hall, towards Jasper's cot. "Crawling like a snake but white like a skeleton. Noises like steel scraping. Never quite went into the light, so I couldn't get a good look." He laughed. "I mean, of course it didn't. Because I imagined it."

Ansehelm had taken the map before the Lamberts could find it. It still seemed impossible, but he could have heard what was happening in the apartments and somehow made it through the tunnels in time to protect their secret. He would have to have been there at just the right time, maybe behind the damp plaster Jasper had stuck his face in; had to have known just which room to go to and which path to take there. Jasper's eyes darted around for the trap door, wherever it was in the dormitory. He'd never checked the map for it, which seemed stupid in hindsight. Was it near his bed? The thought spooked him, not that he had good reason to feel that way. He and Ansehelm were the only ones in the walls.

"Didn't mean to scare you," Ned said. Jasper shook himself loose.

"Don't worry about it."

"It's what I get for having teased Dot about ghosts." He grinned.

"Well, the Lamberts think there's some mysterious intruder, and none of them have head injuries," Jasper said.

"Not that we know of," said Ned.

They got a laugh in before Jasper trudged back through the kitchen, meeting too-gentle smiles from the others. Thorley intercepted him in the great hall to suggest he find somewhere deep in the castle to clean.

"Try to be out of sight for a few hours," the butler said. That suited Jasper fine. He disappeared down the blank halls, wishing to curl up into himself until there was nothing left. Dreaming of arms holding him, he trudged all the way to the back tower only to find Leo wasn't there. And so he sulked along the battlements.

All he wanted was to lay in bed, allowed to do nothing, having his hair pet. He needed Leo to say something comforting and to understand how humiliating that had been.

Leo had to vouch for him with Cordelia. It had all been his idea in the first place; not Jasper's fault he had drawn the parents' ire. He hadn't done anything except be the unfamiliar face. He knew he didn't belong, was too rough, like a gawky, dumb, poor kid, but what could he do about it? This was Leo's plan.

What if Leo had gone to the third tower? Jasper clipped up, relieved to see it undisturbed, still kicking himself for his negligence. He could have found a way to secure it if he had tried, if he had thought about it for even a minute. Heavy air smelled of peony and oil smoke. The mixture had congealed into simmering slick lumps, and he fed the lamp more oil even as he wondered if he should tear the spell down. It was a liability, and it wouldn't help them even if it somehow didn't fail.

Door locked from the inside, the spell could stay for now. Jasper breathed out in the chair, heart still beating too fast. He really wished he could have seen Leo.

He folded the uniform over the chair, down to his undergarments. The Lamberts would notice dirt and, unlike the other night, he wouldn't risk it. He'd have to mind the shoes—combing the tunnels barefoot wasn't an option, even if he did look absurd. Ansehelm wouldn't mind him showing up like that. Better if he had some food to bring, but he could be forgiven that too. He needed to see a friend, and there was no one else.

CHAPTER FOURTEEN

I N THE TOWER CELL, Ansehelm slept prone on the floor until, woken by Jasper's light, he uncurled an arm to ask for leeches.

"No. Sorry, I wish I could have gotten you some more food." Jasper felt a self-conscious pang, sweating in his underwear, disturbing the man's rest because he wanted to talk. He put the lantern to the side to keep the brightness from irritating him.

"Then what did you come up here for?" asked Ansehelm.

"I lost the map."

"I took it, of course!" Ansehelm gave him a big toothless smile, bones creaking to life to reach for the paper. He handed it back, red ribbon and all.

With a thanks, Jasper rested the waxy parchment in his lap. He sat hugging his knees, feet flat so the shoes wouldn't scuff. He should be relieved Ansehelm had somehow pulled that off—he *wanted* to feel relief. Dread lingered, heart in a pit, and it wouldn't slow down. Pinching the meat of his arm, he waited for the bad feelings to break.

Ansehelm folded his fingers under his chin, friendly but serious, and said, "I am sorry they put you through all of that."

"Yeah, me too." Jasper bowed his head, staring at bare shins. "How did you know that was happening?"

"I hear through the walls. As soon as that woman accused you, I feared for the map's discovery," Ansehelm said.

"You knew it was in my bag?"

"You told me yourself that you kept it there."

Had he? Probably, Jasper thought. "You knew which one was mine?"

"Crawling down there and retrieving the map was a laborious task in my physical state, and I would prefer not to recount every detail."

"Sorry, sorry," Jasper said, remembering that he had woken him up. Ansehelm could have recognized the clothes on the bed. "Someone saw you, but he doesn't believe you were real."

"Preferable to anyone finding the map!"

It was, and fortunate Ansehelm had been listening in the apartment parlor at that just the right time.

"Were you following me?" Jasper blurted out.

Ansehelm's lip stiffened. "No, I was not," he said. "I was there because I wish to know as much as possible of what these new masters are planning. Of course, it is exhausting for me to move so much throughout the day; I certainly would not follow you around even if I desired to. You must believe yourself to be quite special."

"Sorry." He winced at the pitch in Ansehelm's voice. Jasper had interrupted his sleep, brought him nothing to eat, and now was accusing him of things.

"No matter," Ansehelm said, warmth somehow coming out of that sunken gaze. "I imagine you are feeling quite anxious at the moment."

"Thank you." Jasper breathed out. It felt like years since anyone had let him off the hook. He lowered himself on the floor and stared into the ceiling abyss, lantern light a faint glow in his peripheral. He could hear the brush of Ansehelm's fingers over the floorboards.

"I really hate those people," Jasper said.

"Did you not before?" Ansehelm sounded charmed.

Jasper had expected to pass by Leo's family unnoticed, not to be humiliated and threatened. He found himself babbling to Ansehelm about every little remark and incident the Lamberts, four of them at least, had inflicted on him since arriving at Kasteel Verlossen. Ansehelm listened like a teacher to the student recounting a lesson. Entitled, bratty, suspicious, ignorant people. Jasper apologized for ever having questioned why he would dump rain water on them.

Ansehelm laughed. "I listen to gather information, but it is burdensome for me to hear their nonsensical prattle. One must find relief."

"Yeah, well, I have to serve them." Jasper dragged his hands down his face. Maybe it would peel off. He twisted his nail under stubble, painful to pick at the hair, but he couldn't stop. Serve them. He wanted to stick his fingers down his throat and retch.

Ansehelm crawled to the trap door, finger to his lips as he lifted it. Just a miniscule amount, and he stuck his eye through for a beat before closing it again.

"She is sitting alone." He beckoned Jasper. "Pick the old chain up and drop it on the ground."

"What? No. It'll—"

"Follow my instructions, you will see." Ansehelm waved a dismissive hand. "I am not strong enough to do it myself."

A bad idea to advertise their presence. Then again, Verna and Elsie had heard him scream on the first day and nothing had come of it. Last time he'd humored Ansehelm, he'd seen real magic, so maybe this would be worth it too. With both arms, he lifted the chain up to his chest and sent it crashing.

Ansehelm watched through the trap door. Flattening down next to him, Jasper saw a jumpy Elsie Lambert staring up. He wanted to snap the door shut, but Ansehelm didn't seem concerned. She wasn't looking at them, instead scanning nervously back and forth. Jasper remembered the thatched beams obscuring the ceiling. Frowning, Elsie settled on her desk chair and picked up a pencil.

"Again," Ansehelm mouthed. Jasper rolled his eyes, but as soon as he dropped the chain, he rushed to watch Elsie's reaction. She was frantic this time, pacing her room for source of the noise. They waited until, without a clue, she had nothing to do but sit back at the desk. Cautiously, she flicked her notebook's pages, easing back into work. As soon as she lifted her pencil, they brought the chain down again.

Elsie yelped, and Ansehelm brimmed with childish glee. It was infectious—Jasper cracked into a big grin. Elsie shouted for her nurse, her maid, her mother, anyone. It was only Verna who answered, head cocked as Elsie cried about thunderous crashes from above.

Perhaps it was the storm picking up, the nurse suggested, and why not lie down?

"I'll show you! It happens when I sit!" Elsie cried and plopped back on her chair. Nothing. She picked the book up, mimed writing. Nothing. Verna insisted on taking her temperature. Scarlet fever could return, unlikely as it was.

"When I was sick, I did not hear phantom noises, did I?" Elsie snapped right before the thermometer went under her tongue. She glared at the ceiling. Jasper remembered Cordelia scowling at his empty pockets.

No fever. Verna promised to send Dottie up with tea, and, if they had any, chocolate. Nurse gone, Elsie curled on her bed in a pout. She closed her eyes. Ansehelm whispered, "Again."

With a shout, she ran from the tower.

Their eyes glinted at each other across the cell. Ansehelm crawled back to Jasper, touching the length of chain as if it were a pet.

"You enjoyed that, I can tell," he said. "And, of course, they will not believe her."

"You can't push it too far." Jasper's attempt at prudence was undermined by his own laughter.

"Naturally. But it is a way to feel some relief while we are both trapped," Ansehelm said.

"Both of us, yeah."

"Once I regain my health, I will tell you what is necessary in order to defeat those who imprisoned me and drive those people out. Then I will have this castle and, if you desire, which I believe you do, you may stay here and learn my tricks."

"I do," Jasper said in one swift breath, adding, "That's a while to go from here."

Ansehelm nodded. "I am feeling stronger."

"When you want real food, you tell me," Jasper said, thinking as he did that feeding Ansehelm would only get tougher. He went unnoticed now because the castle was so big and populated by a constantly occupied precious few, but that could change any day. And the Lamberts were on his case.

"Certainly I will, and I appreciate your continued efforts." Ansehelm knotted twig-thin fingers. "The leeches are still most helpful."

"Listen. The Lamberts, and the other staff here, they go into the town. If they mention noises and mirrors falling…"

"Yes. Yes. I understand. My assailants will only risk entering the castle and upsetting a prestigious man if they believe I have been rescued." Ansehelm grew quiet. "They only wish me to suffer. But they will not act based on the ravings of servants or that man's daughter. I suspect they want as little to do with that family as I."

"In that case…" Jasper shrugged. "Look, don't get caught. But if you wanna pass the time by scaring them, I won't stop you."

"You will participate, even." Ansehelm smiled.

"Can't say they don't deserve it," he said, "but lay off Leo. Mr. Lambert Junior, that is."

"Your master? Alright, if you say so, Jasper." His bony chin titled up. "I thought you might hate him the most."

Master made Jasper wince. It was just how Ansehelm talked.

"No, no, he's okay. And I have to spend a lot of time with him. I don't want weird stuff going on around us, y'know?"

"A fair request." He nodded in agreement. Not too suspicious of why. And Leo wasn't the same as his parents or siblings, anyway.

Would Ansehelm spy on them in Leo's tower? No. Ansehelm wasn't following Jasper, and it would be a huge strain for him to crawl all the way there when the real objects of his ire were in the opposite direction.

Jasper left, apologizing again for not bringing Ansehelm more food. Back in the laboratory, he inhaled dense floral air as he brushed dirt off the shoes. His brain pounded behind his eyes; he needed something fresh to breathe. He stashed the map on a shelf—not safe to have it anymore. If this amulet did form, would he be able to keep it on him without being accused of theft?

The oily clumps in the dish stuck closer together, and when Jasper looked down at them, he caught flares of molten red glinting from their cores. Embers coming to life. He peered closer, smoke not bothering him now, because the spell was working. The red brimmed to the surface, receded, but was back a little brighter each time. Something was growing under the oil.

Even if the garnet did nothing but scare away shadows, it was a feat unto itself.

He couldn't break it down, risk be damned. He would leave the door locked, go out through the tunnels.

He hurried underground, trusting an offshoot to take him to an abandoned room where he could redress. Not worth risking being late, not after what happened earlier. Though he wasn't half as upset as before. Commiserating with Ansehelm had been good, and then, there was the spell.

Tomorrow it would be ready. The headache returned.

░

All the way to the front of the castle only to have to turn around and fetch Leo for dinner, and the first thing Jasper got was,

"My mother thinks you're a thief."

Jasper hunched. "I'm not. They proved I'm not."

Arms crossed, Leo eyed him from the bed. "I got an earful from her about you. And Father took her side, obtuse as he is."

"She doesn't like me."

"You *can* be uncouth," Leo said. "Could you please try to be more delicate around her? I mean, for God's sake, how do you act around your mother?"

"I wasn't—" Jasper threw his hands up. "I was just there doing what Mr. Thorley asked me to. Your dad didn't even think the watch was stolen until your mother suggested it. And it wasn't, not by me or anybody."

Leo sighed. "It isn't like we haven't had a servant nick something before, and it doesn't help that my sister keeps hearing things. Has everyone on edge. You have to be nicer. I can't have them wondering why I hired you."

It was your idea. But what Jasper said was, "Did you tell her I wasn't a thief?"

"*Yes*," Leo said. "Obviously I did. She doesn't *believe* me. Look here, I like that you're unrefined, but I did not expect you to be in such close proximity to my mother, or any of them, and you simply have to be less—"

"I understand," Jasper cut him off.

"When the full staff arrives, you'll barely have to be in my family's presence," said Leo.

Jasper rubbed his temples, remembering he still had bad news deliver. Leo was peeved when Jasper told him about the lie he'd spun for Thorley. There was no choice but to go along with it, though it put Leo in an even worse mood. He didn't understand that the butler had put him on the spot. That Jasper couldn't just wave Mr. Thorley away.

At dinner, to be more delicate, Jasper pretended everyone and -thing besides himself was made of glass.

CHAPTER FIFTEEN

OTTIE AND JASPER were halfway down to the kitchen carrying a punch bowl and gravy boat, respectively, when Cordelia Lambert's shriek reverberated out from the apartments. It stopped Jasper in his tracks. Dottie about-faced and leapt up, punch splashing on the steps. A crowd was gathering as Mrs. Lambert whipped out into the hall.

"Someone has stolen my jewelry!"

She was met with blank stares from her family. Jasper's pulse beat quicker.

"The entire box is gone. Vanished!"

Mr. Lambert's face dropped. "Vanished? My dear wife, what is the meaning of this?"

"The meaning is that it is not here!" Her voice curdled. For a second, she seemed embarrassed to have snapped at her husband.

Florence opened her mouth, closed it, and opened it again to ask, "Mother, your *entire* jewelry box is gone?"

"Yes! And everything I brought with it. The Fouquet opal pendant. Great-grandmother Beaupre's sapphire peacock broach!"

"Not the gold bracelet I gave you last year!" William cried. "You did bring it, didn't you?"

"Yes, darling, and *yes*. It's all *gone*."

"The intruder—" Elsie lit up, and Leo swung his hand out to cover her mouth.

Cordelia tugged at her shawl, tendons protruding from her neck as her jaw clenched tighter. She was already looking dead-on at Jasper. He slid behind Dottie. That looked guilty, didn't it?

"Madame, this is terrible and shocking," Mr. Thorley said. "Please rest assured we will investigate this matter fully."

"We must call the police," she said.

"How?" asked Elsie.

"We ought to see the scene of the crime," said William.

Cordelia bobbed her head. "Yes. All of us. All of you, follow me." She was glaring at the staff, at Jasper. Maja scurried forward and asked if she needed anything.

"Only for you all to see the evidence. Then I am certain we will determine who committed this heinous act."

Maja glanced at Jasper. Irene and Dottie did too, and Mr. Thorley. And Proulx and Frankie. Pity and condemnation. Leo wasn't looking at him at all. Well, maybe that was for the best. If Leo looked at him too sympathetically, it could betray them.

Mr. Lambert led the way, taking his wife's hand as they filed into the master bedroom. She faced the crowd with a piercing eye.

"This is where I kept—" Cordelia fanned her arm in a loop to display the evidence, only to shirk away at the sight of a gilt bronze box resting unscathed on the bureau. Her nose crinkled. She opened the lid, gems and delicate chains popping out.

The four other Lamberts watched her with furrowed brows. There was a flash over Leo's eyes. William and Florence were frowning deeper by the second, but Flo tried to force a soft expression.

"Mother…"

"We need more light in here!" Mrs. Lambert shouted. Dottie rushed out of the room. Cordelia picked her pieces out one by one, sneering at each before setting it down on the bureau. Florence put a hand on her shoulder.

"This was *missing*," Cordelia seethed as she held great-grandmother Beaupre's peacock broach.

"It could have been moved," Leo suggested. He turned on his heels to the staff. "Did anyone move it?"

They shook their heads. Irene was trying her hardest not to laugh. Thorley was pressed so tight he looked like he was going to turn in on himself.

"It was *gone*. The entire box. Only a minute ago!" Mrs. Lambert stared back at her family. "I am not a woman of fancy."

Dottie returned with a haul of candles. Bracelets, earrings, broaches, rings, and necklaces glistened over the bureau and bed. All accounted for. The box looked like it had been squeezed underfoot, lid and drawers jutting out like guts. Cordelia stood in the center, arms at her sides, head titled as she went from livid to despondent.

"I did not imagine this."

"My dear, you have been under stress taking care of a household with such limited resources," Mr. Lambert said. "But all's well that ends well. Nothing has been nicked. And you are correct that it was far too dark in this room before."

"Mother, perhaps you want to take something for nerves?" Florence said. She looked back at her siblings, who offered nothing but squirming glances.

There was a minute where no one talked, Cordelia's eyes cast down, red in the face.

"Well. If that's it, then." Leo took a step back, looking at his parents expectantly.

"Yes. Yes, fine." William shooed him off.

Now he looked at Jasper, mouthing *brandy* with eyebrows arched. Proulx was the first of the staff to walk away, and the rest of them diffused out of the apartments. Jasper picked the gravy boat off the kitchen step he'd left it on. Frankie whistled low.

"It's one thing for the kids to hear noises, but—" He waved his finger in the air. "—*she* can't go crazy."

"How do you think *I* feel?" Maja said bouncing behind.

Frankie swerved and clapped Jasper on the back. "I thought you took it."

"No, I wouldn't," Jasper spat out. Too defensively. The sous-chef was grinning at him. Proulx told Frankie to be quiet. Maja chased down Verna for a nerve tonic, sedative, anything. A bell ringing sent Mr. Thorley back upstairs in a huff. Dottie bent over the counter and buried her face in her arms.

"What is wrong with this place?" she groaned into her sleeves.

"What is wrong with Mrs. Lambert," Irene corrected.

Verna was explaining the use of some substance to Maja as Jasper poured the brandy. Just as he was about to leave, the nurse slid next to him with fist furled around a small brown vial.

"For you. In case they get too much, it relieves stress." Verna flashed a smile and was gone. Jasper pocketed the vial, glancing around as if he'd gotten away with something. Irene noticed but was giving him a friendly look. Not wrong for him to have the tincture, was it? He wondered if Verna gave the others pharmaceuticals too. He had been too surprised to remember to thank her.

Upstairs, he kept an eye out for either the nurse or Leo as he passed through the hall. It was a toss-up whether the man would wait to walk with him. Not tonight. The lights in the great hall were burning down, and it soon grew dark down the corridor. He lit his own candle, balanced in its holder on the tray. The flame reflected in the curve of the snifter.

Jasper found Leo sitting on his bed. The scratchy yellow quilt looked gold under the candlelight. He took the glass with a blank face. The neutrality of it unnerved Jasper, who found himself smiling bigger the more Leo stayed flat. When eventually Leo put an arm around him, relief washed over and he dropped onto the bed.

"We need to get out in the sunshine," Leo said, hint of desperation from the back of his throat.

"It'll happen eventually," said Jasper.

After a shudder, the man eased into his genial self. Jasper contorted to peel the uniform off as they kissed. He remembered being angry with Leo earlier as if it had happened to someone else, an alien feeling he was no longer obliged to contend with, because if Leo was happy, then he could be happy too.

Leaving that night felt worse than usual. Hand in his pocket, he squeezed Verna's tincture. The rubber stopper popped off, and he smelled lavender and lemon against stringent alcohol. Two bitter drops made his tongue recoil. He wafted through the empty halls and waited for his stress to disappear.

Jasper woke to Frankie rocking his shoulder.

"Butler's gonna yell at you."

Groggy, certain it was the middle of the night, Jasper blinked over the dorm. Pulling himself up felt like lifting Ansehelm's chain.

"It's dark," he said.

"Yeah, it's downpouring." Frankie grinned. The bare parts of his lip were discolored. Scars? He told Jasper the time. Late enough to shock him out of bed. He'd be late with Leo's breakfast no matter what, it was just a question of by how much. What about Ansehelm?

Ned waved to him, half-asleep under pelting rain. Outside was raging, the pass between the dormitories and kitchen completely flooded. A full moat had formed around the water pump. He idled on his toes at the edge of the dorm, dreading the thought of stepping outside. The pond must be overflowing, all the leeches and frogs and fish washed onto the ground.

Lights glowed in the kitchen. He bolted in, wiping his dripping face off with an equally wet hand. The chefs were already cleaning up the meal and the maids appeared to be long gone. Earl and Horace milled near the stove, taking in the last whiffs of steam. Jasper downed cold coffee as Mr. Thorley remarked that he'd prepared a breakfast tray for Mr. Lambert, which was ready whenever Jasper felt like doing his job. The tray dinged from a flick of Thorley's finger before the butler clipped upstairs.

Frankie glanced at the drivers. "Bet: which one of them do you think'll hear noises today?"

"Won't hear anything with the thunder," said Earl.

"Nah, nah, it's all in their heads anyway," Horace said. "It'll be the youngest. The fever garnered her too much attention, and now she wants more."

"Now, see, I disagree." Frankie had the affect of a scholarly debater. "It's a family illness. She heard noises yesterday, today it'll move to one of the others. Whoever has the least dignity. Missus, or the middle one. I'll bet a whole quarter."

"You cannot afford that," Proulx said.

"I can!" Frankie ran a coin over his knuckles. "Because I'm demanding a raise and then back-charging the Lamberts for *this*. And you all should too."

"You won't see any money," Earl grunted. The coin was a penny anyway.

"I'll bet you ten cents," said Horace, "that it's the youngest one."

"Deal. I say the middle one. Jasper, you want in?"

No, he didn't.

Proulx glared at his sous-chef. "Watch your talk."

In the hall, Jasper walked past Mrs. Lambert explaining to Dottie that, no, there would not be Sunday service today as there was no one to lead it, and furthermore, the chapel was still in extreme disrepair. Dottie said something about a church in town, but her words died as the thunder rolled. No one was getting down the mountain.

Leo was in bed, hand to his forehead, when Jasper entered.

"Oh, I feared you weren't coming!" He rolled over, bringing the sheet with him, and picked a hard-boiled egg off the tray as the lid lifted.

"Sorry," he said, holding breakfast up. Leo popped berries and bread in his mouth while petting Jasper's arm. Gradually, Jasper slid the tray onto the nightstand, not wanting to pull away. The transition was seamless, Leo ate and held him at the same time. Jasper nestled against him on the edge of the bed. He needed to get Ansehelm something soon. He'd get drenched going outside. Maybe he could get something from the kitchen, but it had to be soft, nutritious, and he had to take it without anyone noticing. And the spell. It was probably ready now. Leo was dragging him into the quilt.

"I don't think I can this morning, I'm kind of tired and, um, busy," Jasper said, but Leo lurched forward and kissed him.

"Lots of cleaning to do, sorry," Jasper said.

Leo's shoulders slumped, and he said, "I suppose," as Jasper left.

The kitchen was blessedly empty. Pawing through food scraps, he found still-good oatmeal and berries he sliced as finely as he could. A sound like a door opening made him jump. He swirled but saw no one.

One finger had smushed into the oatmeal; he licked it off. There was a thump, and he caught a glimpse of movement from the pantry. It was cluttered, almost nowhere to walk since they hadn't found any shelves. All the food sitting on the floor.

A figure behind canvas sacks almost made him scream, but he stopped himself from making a sound.

"You scared me," he mouthed at Ansehelm, crouched grinning from the square hole in the wall. Jasper bent in front of him, stepping over a sack of potatoes.

"What are you doing here?" he asked. The white slime on Ansehelm's skin was the only thing making him visible. This corner of the pantry was dark as night.

"You did not come. I am famished," Ansehelm said. "I feared for you as well."

Jasper glanced behind him. "This is the kitchens, you know that? It's usually full of people."

"But it is only you. If it had been others, I would not have revealed myself."

"Well, you found the food," Jasper said.

"Yes, the raw potatoes," Ansehelm said. "It is unsafe for me here, as you just reprimanded me for. In the time it would take me to find food, I would surely be caught. Fortunately, you are here."

Jasper held a finger up, bouncing to the counter and back with the bowl of oatmeal and fruit. He'd stuck a little silver spoon in it. "Here, I was going to bring this to you. I woke up late, sorry, but good thing you happened to find me here."

"I came for another matter." Ansehelm pointed a finger across the pantry to a row of herbs hung from nails Frankie had forced in the mortar. "Since you are here, you will get it instead of me risking myself. That is wild mint, yes?"

The light was thin, but Jasper spotted a stem of mint, excitement surging as he glanced around to check for witnesses. He twirled the stem when he handed it to Ansehelm, who sniffed the leaves and scoffed.

"No," he said.

"It's mint," Jasper said.

"It is peppermint, not wild mint."

"What's the difference?"

Ansehelm let out a disappointed sigh.

"I'm gonna go," Jasper said. "Yesterday, that spell was starting to work, and it should be finished now."

"Do try to find wild mint for me. As for your little experiment, I wish you luck, although I do not anticipate your success," Ansehelm said.

"Thanks anyway." Jasper backed over a sack of flour. "Sorry I woke up late."

CHAPTER SIXTEEN

J ASPER WAS ALMOST TO the top of the third tower when he smelled smoke and remembered the laboratory was locked from the inside. He sprinted the last leg of stairs, haze coming from under the door accompanied by a smell like a burning pan. If there was a fire, it could destroy the whole laboratory by the time he made it in through the tunnels, not to mention what damage could be done if a blaze got into the walls. The door handle was cool to the touch. Loose too, the lock no more than a gate latch that splintered as he knocked his body into it. With a crack, the latch tore, and he spilled into the laboratory.

No fire.

The lamp was still burning, pumping dry smoke into the room. Charred metal cut Jasper's nose. He snuffed the flame and grimaced at the soot-black stain in the copper. The potion had evaporated completely. No amulet.

Coughing, he unlatched the windows and took in a gulp of wet air. Sheets of rain sounded in his ears as they splashed his face. With the fumes clearing, he faced the copper. He let it burn too long—he should have checked on it last night. Or first thing this morning. Why couldn't he have woken up on time?

Maybe it never would have worked. How could garnet form out of oils and herbs?

The memory came as a sound, a fizzle of acid. Yes, it was possible. *More complicated than it looks*, Ansehelm had said. *More than following material instructions.*

Jasper touched the edge of the copper plate and shirked his hand back. Still hot. Of course, it would be; he didn't know how he could have been stupid enough to do that. His mind was scrambled. A deep sigh sucked dew and smoke down his lungs. Rain was spraying onto Van Hoensbroeck's notes. He gathered the papers to move them to safety when shadows appeared at the threshold, along with the sing-song call of Elsie Lambert.

He dropped to the floor and rolled under the desk, holding the papers like a shield. Forgotten about the door. If only he had checked earlier, he wouldn't have had to break it down. If only he hadn't feared a fire, panicked, lost his reason. Can't think not to touch hot metal, can't remember to close a door.

Three sets of footprints and clipped chatter. Elsie, Florence, and Leo. Jasper sucked in a breath. The false wall was shut but that hardly felt worth praising when he lay trapped and waiting to be discovered. He heard them sigh in awe at the room. How long before they realized the obvious?

"See, I told you!" Voice big with excitement, Elsie clapped her hands.

"We didn't *not* believe you," Florence said. Her retort trailed off as she paced over the floor. "What is this place?"

"The letter I found said it was used for alchemical experimentations," said Elsie.

"You got that from your translation?" Leo said with a light sarcasm that was always accompanied by a certain smile and drop of his eyes. Jasper imagined the face clearly. Time to start thinking of excuses for when they found him. *Just cleaning under here!* The sisters he could sell nonsense, but Leo would demand a real explanation. If not here and now, then later.

"It was in English," Elsie said. "Though, if you must know, my translation is coming along swimmingly."

"Speaking of swimming," Florence said and shut a window.

"Wonder what smashed the door in," said Leo, followed by a scrape like the latch being kicked over stone.

"Do you think there was a fight, hundreds of years ago? Old Van H threw someone against it in a fit of rage!" Elsie said. "Or maybe he got thrown."

"It's rot," Florence said. "Everything here is decayed because of ill-maintenance."

"What is *that?*" Leo asked.

"A medieval cauldron," said Florence.

"No, *that*," he said.

"Well…" Florence sounded like she hated to admit it. "It looks like an alchemical experiment."

Quick footsteps and then Florence snapping, "Elsie, don't *touch* it!"

"It looks ready to use," Leo said.

A cough. "What's burning?" Florence complained.

Her brother sniffed. "Nothing."

"I smell wet books," Elsie said. The other windows closed. Rain muffled, their footsteps were louder. The room felt smaller.

"What a strange place," muttered Florence.

"Let's get it cleaned up in here," Elsie said. "Who knows what we'll find!"

Leo scoffed. "These all look like poisons."

"Yes, they do," Florence said.

"So? No one's going to drink them," Elsie said.

"*You* were about to touch whatever's on that tray!" said Florence.

"I have an inquisitive mind, and I will not apologize for it," Elsie huffed.

Leo said, "No, you don't."

"You're both jealous, because you're cowards."

Neither said anything. Someone walked closer to the desk.

"And you got poor marks at school. I know, because Mother told me. Both of you, absolutely *embarrassingly* poor."

Florence groaned her sister's name. Leo hadn't said anything still, and though Jasper couldn't see, he imagined him surveying the room. Maybe hearing the faint shiver of breath from under the desk. Maybe spotting a strange gap in the wall.

"You're right, Flo, this room is strange," he said. A pause. Jasper wished he could see them, judge the line of their vision and tell the expressions on their faces. What if they were looking at the desk, right now, about to lean over and spot him curled under there like a cockroach?

Thump. The sound was of a rock smashing in the distance.

Florence asked, "What was that?"

"You heard that. You both heard it!" Elsie said. "I'm not imagining it!"

"*Leo*," Florence said in a harsh whisper. Jasper heard a snort, footsteps.

"Excuse me, who's there?" Leo called. The only answer was a loud, singular bang. Elsie whimpered.

"What's that about? Are you worried?" Leo snapped at her. "We shouldn't expect to be alone, this place is full of people."

"Not *full*," Florence said.

"But why won't they answer us?" Elsie asked. "If you weren't standing next to me, Leo Lambert, I'd say it was *you*. Trying to scare me. Or even *you*, Florence. Sister dear. You're not so above it."

Florence squawked in exasperation. When Jasper heard her again, it was farther away, calling for the culprit. The third time the bang sounded, she let out a petrified yelp. Leo and Elsie scrambled after her, the three of them shouting over each other and their own clattering footsteps. The sounds grew faint enough that Jasper risked peering out from his hiding place. The door was wide open, but the siblings were well down the stairs, out of sight. Sliding the false wall back wouldn't be silent, but if he did it quick enough, it would be closed before anyone caught him. Just another strange noise.

Ansehelm was responsible for that banging, had to be, but the figure Jasper saw the other night buzzed in the back of his mind as he sprinted behind the wall. Might have seen, he corrected himself. The false door slammed shut. As he breathed out in the darkness and dirt, voices swelled up behind him. So, they had heard, and it had sent them running back. He could stay here and wait them out, but how long would that be? What if Leo, or Mr. Thorley, went looking for him? And if the Lambert children did spot the false wall, that would be bad, but much, much worse if they found him behind it.

He didn't have a lantern. Forgot that too. There were matches in his pocket, but those wouldn't last long. He'd have to make most of his way in the dark.

If he went down the steps on his hands and knees, he wouldn't fall. He stripped his pants and tailcoat off, tying both around his shoulders and draping them down his front. Feet first, trying to keep the outer part of the uniform clean, he shimmied down the tunnel, cursing himself for all his stupidity that morning.

Now that he thought about it, he shouldn't have hid under the desk. There wasn't a rule that said servants couldn't poke around the castle on their own, he should have pretended he had wandered up out of curiosity like they had. The Lamberts would probably find some fault with it, Leo might be peeved Jasper hadn't gone with him, but it was understandable. Hiding was admitting guilt. What would he have done if Ansehelm had not managed to distract them?

It was Ansehelm making those noises, wasn't it?

Without thinking, Jasper stopped, listening for sounds. Nothing. Satisfied that he was alone for now, he resumed, hands pawing from one crooked plank to the next.

Pure, screaming luck that Elsie hadn't touched the copper. That no one had gone up there at any other time to see the oil lamp burning. Half the Lamberts already thought there was someone living in the castle. Ansehelm had said so many times now that his torturers would only be drawn back if he were discovered. And if Jasper shielded him, took all the blame, he could be fired. Arrested. What was wrong with him that he was so reckless?

At the end of the stairs, he laid over the last plank step for a short reprieve. Now that the others had seen the tower, he couldn't disturb anything more in there, or it would be noticed. They would know. They might figure it out anyway.

Leo had sensed someone else in the room; that the plate, the door, the windows had not been left like that for centuries. If Elsie had felt residual heat on her finger…

Did he hear something? Footsteps? Voices? When he'd slammed the false wall shut, the sound had sent the Lambert children back into the lab. Had they caught on enough to follow the clues? Were they climbing down the tunnel stairs right now?

He bolted, turning down the first offshoot he found, pawing his way through the narrow tunnel. If someone was behind him, they wouldn't catch him. They'd need to trace his path when even he didn't know where he was going.

Not thinking. Jasper paused. All quiet. His heart was racing—ever since walking up the tower steps that morning, he'd been working himself into panics, and it had been bad decision after bad decision. There wasn't anyone following him. Not Lamberts, not mysterious murderers, not even Ansehelm who moved slow and loud, with iron around his neck. And even if anyone was down there with Jasper, the only solution would be to go up. Not get lost in the maze that grew under the castle.

It took Jasper some time to find the main tunnel again, and when he did, there was something unfamiliar about it. A part he hadn't found yet, or maybe he was walking an old stretch at a different angle. He hoped however he was walking would take him outside by the stables. Crawling up there now would be like bathing in mud. But that could work to his advantage—he would say he fell, got dirty, had to clean himself, and that's why he was missing so long. Walk by the stables and make a big show to Earl and Horace about what an ordeal he had.

No, bad idea, that would bring too much attention. Better if they just thought he was dodging work. Once he got his bearings, he'd go out through some small room nobody cared to be in. He shifted the uniform tied around him, letting it fall down his back. Matches gave him occasional light, and between them, he pressed on through the dark, sliding a hand over the wall to check for turns. Cool, soft dirt.

Red mounds on the copper like embers. An amulet just starting to form. It could work, even if he wasn't able to do it yet. Hard to picture how he would get there—wrestling the castle from the Lamberts and evading those evil men. Jasper's fingers scraped the wall. Ansehelm had told him nothing. He didn't trust Jasper not to misuse the information, but Jasper didn't see how he could. Ansehelm found him worthy enough to reveal magic; what about his tormentors was so much more secret?

Loose thoughts slipped in and out. Everything was odd and impossible, so how could he make sense of it on his own? He needed clear answers. It had been almost a week, and the prisoner was doing well enough. There was no good reason for him not to tell Jasper everything.

The tunnel bent. He heard a thump ahead and called Ansehelm's name. No answer back. The match revealed little. He kept on as he had.

After a funeral—Jasper didn't remember for who—he and his family had taken a walk through the cemetery. It was years ago, and he'd asked why some of the gravestones had bells sprouting beside them. *In case they're not dead.* As soon as his father had said it, he declared that he heard them ringing, that there were people alive down there, trapped in earth and wood. Of course, the bells had been silent. He'd been young, and the idea of being buried alive had lit a fire in his imagination. To wake up underground, running your fingers over your own coffin until you found the cord. Waiting to be attended to, like the bells in the kitchen summoned the servants.

Was it strange that the memory was happy? Both of his parents had been there. His mother had been earnest, affectionate. His father had held his hand and told wild stories. It'd been a proper burial too, the grieving peaceful, and the walk had taken them under leafy trees and between lush bouquets planted at the graves.

An odd step; Jasper felt his ankle roll and realized in a split second he was falling. His arms latched into the ground but his legs kept sliding. He was dangling over a ledge, where or how far it went down he had no idea. Nothing to see but darkness nor feel but dirt. His legs knocked against the side; he tried to dig his toes in but couldn't get a foot hold. Arms locked, all his effort went to keep himself from slipping further.

Icy-slick hands clamped his wrists. He heard the clink of a chain. Able to relax his arms a moment, he hoisted his hips over the ledge, groping forward until he could hug the wall and feel flat ground under him.

The match light was feeble. He saw nothing but Ansehelm perched next to him on the ground, pointing towards a pitch black void that sank where the path should be.

"That would not have been good!" Ansehelm laughed. Jasper peered down. The pit. He'd been so turned around, he hadn't even thought of it. Still breathing heavy, he buried himself in the groove of the wall.

"Thank you," he said. "How did you see—"

"I heard you!" Ansehelm wheezed, the old rasp garbling his words. Jasper wondered how much just holding him had taken out of the man.

"Are you in pain?" he asked.

"Yes, but I am glad to have encountered you when I did!"

Jasper rubbed his fingers as the match burnt down.

"You were the one making those sounds. Near the laboratory."

"Of course. It is always me, is it not?" Despite the rough speech, Ansehelm sounded jovial. "It was no coincidence. I crawled that way to see the spell you were so proud of. It ended in failure, as was expected. In addition, you broke the door, an *un*expected failure. The situation had to be rectified. I cannot abide those three children sticking their noses in my books."

"They would have found me if you hadn't distracted them," Jasper said.

"Excellent timing twice, then!"

Dull light behind Ansehelm's eyes revealed them in the pitch. They faced Jasper dead-on. He remembered his questions from earlier, but it seemed ungenerous to needle Ansehelm about his tormentors after being saved two times in a row. He'd try anyway, nicely.

"Thank you. Really, I owe you." He took a breath. "Look, I want to do everything to help you, but I can only protect you so much without knowing what I'm up against. So will you tell me what happened to you? I won't do anything rash."

Ansehelm scoffed. "So you say, yet the events of this morning prove you are not always a prudent man, are you, Jasper? If you feel you must take action, I encourage you to find me wild mint rather than bother me with upsetting questions. It is enough to keep my secret, and the less you know, the safer we are."

Jasper propped himself up, saying, "How can we be in so much danger and entirely safe at the same time?"

The dull eyes darted away then back to him. "I *just* told you," Ansehelm said.

"But I don't even know who I'm supposed to be afraid of!" Jasper paused, but when the man said nothing, he continued, "Is it people from the town? Do they know about your magic? Do they know about Morlen?"

"Yes. People from the town," said Ansehelm. "As for Morlen, he believes me to be dead as well, assuming he is alive himself. As for magic." He was silent.

"Are they afraid of you?" Jasper asked.

"They wish to know magic but do not, and so they turn on me," Ansehelm spoke slowly. "An *entitlement.*"

Dust prickled the hair on Jasper's forearm. He stood with his back flattened against the wall, legs still as tree trunks.

"But," Jasper said, "what are their names?"

"I will not tell you," Ansehelm snapped.

"I won't do anything—"

"Do not ask me. I cannot defend myself and will not risk you making a brash mistake."

"You can trust me—"

"I trust your intentions, Jasper," Ansehelm said. "Not your judgement."

"I know when to not pick a fight," he said, though his self-defense felt awkward.

"So you *say,*" was the rejoinder. Ansehelm didn't believe him. Maybe Jasper did think himself more capable than he was. His mother often accused him of being careless. She could exaggerate, but she wouldn't say it so much if it wasn't true at all. His actions that morning more than proved it. Ansehelm was right about that. The prisoner was uncomfortable revealing the details, and it was his safety, primarily, that was on the line. It must be nerve-wracking to be so vulnerable while some kid insists you put your life in his hands.

"Fair enough, sorry," Jasper said, now feeling bad for having pushed it. "I need to go, but are you okay? You need any help getting back up the tower?"

"No, go, go!" Ansehelm said. "It will take me a long time, but I can do it myself. I have done it so far, exerting myself today. Your failed spell was placed quite the distance away for me, and I will add, bafflingly in the plain sight of your middling companions."

Jasper felt a pang of guilt. "Sorry, must have been difficult—"

"To crawl all the way there, to bang on the walls for them to hear? Yes, it was. But apology accepted. Although, there is one more thing I must take you to task for. I understand you believed you were being helpful when you brought me oats, however, I am now feeling ill. Please continue to feed me as per our original agreement."

Jasper deflated. "They made you sick?"

"Far too rich. My constitution has been severely damaged, and I am not yet able to digest those types of food. It was the same with your eggs yesterday."

"Sorry." He rubbed his temples. Ansehelm still wanted the leeches, then.

"All will resolve, if I am allowed to recover," he said. "I will do you favors, Jasper, when I am able."

Two matches left. Jasper gave him thanks and a smile as he crept by the pit. The light fizzled, Ansehelm's eyes the last thing he saw before it was dark again.

"No harm to your master," Ansehelm said.

Jasper cocked his head towards the voice, "Huh?"

"The one you are charged with, the son. I will let him be, as per your request."

"Oh. Yeah," Jasper said. Instinctively he waved goodbye, as if it weren't pitch dark.

The last match got him through to another offshoot. At some point, his hands brushed wooden rungs, and he felt his way up. He slid open a panel to the dark blue of an unlit room on a rainy day, filled with pews and blotched statues.

The trap door was crouched in the back corner of the pulpit. A conspicuous place to emerge from, if the chapel was in use, rising up behind the priest. Stepping over a hidden coffin. Why was this here—why had they built it like this? He shut the trap and sprung down the ladder. Surprised by his own jump back, Jasper wriggled his shoulders. A sudden alarm that he should not be where he was had overtaken him. Once the moment passed, it seemed cowardly to have bolted only because something felt a bit strange. Embarrassing, but no one was around to see it.

A deep breath took him back up and out into the chapel. He redressed quick as he could, brushing off the uniform and smoothing down his hair. His watch had thankfully made it safely in his pockets, but he shuddered at the time.

No sooner was he outside the chapel than Leo emerged from around a bend, eyes lighting up when he saw Jasper. Ribbon of cigarette smoke around him, he stood with slanted hips, fingers bobbing up and down as he talked.

"Did you hear? We went into that last tower. Downright bizarre. Frightening, almost." Leo talked fast between drags.

"What happened?"

"Flo and I went up with Elsie. It was her idea, since she found some old letter this morning. You should see this place; it's full of poisons and whatnot. Sorcerer's contraptions. A cauldron."

"Like a witch's cauldron?"

"I suppose. I don't know what we're going to do with it. It can't stay like that. When Father said *castle*, I thought Queen Victoria, not..." He furrowed his brow searching for the comparison. "You know what I mean. Do you want to see it?"

"No."

"Ha! We don't have to go there if it scares you. I mean, it's all medieval mumbo jumbo. You know there's no truth to that sort of thing?"

Jasper feigned offence. "Of course, I do."

Leo talked up how unnerved his sisters had been. Loud noises, caused by rain or wind, that's how it was in old places. Elsie had everyone worked up and acting irrationally.

"I half-suspect she's becoming a spiritualist. Billy would be mortified." Leo ran a hand down his chin, casting a glance left and right before saying under this breath, "I missed you quite a lot this morning. I'll take lunch now, in the bedroom, if you don't mind."

As they parted, Jasper wondered what would happen to Leo and him once Ansehelm's plans progressed. The Lamberts could be kicked out, but it would be nice to have Leo here, some of the time. If Jasper showed him what they were dealing with, what fantastic things really were possible, he would understand. Things would be different, but they could still be together.

No fire or candles burned in the great hall. Dottie was alone, resting with her hands against the table. As Jasper walked by, she looked up at him on the verge of tears, saying,

"And now there's a room full of sorcery."

CHAPTER SEVENTEEN

WHEN JASPER EMERGED from the kitchens with lunch, Leo was waiting in the great hall next to his father, stricken with a look of abject disappointment. He explained that, instead of alone, he would be dining with Mr. Lambert this afternoon. Jasper shot him sympathy glances as William patted him on the back.

As a change of pace, they ate in one of the anterooms overlooking the courtyard, safe from the downpour behind tall windows. The rain blurred the view into a smudge of blues and grays. A rather modern round picnic table already resided in the room; Jasper wondered if Ansehelm had put it there. Mr. Thorley had helped him bring up the food and serving cart but left to work on other tasks, and Jasper was alone with the two of them.

Though initially irked due to the storm, Mr. Lambert's spirits seemed to improve the more he bloviated to his son. Serving them both set Jasper on edge, certain he'd make some mistake. Leo looked equally uncomfortable. Was it Jasper's presence, or was he always like this when he was alone with his father? He smoked more than he ate as William prattled disjointed thoughts about politics and architecture. There was an occasional quiz on some issue of real estate, and Jasper could feel Leo's agitation as he trudged through the answers. It didn't register to Mr. Lambert, who barreled over his son with long-winded opinions. There were, perhaps, genuinely interesting kernels in what he talked about, but they suffocated under his diatribes. Most disappointingly to Jasper, he said nothing about Kasteel Verlossen's history.

William was, for the second time, explaining how he had kept his business afloat during the panic of '93, when Florence burst into the room in a feathery orange hat.

"Didn't realize you were here, apologies for the interruption!" She sauntered towards the windows. "Lovely room, if it were a sunny day." She gave something outside a second look before beaming at her father. "You don't mind if I join?"

Before getting the answer, she sat, chin up with a clean smile. Mr. Lambert explained that it was more a men's conversation, to which Leo sucked in a breath. Florence didn't argue, nor did she leave, letting the talk resume. Mr. Lambert brought up construction of the new subway, the scope of what the city envisioned, and how awful it was that Boston had built theirs first. Jasper edged towards the window, cool air on his back as rain splattered over the courtyard. Brown grass, he noticed. It was all dead, in June. Leo tried to excuse himself from the table, but Florence stopped him.

"I forgot, I had something to ask you," she said. "That friend of yours, Bernard Harrison, you invited him to Mother's garden party the other week, and we hit it off so well. I promised to write him from the castle. You do have his address?"

Leo promised in a sticky tone that he would give it to her later. Tapping a finger to his chin, Mr. Lambert said, "Harrison. That family is in coal?"

"Steel," Florence said. "Very good mills, they produce unparalleled quality. They mostly provide for locomotives, but Bernard—he just started working under his father—wants to move into buildings. Wants their name on skyscrapers. He said by 1910 he'll have their steel in every new building in the state, and by 1930, the whole country. Fantastic ambitions."

That secured Mr. Lambert's interest.

"Not married?" He raised an eyebrow.

"No, there's no woman in the picture. Not yet." The brim of her hat dipped. Her father grinned.

"I'm sorry," Leo said. "Suddenly I'm absolutely *stricken* with indigestion."

He pushed the chair out as he stood, leaning with his knuckles on the table as if he really were ill. His father glanced over him with a frown, but his sister's eyes darted around the room.

"*What* was that noise?" Florence said.

"That was my chair, Flo," said Leo. Giving him a look, she shook her head and put her finger to her lips.

They heard raindrops beating on window panes.

"There is no noise!" William Lambert said, but still they listened. Under the rain, Jasper could hear a scratch, as if something heavy were being dragged above them. He watched their eyes circle the room, wondering what they were thinking. Snorting, Mr. Lambert declared that lunch was over.

Leo was quick to exit, bidding his family goodbye as he flicked a finger for his valet to follow. Jasper took a last look at Florence, who smiled at her father between nervous glances at the ceiling. Silent, he followed until they were well away from the family, down a corridor that opened into the courtyard. They walked under a covered path, and water spraying on Leo's side made his cheek glisten. It seemed to refresh him after the lunch. He leaned Jasper against the wall and kissed him.

"The whole time I couldn't think of anything but touching you," Leo spoke into his ear. "Meet me in my room in an hour." He pulled away and was off, disappearing into the castle without another word.

Jasper was left watching the storm soak dead grass. He undid his collar, letting some rain on his neck. Windows he had looked out of minutes before were above him now, through which he saw a dim light. If someone was there, they'd be able to see him, and he didn't want to be seen. He slipped inside the corridor. Nothing to do for an hour. He walked, rubbing his neck.

He hated the uniform. Flimsy, uncomfortable, technically fashionable with its tailcoat and high collar, yet carelessly styled. Like a suit made for a toy doll. The shoes, shiny not long ago, were scratched into oblivion. Mr. Thorley had made a comment about it. How could he work and not scuff them? Especially here, against the stone, over dust and mud. And the heels clicked. He might as well have a bell around his neck. They were so loud through the tall, empty rooms. He hadn't been through this precise part of the castle before, and though he thought he should be excited by someplace new to explore, he wasn't. Walls, floors, ceilings, doors, configured differently but ultimately the same vacant spaces. A castle was meant to hold a village's worth of people. They had brought all this space over, put it somewhere that didn't belong to them, and left it hollow. What was the point? Van Hoensbroeck was obsessed with death; maybe he had liked it that way. A void to bury himself in.

Jasper found himself on an upper level of anterooms, between the courtyard and the armory, facing a series of doors down a paneled hall. He conjured the map in his mind, picturing the tunnels that shot through the walls like trunks from their roots. There would be a secret entrance in at least one of these rooms. He could get inside, scratch at the walls and scare the Lamberts. Tempting to try, but he had already crawled around too much today. More importantly, Leo would want him soon.

He was hungry. He should be eating his own lunch now. Leo hadn't asked for anything to be brought, had he? He tried vainly to remember as he squirreled through the castle. Too late now. He couldn't stomach going all the way to the kitchen and back again. Of course, if Leo asked, he would have to. That was his job, a servant. Bringing Leo meals and sex. The shoes kicked gravel down the stairs as Jasper ascended.

He opened the door to Leo napping. Shivering, he lit a cluster of candles. On top of the quilt, near Leo's hand, rested a daguerreotype of a man. He was handsome with a straight slanted nose and sharp brow, the kind of features Jasper would like to have. The letter B was inked in the corner. Leo opened his eyes and flipped the picture over.

When they were finished, Jasper loitered on the bed tuning his watch. Long since dressed and nursing a cigarette, Leo watched him unabashedly.

"So, before your father, anyone else own this place?" Jasper tried to ask casually but it came out stilted.

"You care about real estate now?" Leo made a face. "You sound like Flo. Please, Jasper, it's *so* boring."

He focused on the watch, feeling eyes on him as he reached for his clothes.

"Do you have somewhere to be?" Leo asked with a little pout.

"Yeah, getting your dinner."

In one motion, Leo abandoned the cigarette and pulled him into a kiss. Jasper smelled his cologne, bergamot and vetiver freshly reapplied. Fingers rubbed the base of his skull, reminding him of the excitement he had felt months ago, when he and Leo had first touched. So much more tender than anyone else before. He let himself melt, hands cupping him as they kissed.

"Little brother!" Florence's voice chimed right outside the door. Leo's fingers clenched around Jasper's head and pushed him towards the floor.

"*Hide*," Leo seethed through his teeth, and waved under the bed. There was just enough room for Jasper to fit; as he scurried, Leo lobbed his clothes underneath. Jasper stuffed the watch into the ball of clothes and kept his breath tight. Cobwebs tickled his naked spine. He saw the edge of a yellow skirt as she whisked in.

"You don't knock," Leo said in his usual flippant way. No hint of panic. All Jasper could see were Leo's crisp patent-leathers and the skirt above Florence's louis heels.

"I didn't drag myself up all those steps to be turned away. Do you have Mr. Harrison's address?"

"Really, Flo?" Leo said. "You're not going to write him; you'll make a fool of yourself."

"In what possible way?" She showed no sign of believing him.

"Bernard hates frivolity."

"You're the frivolous one, and he puts up with you."

After a hurried shuffle of papers, Leo said, "*Here.*" The yellow skirt was out of view, and Jasper heard the door close. As he began to crawl out, the heel of a patent-leather shoe came down on his hand. He snapped back under, squeezing his chest to stifle his cry. He sucked on his fingers until a hand motioned for him to come out. Draped in dust, he faced Leo, who stood stiff with a curdled lip.

"*Hell is wrong with you?*" Leo was quiet, sharp. "Don't you know how to stay hidden?"

Grimy, with only the wad of clothes to cover him, Jasper stammered, "I heard her leave." He shook his hurt hand and, seeing it, Leo deflated.

"I'm sorry." Leo collapsed on the bed and crossed his legs. "But you understand the risk is so great for me. The consequences would be… I don't want to think about it."

He looked away, staring into some shadowy corner.

"Yeah. I understand," Jasper said. What else could he say? He dressed, the clothes gummy on him. If only he could have waited, not crawled out, there would be no upset. He kept feeling Leo's eyes but each time he glanced up, the man was looking away. The memory of being kissed minutes ago lived on his skin. He wanted it back so badly.

Down the tower stairs he caught sight of the wild grounds through slit-windows. He imagined William Lambert shooting him in the head and burying his body in the shrubs. Maybe not even bury—he would he thrown in the overgrowth, barely covered. There would be no one around to protest his murder. He rubbed his swollen, red knuckles.

The weather was taming as Jasper washed off and changed into his old clothes.

"Hurt your hand?" Ned asked as he passed him in the quarters. *Jammed it*, Jasper was quick with the lie. The driver offered him some bandages Verna had left around. Out of Ned's view, he wrapped each finger. There was a crescent dent over his index and middle, deep purple-red and inflamed out to his nails. He winced when he tried to curl them. Gauze hid the bruises. He decided then that he wanted to see Ansehelm.

The prisoner seemed surprised by the visit. He sat with his back against the wall, legs shooting out from under him. Neck bent under the weight of the collar, his head was forced into a bow. Thin clumps of white hair lined his scalp; Jasper hadn't noticed them before. It had been a pain climbing the ladder, but he was glad to have found Ansehelm here instead of losing him in the tunnels. At least he could steal a quick reprieve before he had to serve again.

"What happened to your fingers?" Ansehelm's nose twitched as he asked. Jasper didn't answer but sat, taking some cheese he had brought for himself. Soft, so he offered some only to be declined.

"Did I not discuss this with you before?"

"Yeah. Leeches. I'll bring more. You feeling okay?"

One hand at a time, Ansehelm stretched forward, knees bending under himself.

"I am. Here, take one of these." He produced a damp cigar from the recesses of the cell.

Jasper smiled. "You still have those?" The wrapper was peeling off, but he managed to get it going. There was a faint mildew taste amidst the smoke.

"I do wish you could have brought me another meal," Ansehelm said.

"It's raining," Jasper said, curling in as he heard how meek it sounded. A childish excuse. He'd needed—wanted—some companionship.

"You have no place better to eat your lunch?" Ansehelm asked.

Jasper rubbed the back of his neck. "I—" Smoke swirled around his mouth, making the cheese taste especially salty. Ansehelm extended his legs back; now flat on his stomach, he propped his elbows up and curled his hands under his chin. His spine dipped where the iron tugged down. Jasper wondered how they would remove it. Too dangerous to drizzle acid around his neck, unless they could control the flow, but it would be less fraught if they could use normal tools. The bolt cutters hadn't worked on the chain link, they wouldn't fare well around the thick band. Even trying might break Ansehelm's neck. They would need a blacksmith. The band looked excruciatingly uncomfortable as the prisoner turned his face up.

"Perhaps you are upset about your spell."

Jasper sighed. A clump of ash fell from the cigar. He *was* upset about the spell, on top of everything else. You wouldn't step on a magician's hand, would you? He said to Ansehelm, "You promised to teach me."

"I will," Ansehelm said. "Consider that until I revealed the potion to you, you knew of nothing but your worldly concerns, and now you are over-eager. In my day, we kept our heads straight about these matters. You do not understand, so you try to work it the way you would work a loom or an anvil. You believe your mind does not matter and your soul even less." He snatched the cigar and crushed it under dripping water. "Now it is wet and you cannot light it aflame again, can you?"

"Um—"

"The material answer is no, and a material solution will never produce otherwise. To merely recite an incantation or mix a potion is to wallow in mud. Your mind and soul must be properly attuned."

Jasper's brow furrowed. Ansehelm said,

"You are confused, because you cannot even conceive of what it means to dedicate your soul. You think it is enough to simply want. That if you want it enough, you ought to receive it. That is probably the foolish thought you are latching on to right now, as most men do. No, you are wallowed too deep, and you must first bring your spirit out of its atrophied state."

Jasper pursed his lips. Ansehelm's face had animated wildly as he lectured, freezing after his final sentence into an open-mouthed smile. With the dark hole, along with his indented eyes, his face looked like a mask.

"This isn't about going to church, is it?" Jasper asked.

Ansehelm laughed. "That is another problem. The religious institutions of your time are mockeries as material as anything else. In my day, I would not have to answer such questions."

"Did you used to teach magic?"

"Not to just anyone."

Salt was still on Jasper's tongue. Wild mint. He didn't know how he would find it.

"When will you get the Lamberts to leave?"

"Soon."

"Tomorrow? Next week?" Jasper faced him. "It's not going to rain forever, and once this place fills up with the new people, it'll be harder to sneak around. You need medicine, a real bed, and real food. If you wait too long, you'll die."

The chain scraped the floor. "I am aware I need real food. I desire it. It is not the time yet."

"I saw someone hanging around the castle, late at night. A stranger around the walls, and they didn't answer me."

The eyes flashed up at him.

"And what did you do?"

"I mentioned Mr. Lambert, and they ran away. See, I wouldn't just go fight somebody and reveal you."

Ansehelm frowned into his fingers as Jasper wiped crumbs off his shirt. *Might have seen someone.* He knew he was half-lying, but he needed something to shake the prisoner up. Ansehelm spent his days scheming and spying as he pleased and, agonized as he must be, his confinement had produced an odd freedom. Nothing to answer for, nobody to answer to, and maybe he'd grown accustomed to that. Maybe he didn't want to come out. It crossed Jasper's mind that he could disappear into the walls too. Pilfer from the pantry, make himself into a ghost. Nobody bothered the dead.

But *he* was healthy. Ansehelm couldn't possibly last much longer in this state. He might never make a full recovery, considering his age. How old was he, exactly? Of course, he hadn't said. Besides saying nothing about his plan, or how he had come to be tortured and locked in a secret tower attic, Ansehelm had also kept quiet about who he had been, where he was from, how he came to the castle. Perhaps they were all related: his life had been one trauma after another, and he didn't want to talk about any of it.

Jasper was still parsing his thoughts when Ansehelm said,

"You did not answer when I asked—" He pointed at Jasper's bandages. "—what happened there?"

"Jammed it," he said. Ansehelm held a palm open, curling his fingers in.

"Let me see."

Jasper gave him a blank stare.

"I have knowledge of the healing arts," he said. "It is why I understand what to eat and how to move for my own recovery, even though it does not make sense to you."

Kneeling, Jasper held his hand out. Cold fingers made him shiver. After feeling the gauze, Ansehelm moved down and pressed a thumb into Jasper's wrist. Pressure, a nail on his skin, then pain. He yanked his hand away.

"Apologies!" Ansehelm said. "I was being clumsy."

"Yeah," Jasper said. He had a thin smile on. "Why—"

"Activating the pulse promotes flow of blood, which is essential for recovery."

It wasn't a lot of pain, but it was still there. He took another bite of cheese and massaged his wrist. Ansehelm said nothing, but his gaze lingered. Jasper looked down to bits of rind falling from his mouth. He heard pages being turned and Ansehelm, book in his lap said,

"Here. You can make a healing rub with fennel root and St. John's wort."

"Thanks," Jasper said, doubting he would find either of those before it healed on its own. He had no concept of what St. John's wort looked like. He stood to leave.

"You have had your meal, but I am quite hungry," said Ansehelm.

Tired as he was, Jasper promised to bring him something then. His fault for coming up here with only food for himself. Ansehelm stuck his chin out and said, "Please, the leeches still."

Jasper paused at the tunnel crossroads. The path that lead back to the third tower had two wooden planks pinned near its arch, while the one that ended by stables had a shorter mouth than the others. Visual cues he memorized to tell his way, but the intersection still confused him. The other opening was wide and warped, looking like two, and bled into the others. That's where the pit was, running under the chapel and ending where, he did not know.

Scrambling all around the castle was exhausting. He understood why Ansehelm did it, despite the pain and what he guessed was an appalling length of time to get anywhere. Desperate to hear and see what you can, to break from the monotony. But there was something uncomfortable about it whenever Jasper saw him outside of the tower.

A pool of mud had formed in the tunnel exit near the stables. He resigned himself to the mire as he pulled himself onto soaked grass. The rain had faded to a drizzle. He kept against the wall, not wanting to be too visible to anyone who might be looking out a window.

For all his grievances, Ansehelm often seemed unconcerned with his own plight. That's what made Jasper uncomfortable. He was happy to exert himself to gather information, to tease the Lamberts. Get revenge on Jasper's behalf. Terrified then unbothered. Too content with eating worms.

The pink stalk of the berry bush was fabulously bright under the clouds. The pond water spilled over, washing torn lily pads into flower beds, but the leeches rested deep down. He scooped them with his good hand while staring at swollen red skin peeking out from under gauze. There was a thumbnail-shaped scratch on his wrist.

Nobody in the armory or the third tower. He'd worried it would be full of Lamberts excavating its secrets, but it seemed everyone wanted to leave it alone. Jasper found a laboratory contraption to sacrifice—a thin cylinder that stuck into the pulleys of the false wall. Now it could only be opened from behind, from the tunnels themselves.

If he disappeared into the walls, he would leave his mother, his family, Leo, everyone behind. Thinking about that didn't make him sad; it was more like relief. And if he learned Ansehelm's arts—it was real, even if Jasper couldn't wield it yet—that would be enough meaning for a life. He wouldn't need anything else.

His hand hurt less going up the ladder again. Ansehelm slept in a clump, one knee bent in, a leg curled behind, waist twisted to the side of his hips. It looked like he had been dropped from above and froze how he had landed. Twisted up and too tired to move. He could keep himself crawling through the tunnels for long enough, but it must drain him. His eyes opened to the sack tossed in front of him.

"If you want to get better, you need more food than this. I know your teeth…" Jasper paused in anticipation of being cut off, but the prisoner listened patiently from the floor. "I can get you food you can eat. Soft bread, sugar, that kind of thing. You have to work up to eating it."

"Sugar, soft bread," Ansehelm muttered back. "Why don't you come tomorrow with it, then."

"Oh. Good." Jasper hadn't expected easy progress. Ansehelm had put the sack to the side, unopened.

"And think about when you want to tell me what happened to you," Jasper said.

"*When?*" Ansehelm said.

"Yeah. When."

"You know I dislike being asked, so I see you have skipped and gone straight to demands!"

Jasper held his palms up. "I need to know what, and who, I'm dealing with. The castle won't be isolated forever. What if someone else finds the tunnels? I'm at risk myself, helping you. I deserve to know."

Ansehelm's brow fell. "I must say, I do not appreciate this attack when I am so hungry and tired. But you have a point. I will think about it. Do not inquire when I see you next. I do not need reminders."

Jasper waited, prepared for another lecture, but just like that, Ansehelm was asleep before him. As he left, he watched the sack wriggle, inside it twisting braids of leeches.

⧓

Jasper rushed to change back into the valet's outfit in time to fetch his charge for dinner. The gloves hid his fingers. He spoke to Leo like a servant, and Leo acknowledged him much the same way. They walked in silence through the castle expanses. Jasper found himself listening for scratches from the walls.

They entered the great hall to find an unexpected visitor. A stout man with bifocals that seemed too small for his eyes spoke to Mr. Lambert near the arched entrance. Leo pounced beside his father while Jasper tried to hear them, drowned out by Dottie and Maja's theories on who it could be.

Everything would be recounted over dinner. A Mr. Shaw, prominent figure in the town apparently, had gotten word of their situation and came as soon as the rain let up. The problem was Robert Morlen: the fact that he hadn't been seen or heard from was worrisome. Despite the late time of day, Shaw wanted to check the groundskeeper's house, which was so close to the castle property it was practically inside it. He was surprised the Lamberts knew nothing about it.

As for the new help that was supposed to come, Shaw couldn't say. Mrs. Lambert offered him dinner and was relieved when he declined. He put his horse in the castle stables and headed off to Morlen's house on foot.

"The groundskeeper's dead, I bet." Elsie cocked her head with a sly smile and bounce of her hair.

"*Elsie Lambert*," Cordelia said.

CHAPTER EIGHTEEN

DULL PAIN THROBBED through Jasper's hand as he cleared the table. The family milled in the hall after dinner, except Leo, who had slipped away as soon as it was acceptable. Jasper stacked as many plates as he could at once, wanting to keep himself downstairs with the dirty dishes. He wiped scraps off while the others buzzed around him. The maids pined for the townhouse kitchen, with its lift for the dishes. Frankie scrubbed cutlery in a distended tub, muttering, "See, this is the kind of thing that isn't my job."

Elsie had left a slice of mutton on her plate, and it crossed Jasper's mind to eat it. All he'd had today was that cheese in the attic cell. He eyed Proulx still slicing meat, hoping it was for the staff's dinner.

"The new people will be here soon," Irene said.

"Will they?" Maja grimaced. She took up scrubbing, and Frankie gladly stepped back from the tub.

"Clearly someone can get up the roads," said Irene, rag drying plates and stacking them on the counter.

"I don't like this business about the groundskeeper," Dottie said. She rearranged the dishes Irene had put down. Distant noises simmered under the kitchen clamor. Mr. Thorley appeared on the steps with deadly serious eyes. He pointed right at Jasper.

"Everyone up. You first."

Jasper put a plate down and followed the butler, sweat beading under his clothes. The others shuffled behind him. His first thought was that they had found Ansehelm. Maybe the tunnels, that they knew he had been keeping a secret. Or it was about him and Leo—but no. If they ever found that out, they wouldn't make a public show of it.

Thorley led them into the apartments where Leo was laid out on the parlor couch, Verna at his side. He was covered in red, round, bleeding marks.

"Oh, god." Jasper knelt by the couch under a wave of murmurs. Resisting the instinct to take Leo's hand, he hovered his fingers above, staring at the wounds. Blood trickled out from rings of tiny punctures that dotted Leo's exposed skin: hands, neck, and, mostly, his face. Verna padded them with a steaming cloth under the family's worried faces.

Irene was the first to ask what happened. Bumping the nurse, Leo sat straight up, eyes glaring at an empty spot on the wall.

"Something attacked me," he spat. Fists of greased hair shot from his head. He was pale from fright and blood loss, and it made the marks look boiling red.

Silent, Mr. Lambert shuddered. Mrs. Lambert, fingers twisted in the breast of her dress, urged her son to continue.

Leo always walked the same route from the great hall to his bedroom, he explained, around the courtyard's left and turning past an old suit of armor. It was the first of them before the armory, more robust than the others even if it was missing a shin plate. Tonight he'd walked by it same as he had many times since arriving at Kasteel Verlossen. The sun was truly down by then, and he'd paused to light a candle. So used to the sound of rain, he had not noticed a scratching from the walls until it was too late.

They'd dropped from above. Sliming, wriggling leeches, slithering over him, sticking their suckers wherever they could. He'd wrenched them off, but there were so many, all hooked into his flesh. A fist had knocked him off balance and then, standing over him, was this *thing*. A phantasmagoric man, emaciated with a ghoulish cackle. He'd tried to get up, but the man had pinned him down. It must have only been a minute, but it had felt so much longer that he was forced to lay there, being bled by dozens of parasites, frightened to death. Then the man had picked the leeches off and stuffed them, alive and full, into a sack. Leo had seen him put one in his *mouth* before disappearing into the ceiling. It was over. He ran back. Of course, in the castle it was long before anyone heard him scream.

He was panting when he finished the story, and for a few moments, it was silent except for his breathing. Wounds on his cheek and neck had opened, blood dripping on to his shirt.

"I would have chased him if I had a clue where he had gone," Leo added.

Jasper bit his lip. Despite himself, he felt a smile coming on. He shuddered at that, ashamed of the jackal grin sliding on to his face. He turned the urge to laugh into a gasp. That was how he really felt anyway: concerned. Of course he cared, but Leo was so serious, and so clearly exaggerating. That's why the smile was creeping in.

Ansehelm hadn't really eaten them off of Leo. Hadn't pinned him down either; Leo had fallen and been too scared to do anything. Jasper offered to bring him something, a stiff drink or hot tea, anything. A scotch. Briefly, the blue eyes looked into his, and the fright in them made Jasper wince.

Glad to be a servant at that moment, he hurried to the kitchen. Alone, Jasper laughed even as a hot, tight feeling cinched his chest. He poured the whiskey and downed some himself. Smoother than he expected. The burn cleared his senses. Leo was exaggerating, yes, but it was too odd a prank—Ansehelm had begged Jasper for leeches all day only use them like this? Jasper doubled over, suddenly light-headed, and he stuffed fatty slices of meat from Proulx's carving board into his mouth.

Before Jasper went to sleep tonight, he would talk to Ansehelm. The man didn't seem to care about being noticed. Or perhaps Leo Lambert irritated him past concern for his own safety. Regardless, it was time he gave a real explanation of what had happened in the castle.

Another gulp of scotch for himself, and he poured the drink for real. He wiped the grease from his lip off the rim.

Upstairs, the parlor fire roared under Dottie's nervous tending. The rest of the staff clumped in the corner behind Mr. Thorley, and Jasper felt them jump when he entered. The Lamberts' voices were already raised over each other. He only got as close to the fray as needed to serve the drink.

"None of you believed me! You told me it was my imagination, but you believe him!" Elsie screeched.

"I won't have this right now!" her father shouted.

"I don't believe him either," said Florence.

"How dare you!" Leo jabbed a finger at her from the couch. "I need a cigarette."

"If my croquet set unpacked itself, then those leeches must have attacked you on their own." Florence crossed her arms. "I bet you fell in mud in the courtyard. Really, a man leaping out of the ceiling."

"It sounds exactly like the face I saw!" Elsie declared.

"*Cigarette*," Leo groaned.

"Father, why couldn't you have bought a *normal* estate?"

"Please, do not talk to your father like that, Florence," Mrs. Lambert said.

"Dammit, Jasper, a cigarette, by *God!*" Leo snapped his head, looking like a sneering demon, shadows from the fire flickering over his bleeding face. Jasper took in a breath.

"I think they're, uh," he tried not to say too loudly, "in your pocket." Leo's eyes still burned at him as he felt the silver case inside his vest. His sisters watched him smugly. Florence jutted her hip.

"I worried there was a stranger in this house, and I was convinced otherwise. Now I believe my brother is making up a tale to exploit us."

"Flo, you turncoat," Elsie said. "I believe him, and furthermore, it proves I was right from the beginning."

"Now, girls, please," Mr. Lambert said. "Your brother is not prone to stories."

"He's prone to drink."

"*Florence.* Your brother is injured, and you will show some concern." William was stern. "We cannot say that this incident explains every odd occurrence that has happened, but it is now clear to me that we must take serious precautions. All of you children will sleep in here tonight. Elsie, that means you too. Verna will be here. When that Mr. Shaw comes back—he hasn't come back yet?"

"His horse is still in the stable." Frankie scratched his lip.

"Make sure he doesn't leave without speaking to me. Tell the drivers to stand guard until he arrives for his horse."

"We need bodyguards," Leo said. Mr. Lambert eyed his staff.

"Perhaps Proulx can spend the night here, and the young ones. The other cook and the driver. And your man, Leo."

The chef grunted, if not in approval, in acquiescence.

Having been whispering with Irene, Mr. Thorley spoke up. "Sir, the maids are concerned about the safety of our quarters. Earl and I aren't as young as we used to be, and Ned is still unable to walk…"

Mr. Lambert considered for a moment. "None of you have experienced an attack. It is clear that *we* are in danger, if anyone is."

Maja crossed herself. William grunted, signaling the matter closed, and it was Cordelia's turn to give orders. Everything was to be rearranged for the whole family to stay in the apartment. Florence huffed and sighed as Elsie was moved into her bedroom. The empty one went to Leo. Jasper was sent all the way to the tower and back for his bags. He took the route past the suit of armor, expecting to see a pool of blood or dead leeches or Ansehelm, but nothing. Not even a sound. On the way back, he went downstairs for extra blankets, and saw the maids moving into the dormitory with Thorley and Ned. Earl took a bottle of wine with him to the stables, waiting for Mr. Shaw.

Inside the apartments, Proulx, Horace, and Frankie stood awkwardly with their rifles around the parlor. Once Jasper was in, the chef latched the door.

"What will we do if we need something in the middle of the night?" Florence asked, looking at her mother. "How can any of the maids get in?"

"I agree. It doesn't matter, since the man can climb through walls," Elsie said, prompting her sister to storm off to bed.

"Let's get you to sleep, Mr. Lambert," Verna said to Leo. She guided him, Jasper close behind, into a small room opposite his sisters'. The bed was perfectly made, with a battalion of pillows across the headboard. The nurse pulled the sheets back while Jasper unpacked a dressing gown. Leo gave him a look he couldn't parse.

"I'll be right outside the whole night," Verna said. "The cuts are not that deep, and I don't see any sign of infection. Rest and cleanliness is the answer."

"Yes," Leo muttered, looking off in the distance. "Jasper, stay in here the night."

The nurse left. Leo changed into the dressing gown. The marks on his neck stopped abruptly where his shirt collar had been buttoned. Mechanical, he pulled back the covers and climbed in. Jasper took a step towards the bed.

"No," Leo said.

"Oh. I should…"

"On the floor, yes."

There wasn't even a rug. As if he wanted to sleep next to Leo in a mood like that. He thought Leo expected it. He was trying to be kind. There was a sheet he could smooth out, not that he could lay down yet.

"Will you be ready to bring me something if I need it?" Leo was stock still, voice hollow.

"Yes," Jasper said from the foot of the bed. Leo snuffed the candle, leaving him standing in the dark. He wanted to walk right back out the door, but he couldn't be heard leaving. He waited in the shadows until he heard a faint snore. In the parlor, embers burned down as the others dosed. Only Frankie was alert, having taken first shift. He sat on a dinner chair by the door, legs crossed with the gun over his lap. Jasper concocted a lie about where he was going but never had to use it. Frankie even opened the door for him.

In the great hall he let himself breathe. He had a fresh candle in a tin holder that he wouldn't light yet. Safe to be in the dark. If Leo would make him sleep on a floor, why not out in the castle, out in some secluded room? He would rather sleep on bare stone if it meant he could be left alone, instead of in that bedroom. Sequestered in the apartments with the Lamberts bandying him around. He scolded himself—he should be more forgiving. If to no one else, then to Leo, who really was scared and hurt.

Jasper was hurt, afraid, tired, upset all the time. That's how his life had gone. He didn't put it on anybody. One bad thing and Leo let himself shatter, knowing someone else would be there to clean it up.

Maybe Jasper would start dumping bugs on their heads. What could the Lamberts do about it, if they didn't know it was him, if he attacked them from the secret tunnels? Nothing.

Which way to go in? He cycled through possible entrances before remembering the central tower was empty. At least of Lamberts. He closed the door to its staircase behind him, starting the candle only then. The tower room looked ransacked, with half of Elsie's things left behind, empty boxes, books and stockings strewn over an unmade bed. The cabinet to the old desk was wide open, papers spilling out. She had been working on her translation, he saw. On the open page of her notebook was a column of Dutch words with the English beside it.

Age. Church. Day. Old-lord? Life. Talk. Servant/serf. Bile. Painter. Eat. Start. Secret. Loathe. Dig. Mountain. Rose bush. Teeth.

The journal she was translating was filled with blotted writing. He flipped through the pages but saw no occult symbols. Without much thought, he slipped the dictionary into his jacket pocket.

Out of some sense of propriety, he knocked on the trap door before opening it. "Ansehelm," he whispered as he stuck his head up, thinking he saw him before realizing it was just the chain hanging from the bolt. No one there. Rot whiffed out from the tower attic. He hoisted himself up. The back corners, behind where Ansehelm always sat, were illuminated now. Cigars, books. His heel squished a moldy peach. It had been rolled next to the sack of table scraps he had brought days ago, old vegetables and now-curdled beef. Ansehelm feared for his digestion, but it seemed an extraordinary power of will that he had resisted cooked meat. In the times Jasper had gone hungry, he could not imagine foregoing food like that, no matter the consequences. Maybe he didn't understand. He had all his teeth. The patch of floor was wet. Pinching his nose, he crouched, but it was water. There was a sizeable pool of it; from a leak, probably, though the rest of the floor was dry.

He needed to find the prisoner, but how? Perhaps he would meet him in the tunnels. He managed down the ladder with the candle holder and through the split. He didn't want to shout for Ansehelm; the thought of it made him feel exposed. Someone could hear him. Leo would recognize his voice through the floors. He would have to keep his eyes peeled. Damp permeated the tunnels. Ground and air felt the same down here, like breathing earth. Did new air flow in? Maybe each breath he took down here left him less next time. It was all being sucked up. Soon he would suffocate, and Ansehelm too.

Without realizing it, he was heading to the laboratory. It was where he wanted to go, ultimately, and pursuing

Ansehelm wasn't working. He'd heard no scratches, seen no footprints not his own, so he would rest. The false wall slid back. There was the cauldron, the lamp under the copper plate. Little had been touched. The door rested in place, cracked open a few inches.

Total dedication. What did that entail? He couldn't conceive of it because his soul was degraded, or something like that.

That green jar he'd despised glowed at him. He wanted to know what the gel inside did. There had to be more he could suss out on his own. Leafing over the shelves, he picked up a spineless volume and a few badly bound pages fall out. The front bore the name Pieter Van Hoensbroeck, some title scrawled underneath. Latin or Dutch? Collecting the manuscript on the desk, he consulted the dictionary. The first word confirmed, Dutch. Nothing to write with but dried quill ink, he committed to remembering each translation. The words in the title were: Transform. And. Submit or Submission. Of. Immortal. It was dated 1701. Only a few pages were filled in before it abruptly stopped. The sheets that had fallen out were blank. Sticking them back in, he lingered on the very last sentence. Not. In state. Eat. Carrion? Weak but. The body, or, the corpse. Continue. In. Life.

That was the best he could do looking up each word on its own. Ansehelm said Pieter had never raised the dead, but had he tried? Perhaps he was claiming he had or to have something that couldn't die. Jasper could try looking up the whole journal with the dictionary, hoping the meaning would shine forth from a garbled translation. Had the groundskeeper known what it said? He stared down at "*leven – life*" on the dictionary page, as if it would suddenly yield him an explanation. Fire growing from sludge. He had the sense that in the back of his mind, an answer was being figured out, but he didn't even to know to what question. Flimsy thoughts disintegrating at the slightest pull, whiffs of ideas with no words for them.

What had stopped Van Hoensbroeck's writing? Had his dedication floundered? Maybe, like Jasper, he'd glimpsed a possibility only to have it shrivel before his eyes. A person spending their decades working towards something only to have it never come to fruition. Staying on track, living the same way year in and year out. Dull even for an alchemist. How frustrating it would be to never, ever turn lead into gold. What could you do? Jasper had always just accepted what life offered. He could agree with Ansehelm, in some respects, that things were what they were regardless of what you wanted.

If Van Hoensbroeck had made any real breakthroughs, in his alchemy or necromancy or whatever −*my*, he would have kept it locked up. Jasper felt around the back of the desk. There was the compartment with the key, just like the other, which opened the drawer. Nothing inside except a velvet pouch, the kind that might hold a ring.

He heard the clank of a chain swinging. Ansehelm stood in the entry of the false door. Jasper slipped the pouch into his pocket.

"Snooping?" Ansehelm stepped towards the desk. Strange to see him walk. His bones looked like they ought to break under their own weight. He staggered, bending his knees as if he were catching himself at each step. Despite that, his gaze stayed fixed on Jasper.

"I can't read Dutch," Jasper said, closing the drawer. "What happened tonight?"

"Did you enjoy it?" Ansehelm asked. His skin—still pale as death—looked drier, free of its slime. He could nearly hold his shoulders back, and when he was right in front of the desk, he leered down at Jasper, who did not know what to say.

"Consider it a thank you for all of your assistance. He deserved it for how he acted towards you. That was no way to treat a lover."

For a second, Jasper's heart stopped. The pinpoint eyes peeled over him from deep under Ansehelm's brow, beady black and green. The colors of the mountains.

"Do not look so startled," Ansehelm said. "I have not lived my many years and not encountered a sodomite before."

Jasper heard his own nervous laughter outside of himself. The enclave in Leo's tower. Windows around the courtyard. Did Jasper think he couldn't be spied on? He thought of what his mother would do while he languished in prison. The Lamberts could afford lawyers. If he were arrested, he wouldn't get out.

"You won't tell anyone?" His throat was hoarse.

"No, as you have not told anyone about me. We are friends, are we not?"

Below the fear, deep in his gut, was a sorrow that sucked away at him.

From the decrepit remnants of a shirt sleeve, Ansehelm pulled out a leech. "Yes, we are friends."

"I asked you not to—" Jasper's words died mid-sentence as the pinpoint eyes moved from the leech to him. He took a breath. His thoughts moved too slowly. "You didn't eat those things off of Leo."

"Is that what he said, in his cowardly ravings?" Ansehelm treaded back, warp-limbed, with a gummy smile. "Enjoy the old books."

"Wait." Jasper bit his dread down and tried to conjure an argument. "I know you told me not to ask, but with everything, the Lamberts might leave tomorrow. If you tell me who did this to you, I can help you. I won't tell anyone else, just get you help before you're abandoned here again."

"You are correct, I did tell you not to ask." His tone was amused. "I appreciate your continued concern with my health and safety. As you can see, I am doing much better. It occurs to me also that at this point, your masters may dislike it if they discovered you had been harboring me. Consider that we both protect ourselves by keeping our secrets." He crunched the leech between his gums. Coppery-putrid scent hit Jasper's nose as it punctured.

As soon as Ansehelm was gone, he slammed the false door shut. The wall of the tower room looked solid again. Arched over the desk, he dug his nails into the wood. A thousand strange and sinister possibilities wriggled through his mind. The anxiety balling up in him was stronger than any single thought. It quieted, just slightly, when he thought of telling someone about Ansehelm.

Not the Lamberts. Shaw, or someone else from the town. He had to be careful. Ansehelm kept secrets, but he hadn't chained himself up. Maybe he should get a confidante—Frankie or Proulx. He should be ready with his own lie. Anyone he told would question why he kept it a secret from the family.

And if Ansehelm retaliated by telling them about him and Leo? He could deny it, of course. He could deny a lot of things. Dizzy, he crumbled into the claw-foot chair. If he did nothing, Ansehelm would do nothing, right? Acting without a plan was the worst thing to do, and he shouldn't push himself to make a choice now when he knew it would be the stupid one. Like running and telling somebody the whole thing. Or going up to the tower in the morning and snapping Ansehelm's neck.

Murdering an old man. Jasper shook the repulsive thought away. He couldn't do that. Not to protect his own secrets. For someone else, maybe, but that wasn't the case. Ansehelm might dislike the others, but the only person who had been hurt was Ned, and whose fault was that?

Leo was injured, technically. He would be fine. Ansehelm's actions were unnerving, but he was too weak to pin a grown, healthy person. Leo wanted an excuse for why he had been bested by an old man. And he wanted everyone to be terrified for him. Always had to seem more put upon than he was.

Suppose he was awake right now, screaming for this and that. Jasper left the tower. How absolutely livid Leo would be if knew about any of this. How out of his mind with anger. When they were alone again, Jasper would use the word: sodomite. He'd bet Leo would explode just at that. The more he thought about it, the more he liked the fantasy, despite the way it clawed at his chest. He never talked about it with anyone explicitly, not any of the men he'd been with, not ever. All of his fears and desires and joys mulled inside his head. No one wanted to hear them. Leo wouldn't. But suppose Jasper just did what he wanted instead and watched Leo scramble in the aftermath.

In Leo's tower, he bundled the yellow quilt, holding it up for Frankie back at the apartment.

"He needed this," Jasper said with an eye roll.

Frankie cracked a grin which turned to a yawn. The fire was out in the parlor. Leo was snoring when Jasper curled on the floor, still in uniform, a sheet under him. Tomorrow he would do something about Ansehelm. Or the Lamberts would leave, taking the whole crew back to the city, and the ordeal would cease to be Jasper's problem.

CHAPTER NINETEEN

JASPER WOKE FULL WITH the visceral memories of a dream, a world that felt true even as its details diffused into nothingness. Gnawed by the fragments that remained—an image of a tree, a sense of trepidation—he wanted to relive it, but trying to remember dulled the whole thing. Reduced to its literal events, the crux of the dream was stripped away. There had been a feeling, something like awe and terror blended into such a tantalizingly good form he had to chase it into his waking life. Too slippery. A memory of an experience he had not actually had.

He opened the shutters to a bland morning. In the new light, the pocks on Leo's face looked rose-pink.

"Tea, right away, and have breakfast started."

"Good morning," Jasper said.

"I'm positively famished."

The chef and sous-chef slept soundly in the parlor, and Jasper didn't feel much like waking them. Breakfast would happen when it happened. He brought the tea. Leo had unfurled by then, half-smiling at Jasper's return. He managed to say thank you as he stirred in a sugar cube.

"I had the most horrid dream," Leo said. "Truly disturbing. It's not my style to be disturbed. At first, I thought it was a lark how depressing this place is, but… I don't like you looking at me like that, Jasper."

"At you like what?"

"Like I'm mad. I know it sounds odd to say there's a strange man living here, but, really, it would be odd if there wasn't. None of us have even seen the whole place yet. There's no one else around for miles. No security to speak of. I'm surprised there isn't a whole town in here, so don't look at me like that."

"Sorry."

"*No* security to speak of. Flo's right about one thing: Father was absolutely mad to buy this. He always does things just to brag about them, you know? All of it so that the night before we left, he could sit in the club parlor and tell Van Wyck, *we're going for a stay in a castle*. Ridiculous. I'd go so far as to say irresponsible." He twisted his mouth. "You believe me, don't you?"

Jasper almost said no. The idea of it was delightful. But he nodded yes. Birds chirped outside, no hands or feet or iron bumped the walls. Wherever Ansehelm was, he could get himself breakfast today. He wished he could say as much to Leo.

"Anyway, I hate staying in these close quarters." Leo knocked the spoon around his cup. "Oh, and I have a job for you, while you have an excuse to be poking around the apartments. I don't want my sister writing Bernard. I gave her his calling card, so I need you to steal it back. It's a cream color with bronze trim. I don't know where she put it, but I'm sure it's organized well, being how uptight she is. My God, Jasper, you're filthy."

Dirt covered the uniform jacket, again.

"I had to sleep on the floor."

Leo's face scrunched, and Jasper said he'd check on breakfast. Both cooks were still asleep. The front door creaked as Mr. Thorley brushed into the apartments, not quite dressed. He noticed Jasper with a nervous bristle.

"Is Mr. Lambert awake? Senior, I mean."

"Haven't heard him."

Thorley got close enough to whisper.

"That man, Shaw," he said, "apparently he never made it home last night. There's a group of men outside. His horse is still in our stables."

"My God." Jasper pointed his thumb over his shoulder at Leo's room. "Did you tell them about—?"

"About what? That?" Mr. Thorley shook his head. "No. Not yet. I don't know. You don't have to worry about it; worry about keeping him happy. If you have the chance, start packing. And clean up. Where did all that dirt come from?"

He clapped Jasper's sleeve once then pivoted, knocking on the master bedroom door.

╫╫

Hours later, Leo was feeling better, though everyone else's moods had turned. The men from the town were combing the property and the woods around it, now looking for two missing people. The Lamberts' attitude was that the men should be helping them find the culprit who had attacked Leo, but they were, for some reason, more interested in their missing neighbors. Mrs. Lambert discussed with Verna about whether it was wise for Leo to travel. Either way, they were down a driver. Mr. Lambert would have to go back into town to make all the plans for their departure. They would have to cancel the new staff that was to be sent up, among other things. Eager to get away, the women took the trip with him, leaving the apartment near empty.

"Verna, you ought check on the injured driver," Leo said as she ran a cloth over his hands. "Really, I'm fine for now. Jasper will fetch you if I need anything."

The nurse was happy enough to do that, leaving the two alone. When she had, Leo's mouth crawled into a sly little smile.

"I hope you don't find these marks repulsive," he said. Jasper shook his head no. "Why don't you undress for me?" His tone dipped. "You really are dirty. That can't be all from the floor."

"I…." Jasper shook his head. "Can't we wait?"

Leo snorted in derision.

"Really?"

"I'm—" He shrugged. Tired? He was always tired. Busy? He worked for Leo. After everything since yesterday, the way they had spoken last night, it seemed gross. Surprising that it had been suggested at all. Was Leo not angry with him anymore, or was that unimportant?

"I thought you always wanted to," Leo said matter of fact. "Isn't that the way your kind is? Working so hard all day, building up an appetite, so to speak."

Taken aback, Jasper did nothing but stare at him, leaning against the headboard with teacup in hand.

"Oh, you know." Leo laughed a bit. "Well, everyone says you people can be like animals."

Jasper clenched his jaw to keep it from hanging open. He swallowed before speaking.

"Is that what you think?"

Leo shook his head with a huff. "You know what I mean. I'm not calling you an animal. But that suit I bought you is the nicest thing you own, and you managed to cover it in mud within days. Honestly, even being a domestic is too genteel for you, but that's to be expected; it's nothing to get flustered about. So what if it's not a good use of you? Your talents are *elsewhere.*"

Leo slouched, perfectly at ease, while Jasper flushed under the starchy collar.

"What is it?" he asked, reaching his hand towards Jasper's hip. "Come on, don't be so sour."

Instead, Jasper suggested, it was the perfect opportunity to steal that address back from Florence. With a frown, Leo agreed.

"Come right back so we have some time before they return," he said. "Really, Jasper. I mean, I'm up for it, and I was brutally attacked last night."

Jasper pulled away from his hand.

The girls' bedroom had been split down the middle, one side piled with Elsie's necessities and the other primly organized. On Florence's nightstand was an address book that opened right to H, with Bernard Harrison's calling card serving as a bookmark. Jasper hadn't expected that task to be so quick. He didn't want to go back now. Servant, lover, animal, as Leo liked it.

This room must have a secret entrance. He scrutinized the wood until a ridge in the wall on Elsie's side told him he might have found it. In the corner, near a dresser, he pulled a panel back. There was just enough room for someone to fit through.

"Dorothy, are you going into my sisters' room?"

He heard Leo speaking as loud as possible.

"I have the rest of Miss Elsie's clothes," Dottie said. The door handle turned. Just as she entered, Jasper ducked into the wall.

He could stand, but it was a narrow fit. Heavy dust swelled between the planks. He could wait her out, choke on dust, then scurry back to Leo to pleasure him. Instead, he shuffled left, left, right, until wood gave way to stone. He must be around the great hall now. Stepping carefully, he eventually felt the rung of a ladder underfoot. It took him down to an offshoot and back out to familiar packed dirt. One match, and he recognized the main tunnel, the one he always walked from tower to tower. Tossing Bernard's card, he made his way towards the back of Kasteel Verlossen. He hadn't written his mother. If she didn't get a letter postmarked from the castle, he wouldn't hear the end of it, even if he was back in the city tomorrow. She couldn't stand not being a priority.

Memories of her interjected themselves. Yelling, sobbing. More came of men he'd been with, ones he didn't like remembering. A cacophony of others bearing down on him, words, rough hands, heat under his cheeks.

Outside was gray but bright, so that he had to shield his eyes. It was moist, the smell of fungus, leaves, and flowers infused the air. A sapphire blue dragonfly zig zagged across his face. Leo would be missing him and certainly wonder how he had gotten out of Florence's room. The mere thought of pulling out all his excuses sapped his energy. The shoes rattled his feet so he took them off and walked into the overgrowth.

His vision was all meshed browns and greens cut with saturated wildflowers. The remnants of the coffin, half-buried and weathered from the storms, had become an almost natural extension of the thicket. The back gate was wide open; through it lines of boot prints lead in only one direction. The search party must have come this way. A twig dug into the underside of his foot, but he didn't want to put the shoes back on. Enthralling to feel the woods under his bare feet. A slice of the dream flashed by.

The forest shivered with life. High-toned trills and deep caws rung from the canopy; branches were rustled by wings he could not see. Spikes of roots were awkward to walk on, but moss felt like quilting under his toes. He caught more boot prints next to hooved tracks. A chipmunk ran past, leaving the light mark of its paw in the ground. Through the trees, he glimpsed the hills, some nearby slopes of green. Others, blue, stood sentinel in the distance. The land sloped haphazardly, bulbous rock jutting out in pits and inclines. Out of a crevice, a trunk grew sideways, curling around a boulder before angling towards the sky. From its base, gleaming red discs of mushroom fanned like steps. He took a large breath that ran cool down his throat. There was more inhuman than human in the air here, unlike anything he had ever breathed. It kneaded out his tension as it parsed through his lungs.

His feet rolled over rocks as he worked his way up a slope. A brief look down, and he saw it was steeper than he had realized. Easy to lose track of the land and plenty to catch the eye, to pull you further in. Anything here could be an ingredient in a spell. Were any of them mint? He wanted badly to know what Ansehelm would have created, but he wouldn't now. Things had gone too far. His chest seized up as he remembered *sodomite*. He hadn't repeated it. In the morning it seemed absurd to, but now he took some pleasure in the idea again. Jasper could force Leo to hear it. Make him shatter on purpose.

At the top of the hill, he slid over a fallen trunk and caught the edge of a brick wall through the trees. Pungent smoke rose over them, he gagged, remembering men slumped in alleys and suffering in the corners of his tenement. Piss, shit, and disease, it was all over the city. It had been a week since he'd smelled anything like it, even in the tower cell. He thought of it, blotched with pools of water, moldy, but not smelling of anything else. No other odor to Ansehelm, either.

Those thoughts were stopped by a hand on Jasper's chest and a glowering, gray-bearded man.

"You lost?" He was lanky, untucked shirt billowing over him. He held a rifle.

"No. Taking a walk." Jasper was nervous, and it sounded like a lie. The man's eyes went to his feet. He threw his shoes on. "Didn't want them to scuff."

The man looked as if he'd eaten something distasteful.

"You're with the new people at Verlossen."

"You searching for Morlen? And Shaw?" Jasper asked, sizing him up. Was this the type of person who would have locked Ansehelm away?

"Found *some*one." The man pointed at the brick. "That's Morlen's place. *Some*one's in there."

Without another word, he marched towards the house. Jasper hung back at first, but then followed, hoping to glean what he could. It was nothing more than a hut, chimney spewing thick smoke. The whole place stunk of sour meat. The man knocked, calling for the missing people. No answer. He moved to the window, bending his knees as he peered in. With a jump he reeled back, gasping out an incoherent cry.

"What is it?" Jasper said.

The man steadied himself on Jasper's arm, pointing at the window.

Stretched out on a table was Shaw, bifocals dark, blood caked over his stomach. He didn't move. The blood was dry. He was missing a leg—the right, cut cleanly at the knee.

Jasper's fingers dug into the windowsill. He could sense the man behind him, quivering. Someone was working at a stove in the corner. All he could make out was the back of a coat and mottled hair until the figure turned, revealing a sagging profile. A hand clutched Jasper's shoulder.

"That's Morlen," the man whispered.

Robert Morlen pulled a tray from his oven which held a human leg. With a knife he sliced off a toe, blew on it, and popped it in his mouth.

Jasper wretched as he was pulled to the ground, out of the window's view. The man was panting wildly, but he held Jasper secure and looked him in the eye.

"Run back. Get to town and tell the sheriff."

Jasper ran. The man collapsed as soon as he let go, barely holding back vomit. Morlen burst from the hut, knife in hand. The last thing Jasper saw was the man standing with his rifle, before the woods obscured the scene. A gunshot. He hoped the man hadn't missed.

He stumbled over rocks and thorns, pulse churning, back through the gate, past the garden, along the side of the castle. As he peeled around to the front he was faced with a carriage, just arrived, Horace helping Mrs. Lambert down. They all turned as he finally stopped running, doubling over in exhaustion. Mr. Lambert harrumphed.

"What the devil is the matter with you?"

CHAPTER TWENTY

RAINED, JASPER SUNK into the stone castle steps like they were pillows. He sat looking straight ahead at the rising mountain peaks, drowned by his thoughts. A whiff of that dream-feeling, and the smell of the smoke. He searched for a neutral memory—eating with Ned, but as he recalled it, the pecan in his mouth turned into a toe.

He hadn't told them about that part, not for any reason other than that he had not wanted to speak it aloud. Doing so made him feel complicit. *Murder* was more than enough to send their tails spinning. *The groundskeeper, he killed Shaw, he's a murderer.* They had bickered about whether to flee the place now or after supper. Jasper was left to wait for Horace, who could lead him into town to get the sheriff. It would be quicker if Leo drove them in the car, but it wasn't his place to suggest.

Jasper hadn't seen him, hadn't gone back inside, and *he* certainly hadn't come out. He could use a comforting hand, but did he think he would get that from Leo? Better to sit alone. No one to suck up all the air.

Heavy footfalls from around the castle side shook him out of his daze. What if Morlen followed him? He stood, ready to face whatever came around the bend. It was the bearded man, followed by another person—young, whose face was red from tears.

"Thought I told you to get the sheriff?" the bearded man said.

"Morlen's dead?" Jasper asked.

"No," the man said, quietly adding, "I missed. He ran off. The others out there know, but we have to get back. I'll get the sheriff, you being so slow and all. Need to tell the rest of the family." He glanced at his companion, then took Jasper aside. "That's Shaw's son. Do you have anything for nerves? He needs something. Your people are hospitable, right?"

Watery-eyed, the son stared at the ground with broad shoulders curled in. He never looked up but let Jasper guide him around the side of the castle. The bearded man dealt with Horace and the stables as the two continued inside.

"I'm Jasper, what's your name?" he asked.

The man blinked, as if just then realizing where he was. "Tom."

Meat sizzled in the kitchen. The chefs looked at them as they spread over a countertop.

"What do you like, Tom?" Jasper put scotch and the tincture in front of him, hoping Verna was around. Tom gulped the whiskey straight from the bottle.

The butler was there now too, frowning at them from across the kitchen. Jasper walked up to him, explaining who the younger Shaw was.

"*Alright.*" Thorley was annoyed. "Did you tell Mr. or Mrs. Lambert he's here?"

"No."

"Jasper, you cannot invite strangers into their home and serve him their food and drink without asking."

He thought to laugh in Thorley's face, though his composure held. The butler left, perhaps sensing he couldn't do anything more to sway Jasper. Frankie asked, "Does he need something to eat?"

Jasper smelled the charred fat from the pork. "No...not right now." He led Tom into the dormitories. Only one wing was occupied now, where those who hadn't spent the night in the apartments had bundled together for safety. Jasper gave Ned a small wave before leading the man into an empty room. Better to have privacy. Tom slunk onto an unmade cot, and Jasper sat facing him. He was probably Jasper's age, wearing an undershirt beneath a worn leather jacket. Mud fell from his boots onto the bed where he'd sprawled out, one hand on his forehead, the other on the neck of the bottle. Big eyes darted back and forth, eventually settling on Jasper like he was coming out of a daze.

"Thank you. I just need to rest a little, and I'll be on my way. Gotta compose myself. I don't want to be like this when I see Ma." His voice cracked. "You saw him? Garett said you did."

Jasper nodded.

"You saw the *whole* thing? You know, I made Garrett tell me what happened, the whole thing, and I regret it."

"Yeah, yeah, I did," Jasper said. He thought of toothless gums eating slugs. Tom stared at the ceiling, and Jasper did too. Both of them filthy from the woods and sweat, laying on fresh mattresses. When he noticed Thorley, haggard in the entrance, he assumed it was to chide them about that. Using the Lamberts' beds without permission. Resting on the Lamberts' time without permission.

"Have you seen Ned?" Mr. Thorley had a hint of panic in his voice.

"Yeah, I just passed him."

"He's not there now."

"Leg's feeling better?" Jasper swung up.

"No. Not last anyone spoke to him about it, anyway. It certainly wasn't healed, and he could not have gone far on it."

"He must be around. Maybe just got antsy," Jasper said. A pit was growing in his stomach.

"*You* need to get back up there. The other Mr. Lambert is clamoring for you."

"What does he want?"

"*You*. Attend to him, for God's sake." Thorley tapped his foot. "He'll fire you like he fired Charlie."

The butler was gone, and Tom Shaw pulled himself up, resting his head in his palm.

"I didn't get you in trouble, did I?" he asked.

"What? No," Jasper laughed.

"Good. Thank you. There a place I can wash my face?"

He gave directions to the water pump and offered to walk him there but was declined. Tom staggered out, and Jasper examined the scotch—between last night and now, it was almost drunk down. If Leo wanted any, that would be a problem. There'd be no more until they got back to the city, not that that was so far in the future. It could be tonight.

What would Jasper do then? It was decent money doing odd jobs for rich people, but he couldn't go back to the Lambert house, and so much for the reference. He'd get some other line of work. Someone would be hiring, eventually. Even if it was hard, or monotonous, he just needed to find steady work in a normal place. A place where the richest person he had to interact with was the foreman, and for all the disease and suffering he might witness, he wouldn't have to feed anyone leeches. He'd meet a girl he got along with, and they'd get married. He'd have his own kids, a family that would stay together, and it would be better at the end of his life than it was at the beginning. Next year, he'd see Florence and Bernard Harrison's wedding announcement in the paper and know Leo was seething. Drinking scotch, remembering the bottle from upstate so cruelly stolen from him by a servant and a boy whose father had just been murdered.

Why had Jasper agreed to come up here? Because he thought he was important to Leo the same way Leo was important to him. Because he didn't think he'd ever find another lover.

Jasper felt the little velvet pouch inside his pocket. With everything going on, it had slipped his mind. He could look now, in the privacy of this place, and then go upstairs to face whatever was happening. Maybe it was a jewel. Wouldn't it be funny to find treasure after all? He heard light clinks as he overturned the pouch and dropped the contents into his palm.

In an instant he overturned his hand, scattering them on the cot. Teeth. Calcified, with deep gray streaks along the roots. Undeniably human, at least thirty of them. Two were fangs. Curved, nearly an inch long. Jasper pressed the tip of one and felt a point sharp as a knife.

He didn't realize how quickly he had fled until he was back in the kitchen. He had left them there—the teeth—for anyone to see. It hardly mattered. His gut twisted, knowing something he would not allow his brain to acknowledge. He had to tell somebody about Ansehelm.

Tom Shaw had gone upstairs, Frankie said, and Jasper raced after him. The hall bustled with orders and bickering, luggage spilling out from the apartments. He spotted Shaw at the other end, about to leave through the vestibule.

Ignoring someone calling his name, he rushed to catch Tom. Grabbing the man's arm, he lurched to exit, but the vestibule and steps were cluttered with Lamberts. Behind, Thorley shouted for him. With barely a word he pulled Tom down a corridor, the only direction free of people. They sprinted further into the castle, stopping eventually in a secluded room where uncovered windows let in dull sunlight. Jasper apologized, listening for the distant sound of the Lamberts or their staff and, hearing nothing, began.

"I need to tell somebody about this. One of you, from your town, I mean. Not them." Jasper pointed back towards the hall. "There's someone living in the walls of the castle. I found him locked up here, starving, and he's too afraid to leave. Wouldn't even tell me who had done it to him. Now with what I know about Morlen—"

"What's his name?" Tom asked, red eyes wide at Jasper.

"He said Ansehelm."

That meant nothing to Tom, who watched him now with precision.

"Look, I'm sorry to lay this all on you now," said Jasper. "Someone else needed to know, and I didn't tell them, because I didn't trust them to handle it, you know?"

"No. I don't understand," Tom said.

"That's just how it happened. He begged me not to tell anyone but now—"

"You don't want to confess to your employers that you let a man live in their house without telling them?" Tom smiled. Jasper couldn't tell if it was commiseration or a threat.

"He said if anyone knew about him, the people who had tried to kill him would come back."

"And now you think Morlen is responsible?"

Jasper's tongue tied. No, he didn't think Robert Morlen had chained Ansehelm in the tower. There was something else. It came to him like slices of the dream, so clear a feeling but no words were with it, and then it was gone.

Scratching. Behind Tom, the wall moved. From inside, a spindly face looked at Jasper with a finger to its lips. Tom turned, and as he saw it blurted out a wild cry. Frozen, they both stared at the creature in the wall. The quiver of Tom's foot betrayed that he was about to shake loose and run. Clouds rolling over the sky darkened the room. Ansehelm only needed an instant. He sprung, clutched on to both men and sucked them into the wall before the clouds moved again.

Jasper thrashed, trying to wrench free, but the grip dragging him by the collar was too strong. They moved too fast. There was no pause, though Tom screamed enough to shake the stones as they descended. He clutched the dirt, trying to anchor himself, but he and Shaw were bounced over ground and each other like tin cans on strings.

They stopped. Jasper, bruised and dizzy, lurched away, but a weight pinned his ankle. It felt small, like a foot barely curled over his leg, but he could not budge. He might as well have been trying to crawl out from under the mountain itself.

Tom's screams had turned to moans.

"Ansehelm!" Jasper shouted.

The noise from Tom grew fainter until it stopped altogether.

The hand that clamped his mouth was ice cold, but the blood that coursed down it was warm. Tom Shaw's. Some dripped in his mouth. He squirmed, but it didn't loosen

Ansehelm's grip. Another hand lifted him up by his back, pinching some flesh with his shirt, and tossed him.

The thud of the fall rattled his brain, but he recovered in a moment. He picked himself up, spitting out earth and scrambling for a match. In the small light, Jasper saw the vampire beaming down at him from the top of the pit.

Ansehelm jumped down in a blink of an eye. He might as well have appeared in front of Jasper from a puff of smoke. There was flesh on his bones now, filling out the scraps of clothing he was still caked in. The face was fuller, hair grown into long strands. Bony white nubs poked out from the gums.

"I had asked you not to tell anyone," he said. He snatched Jasper's wrist and cut the skin with the slim edge of a fingernail. Jasper heard his own shallow cries apart from himself, his body a whimpering animal. Blood bubbled out of him. Ansehelm's lips circled around the wound, ice-tongue lapping, slimy gums pulling the broken skin.

He let go with a pop, and Jasper stumbled to the ground. The match died in the air, leaving them in darkness.

"I admit, I have wanted to try that since I met you." Rasp vanished, Ansehelm's words flowed melodically. "The taste is charming. A little weak."

"What are you?" Jasper said. He knew; he wanted to hear Ansehelm say it.

"Bah. You and your questions."

Pounding from his skull to his toes, Jasper careened up. All he could make out was the glisten of the monster's eyes. He didn't know he was about to attack Ansehelm until he did. He was on him for a second, squeezing a neck encased in iron, before being swatted off like a fly.

He heard scuttling in the dirt, and lost track of the eyes.

"*Ansehelm.*"

The monster was already gone.

Jasper ripped a tail off the uniform jacket and bandaged his wrist, yelling for help. They'd be able to hear through the floors—they had to—if he screamed as loud as possible. But he was too far down, at the bottom of a pit hollowed out below a secret underground tunnel. His voice cracked as his throat soared. Backing into the side, his knees buckled under him, and he dropped to the ground. One hand landed on something smooth and hard. He felt along it until his fingers dipped into sockets. With a shudder, he knocked the skull away. Every nerve on fire, he sat.

He laughed. He didn't know why, but it kept going. It turned to a wheeze then mounted into a ferocious, strange screech. That shifted to frenzied chatter, then back to calling for help, but this time the words came out as laughs. Of course it was funny, he thought, funny that he had been so witless, funny that he had expected anything special or nice or lucky. Didn't he know who he was? There was no stopping it—the laughter spewed out from some place so deep within him he had not known it was there.

✚

The sounds died. The fires on his nerves went out. Heart sunk, the pain set in. The hand that had been stepped on, his right, still in its gauze, hurt again now. His right wrist had been drunk from, and that side from nails to elbow all stung in tandem. The rest of him pulsed with sore spots where he had been dragged and flung. Lying flat on the ground was all he could do, thinking of how nice it would be to fall into a deep sleep.

They knew someone lived in the walls. Leo knew, and he wouldn't let himself be questioned. Even if they weren't looking for Jasper, they'd look in here. The pit was by the base of the tower where Elsie had seen Ansehelm. Not far from the corridor where her brother had been walking when he was attacked. If they found the tunnels—and they must soon—they would come this way.

But, no, the Lamberts would be gone by now. The townspeople were hunting for Morlen.

They would look for Tom Shaw, wouldn't they? No one would look for Jasper, but they'd look for Tom Shaw. They would have to search the castle. He couldn't see a reason they wouldn't search the castle.

He wished Tom was okay even as he knew Tom was dead. He hoped anyway, as if that alone could upend reality. Tom Shaw had just needed a moment of care after what happened, and Jasper had gotten him killed.

It had been stupid to keep the secret so long, and selfish. Yes, selfish, because though it was gross and tiring, he liked feeding Ansehelm. Having something that the rest of them didn't.

Long enough in the dark and his eyes began to sense miniscule shifts in light. In time, he could move again. Another match burned long enough for him to see there was no obvious way out. The pit was all solid ground except the twelve-foot high mouth that opened from the earth. He dug his hands in the wall under the lip, but the dirt crumbled under him. He latched onto different spots, jumped, scoured for footholds. It wouldn't work, climbing out, but he tried anyway for hours before collapsing into sleep.

Two thumps then another resonated over the pit floor. He saw the glisten of the eyes. The makeshift bandage was unwrapped, and his wound reopened. Shallow incisors clamped over his arm as his blood was sucked.

On the ground he felt for the cloth, thankfully intact, and resealed his wrist. He was lightheaded, but there was plenty of blood left to leak out of him. Something had been put at his feet after he was let go, and by match light he saw a sack stuffed with dinner rolls and half-green peaches. He stuffed a roll in his mouth, suddenly aware of how completely famished he was. It was as if, with no hope of food, he had been pretending not to be hungry. Next to the food was his canteen, the one he'd brought with him from city, filled with water. He had barely finished chewing as he guzzled it down, interrupted by a violent coughing fit. He drank more to soothe his throat and broke open another roll. His nose crinkled at the smell of rotting meat. It wasn't from the sack.

Two bodies had been dropped into the pit. Tom Shaw and Ned. Bloodless eyes bulged out of their sockets. He dropped the match and scooped up the sack to huddle with it in a corner. He whoofed down the peaches, biting through the hard, unripe parts too. Sugary juice splashed into his nostrils.

There were three more thumps the next time. Ansehelm brought food and drank from him. Jasper let it all happen in a daze, and when the monster was gone, he lit a match to see who had been taken. Earl, Horace. Another man he didn't recognize. They had not left the castle, but no one had found the tunnels. The stench was excruciating. He had no choice but to bear it.

CHAPTER TWENTY-ONE

THE EYES WERE BACK again, gleaming from the top of the pit.

"I have a gift for you," Ansehelm said. Jasper heard the thump along with muffled cries—alive this time. He dashed towards the noise, but a stony grip held him back.

"You will have him soon enough." The monster unraveled the cloth, stiff with dried blood, from his arm. Jasper took it with a wince, as he had done before. When it was over, he waited for food and water while his dizziness subsided. The sack fell at his feet. The eyes were gone. Someone sobbed in the pit.

"Leo?"

"Jasper? Is that you?" His voice was ragged with fear. "What is that horrible smell?"

Following the voice and faint outline of his body, Jasper crouched at his side.

"Are you hurt? Did he drink from you?"

"No. *Drink from—*" Leo whimpered, reaching for Jasper's hand. "No. He's using me. He needs father to comply. To give him the castle."

"What happened? How long has it been?" Jasper wrapped an arm around him.

"Days. A few days. I called for you. Thorley saw you with that man from the town, and then you were gone." Leo's palms were clammy. He continued. Ned had disappeared that day too. The sheriff and townspeople were crawling all over the place looking for the murderer. They found more bodies in his hut, but there were still people unaccounted for. They searched the whole castle, and all the woods around it. The Lamberts kept trying to leave, but things went wrong. Carriages broke, horses died, the auto was destroyed. The other drivers disappeared—that was yesterday. Everyone was in a panic. Today they had ordered more transportation, carriages that would arrive from the town to take them away. No chance for the vehicles to break that way, but it meant the earliest they could leave was tomorrow morning. The townspeople thought Morlen must be taking victims on some other part of the mountain and decided to move their search. At sunset, an hour ago, they said goodbye to the Lamberts, assuming none would see each other again. Then the family had sat down to dinner.

That was when the creature had come. It overpowered them. They saw it kill. It made demands of Mr. Lambert—it wanted the castle, maybe more. It wanted them under its control. Leo thought he was going to die when it put its claws on him, but it took him as collateral. William Lambert would get his son back if he complied.

Leo had one cigarette left. He lit a match and the corpses stared at him, necks and limbs lying twisted where they had fallen. He screamed, losing the light and tobacco on the ground. Jasper held him as he panted, gagged, then fell over vomiting. Rubbing Leo's back, Jasper suppressed a wretch at the new smell.

"Why aren't you dead?" Leo asked. Jasper felt himself flush, but he couldn't be seen. It soothed him a small bit that his expressions were hidden.

"I don't know. He's been feeding off me."

Leo pulled away, and Jasper heard him kicking at the wall.

"We have to get out," Leo said. "Here, help me climb."

"Give me some time." His right arm tingled.

"*Now.* We can't stay here," he barked.

"I tried that already, and it didn't work," Jasper said. "I've fallen so many times. My blood is being sucked away."

"Hold me up and I'll climb out."

"My hand hurts. Somebody stepped on it."

The kicking stopped. Leo said, "That was days ago."

"It didn't heal."

"I lost blood too. That creature is the same thing that attacked me before, or didn't you know?" Leo's pitch was rising. "It's targeting our family. What if it kills my father? Or my mother and sisters? It needs me, it doesn't need Elsie or Florence. What if it—"

"Maybe it'll just eat the help," said Jasper, picturing Ned's bloodless, bulging eyes.

"Maybe!" Leo sounded too chipper. As if Jasper had meant to console him. As if it were a relief to imagine more bodies piled up in here. How could he call himself a target while surrounded by the corpses of those Ansehelm had killed? Didn't he care that Jasper was being eaten alive?

Jasper could spot his silhouette easily enough. Walking over he cupped Leo's face, feeling his nose and chin. As he had done so many times before, kissing, in bed. He knew Leo couldn't see the fist coming. He hooked him under the cheekbone, sending him sputtering back. Jasper nursed his stinging knuckles with a laugh.

Hell was the only clear word Leo said as he charged him in the dark. Jasper dodged, finding safety against the wall.

"You sniveling little shit, where the hell are you!" Leo shouted with such exasperation one might expect him to pop.

"I'm sorry," Jasper said. It had felt good but perhaps was not so smart. "I've been in this pit too long. Come on, we can scale the wall together."

Between heavy breaths, Leo said, "I don't trust you now. I'll do it on my own."

"Okay," said Jasper, "but even if you get out of the pit, you won't be able to get out of the tunnels."

"Tunnels? What are you talking about?"

"The tunnels. The spaces in the walls." Jasper spoke about it like it was obvious. "How do you think the creature gets around?"

Low-voiced, Leo asked for an explanation. He grew demanding when met with silence, the pit filled with his singular question until, chest tight, Jasper capitulated.

On the first day, he had discovered the tunnels and a dying man in the tower. Easier to admit with his words disembodied by the dark. He had feared a mysterious gang—such a foolish lie to believe, but out loud he only talked about how scared he'd been. Nor did he mention the leeches, or the potions, but he did tell Leo that he had smoked one of William's stolen cigars. That he had known what has happening when they heard scratching from the walls.

The more he talked, the closer Leo stepped. Vomit still clung to him. His breath was hot.

"Are you telling me that you let a monster torture me and my family?" His hands hovered around Jasper's throat. Before they had a chance to squeeze, Jasper knocked his head into Leo's and shoved him away.

Leo's just-distinct form swayed back and forth. Jasper kept his eye on it, ready as it marched forward again. When Leo was close enough, he cut him under his jaw. There was a cry, and the form was on the ground.

"You goddamned worm," Leo spat. "You damned cretin, you—"

"Shut up." Jasper spoke it with a burst of air. "You're a selfish, whining louse, you know that, Leo?"

A wheeze, and Leo said, "Better that than a traitor."

"I was trying to help someone, and he—it—betrayed me. It wasn't my fault." Jasper swallowed, hot under his cheeks. What he hadn't admitted to buzzed under the surface. "I was trying to save someone. You wouldn't know anything about that. You dragged me here because you wanted someone to fuck who you could treat like dirt. You think you matter more than anybody else, you and your sisters and your parents. You weren't tortured. It's those people, those bodies over there, who were murdered. I've been trapped alone here for days. He comes and drinks my blood. Don't you care at all?"

"I care." Leo's voice was flat. "But it is not *selfish* or *whining* for me to be more concerned about my family than *you*."

They both panted in the dark, pit crowded with bodies, vomit, and rot.

"I had four sisters die." The words popped out of Jasper's mouth.

"So what? They're not here, are they? I assume they died a long time ago, and it's no longer worth bothering about."

Nell and Annie, infants, Matilda, five, and Ellen, thirteen. He didn't know why he had said it. For so long, he hadn't thought of their names or faces, only to blurt it out here and now. It felt like he'd exposed himself. Clutching his arms over his chest, he mumbled, "No one cares about them."

"Did you unleash a monster on them too? A monster in the walls of whatever squalid rat's nest you live in?" Leo spat. "I always treated you well, Jasper, like a gentleman, and it turns out you're nothing more than a greedy, dumb, violent animal."

Jasper heard Leo's fingers scraping the ground.

"What's this?" Leo's tone was somber.

"A skull," Jasper said. "You won't die down here, but I will." He laughed, and after a moment the other did too.

"I hate that I want you," Leo said. "You come to me after having fucked God knows what, dirty my sheets and drink my liquor. I wish I could be different, so I didn't have to be around the likes of you. It would be one thing if I could be with a refined man. Not perverted."

"Perverted," Jasper murmured.

"Yes. You are. Don't think I can't tell. If it was women, you'd have already gotten a dozen pregnant and left the infants to starve. You know no woman of my caliber would ever touch you, but since we are what we are, I had to settle. It's not fair. Now after everything I've done for you, you've let this monstrous creature loose in my home."

"It's not your home," Jasper said.

"Isn't it? I own it, don't I? My family and I own it!" he shouted.

Jasper said *sodomite* and slunk to the ground. He felt a little twist in his gut, a feeling that he had betrayed something. It was worth it a moment later. The sound out of Leo was between a shriek and a bellow, spewing insults as he reeled into a hateful diatribe. Jasper stretched his legs out. If he focused on the outlines of the bodies and the horrid smell, he could tune out the rant. He didn't need to hear the vitriol; it was enough to know that Leo was in pieces. His heart pounded louder than the screeching.

Henry. That was the name of the brother who he had played the game with. They pretended to be grown-ups, Henry always dictating the scenarios. He went at nine. Same disease that took Matilda. But Nancy—Nancy was alive, living by the pier with the kids she must have by now. If Jasper made it out, he would go there first and talk with her about everyone, their parents and all the siblings. He wanted it so bad, he would beg Ansehelm for it.

He wondered if Leo would kill him in his sleep. He could do the same, he supposed.

The pit was silent. At times he dozed, at others, he heard Leo's slow breathing. He tried to piece together how much time had passed, but the track was easy to lose.

A yellow light glowed like a star from the top of the pit. Through half-sleep, he saw it, and it shocked him awake.

"Hey!" he called. "Hey! Down here!"

Leo stirred. The glow was enough that Jasper could make out his face, bruised along the cheek and mouth, with a fat lip. There was still some shine to his hair, the grease caked in deep. They glanced acrimoniously at each other as they converged under the light.

A haggard man held up a lantern, and Jasper recognized the jeering mouth. He'd seen it eat a toe. Robert Morlen leaned his head down to gander at them. Twigs stuck out of his hair. He tossed a line of rope down. Leo leapt for it—Jasper wanted to warn him, but he shirked away to scuttle up the rope. It might be their only chance to escape, regardless of who was helping them. With a weak arm, Jasper climbed slower. He tried not to look down at the corpses.

Morlen waited patiently, tight-lipped under Leo's demands to know who he was. He furled the rope up once Jasper was out, watching them with waxy eyes. He had an old musket, the kind that ended in a bayonet, and when he had his rope back, he pointed it at them.

"What kind of rescue is this?" Leo fumed.

"Take it you're the son," Morlen said. He looked from Leo to Jasper. "You still have blood in you, so you're coming too."

"Where?" Leo demanded.

"Don't get all excited." Morlen jabbed the bayonet in the air to usher them forward. "He wants you. I'll hide you where he won't find."

"What for?" Jasper asked. The man hopped forward, waving the musket in his face.

"So I'll have what he wants!" He bared rotting teeth and ordered them to walk, rusty metal poking at their sides. They complied, walking back towards the central tower and the main tunnel stretch. Jasper glanced at Leo, who avoided his eye. Behind, Morlen cackled to himself.

"You have to be careful. Not much can kill him!" Morlen said. "Would be nice to be that way. He's been alive a long time. That's what *I* want."

"Oh, do you?" Leo sneered.

"Yes! And I'll get it soon. Crack his secret."

The lantern swung from side to side, shifting the shadows with it. The bayonet faltered. The old groundskeeper was only half-minding them. In one motion, Jasper stepped back and slammed Morlen into the beams, reaching for the musket. He got ahold, but Morlen tugged back, Jasper dodging the point of the bayonet as he pulled. Leo had spun around and grabbed Morlen's arms, but Morlen jammed the butt of the gun into his side. He doubled over as Jasper lost his grip. The bayonet stuck under Leo's chin.

"None of that. You want to make it out of these tunnels, you'll follow me." Morlen swung the point to threaten Jasper too. "He's sleeping now, but it's close to sunset. Won't be safe here at night."

Leo stood and, after a prod from the musket, kept walking. Jasper fell in line. Morlen was marching them through the main tunnel, but they were coming up on one of the offshoots. Jasper knew he could lose him in its bends. Leo rubbed his side. Still in evening wear, splotched and torn, skin inflamed with pink sucker marks. The bruise on his cheek was deep purple. Jasper's left hook wasn't so bad. He finally caught his eye and titled his head to the side, towards the offshoot. Leo edged closer to him.

Jasper shored himself up, ready to move as fast as possible. He pulled Leo by the sleeve, releasing him once they peeled into the bend. Jasper was prepared for the narrower tunnel, but he heard a grunt as Leo knocked into the wall. Lantern light was dim behind them. He pressed on through the darkness ahead, turning whenever he felt a corner. There was no light now, and though he suspected he'd lost Morlen, he didn't stop. He twisted through the maze until he spilled back into a wide tunnel, a rancid smell letting him know the pit was near. One match left—all he needed was a glimpse. The slope towards the central tower flashed before him. Just the memory of climbing it made him shudder. Now he could be sure where the tunnel paths would take him, and he sprinted until he was squeezed out onto the grass.

CHAPTER TWENTY-TWO

THE AFTERNOON SUN was blinding. Hunched over on the ground, Jasper covered his face and wheezed in the heat. He crawled into the shade of the stable wall and, blinking, began to adjust. Lime-colored grass stretched out to the bushes, insects buzzing through pollen-choked air that made his eyes water. The castle wall sizzled. Leo wasn't with him. He tried to think back to when he might have lost him, but it was all a blur. Jasper couldn't go back in the tunnels, not now. Leo would be safe, or at least not dead. Morlen and Ansehelm both needed to use him. He was too important.

Wet blood seeped through the cloth on his wrist. He threw the jacket off and tore away the other tail for a fresh bandage. It was a clear, blue day, and he could see every grisly detail of the wound. A crisscross of bumpy ridged skin ran down his forearm, cuts that had started to scab and then been ripped open. Between the scars fresh blood pooled out in ruby red dots. He was thirsty. There was water in his canteen in the pit.

There were no horses in the stables. Carriages lay in pieces, wheels and sides smashed apart. Wires splintered out from under the car, the smell of gasoline soaking in hay. The water pump glittered copper in the sun. He could see into the kitchen and servants' quarters; all the doors had been left open. Blankets and pans and food and luggage sat idle. There were no people. By the cots, bags were packed except for sleeping clothes, laid out in expectation of one last night. His bag had been moved next to Ned's. He scraped the reeking uniform off.

Naked, he ran the water at the pump over himself, drinking as he washed his head, then relaxed into his old clothes. On his way to the kitchen he grabbed a rifle. He was ready to fire it as he poked around, eating what he could find. Most of it was fresh enough. He peeled withering skin off a chicken breast before taking a bite.

He could go down the road to the town. He didn't know the way, and even if he was fast, it would still be at least another night before he could get any help. Ansehelm would kill again if the groundskeeper didn't beat him to it. Everyone was expendable except the Lambert men—that's how Leo had made it sound. Jasper should save who he could while he had the chance. He gulped more water before circling around to the front. No one on the steps. Down the drawbridge, the was gate locked. The two mountain peaks leered at him, bright green against a cloudless sky.

Fighting Morlen was one thing, but what about the vampire? Jasper's heart dropped. Someone had rendered it harmless, but he had undone all that. It seemed cold then, even in the sun.

Whoever was still alive would be kept prisoner, somewhere in the castle depths. Jasper told himself he would go back into the tunnels to find them if he had to, though the idea of it made his blood freeze. *Had* to. Punishment for his dense selfishness.

The big double doors were locked, and as he rounded back towards the kitchen, he saw a flutter of movement down the other end of the castle. A person, he was almost certain, they dashed away before he could see much of anything. He followed, preparing for Morlen or one of the townspeople. Or Leo.

Around the back, a breeze blew, and nothing moved in the windows. Bees whizzed towards the clusters of garden flora. He hovered outside it, brushed by peach branches. There was a rustle from within the garden, and he stepped in, rifle first. A blonde head shot out.

"You!" Elsie cried. Jasper put a finger to his lips and shooed her back behind the wall. It was cooler under the canopy. Her lavender dinner gown was marred with grass stains, skirt spilling over her feet. She had taken a petticoat and wrapped it around her bare shoulders, which she balled behind her back when she saw Jasper.

"What happened? Do you know where my family is? Did you see that beast? Where were you?"

"Don't shout," he said. He fanned his hands down, and she fell silent. They sat in the iris bed, Elsie rubbing the petals of a purple flower by her knee. She looked at him with a child's glazed fright.

"The groundskeeper is around, Morlen," Jasper said.

"The murderer?" she whispered.

"The cannibal."

Her hands flew to her mouth to cover her shriek. It was a little mean of him, he thought, noticing the panic rise in her eyes.

"It's okay. He's not that strong. But he can walk around in the day."

"As opposed to whom?" She clutched his forearm in satin gloves, one finger needling his wound.

He jerked away. "Tell me what you know."

"Nothing," she said. "I've been out here since last night. That monster. He's unbelievably strong. He said he had business with Father. It was at dinner, the chef and the others came up with guns. Mother told us to run, and I did, but no one else was behind me, and I heard gunshots. I saw that man kill someone with my own eyes."

"Who?"

"I don't know who."

"You don't know?" Jasper glared.

"I hid in here. No one has come out. Are they…" Her face pinched. "…dead?"

"Leo isn't. Your father is probably alive, but I don't know for sure. Ned, Horace, and Earl, they're gone, along with two other men."

She bit her lip. "And where were you?"

"In a pit. Filled with corpses."

She shrieked again. "What do those awful men want?"

To eat us, he thought. She looked at him, sharp, despite the tears in her eyes.

Her voice dropped. "Why aren't *you* dead?" His mouth hung open before cracking into a smile.

"Your brother asked me the same thing."

"You saw him? You talked to him?"

"Yes. No more questions," Jasper said. She huffed and asked what they were going to do.

"That's a question," he said, and she made a sad, scared sound from the back of her throat. He sighed. "Look, we'd have to walk, but we can make it to town and get help. But if we do that, no one will save the rest of them until tomorrow."

She thought about that and asked, "Do you think they'll survive the night?"

He didn't pick on her about questions again, though the temptation was there.

"Honestly," he said, "no. He'll kill at least one person."

"He has business with Father. You said Leo's alive; is he keeping him alive?"

"Yeah, he wants him alive."

"And surely Mother and Florence too, right?" She grew frantic. "He needs us for something, that's why he wouldn't let us leave. They'll be alright for now, won't they?"

"He'll kill *somebody*," Jasper said.

"But not us. Not my parents, or my brother, or sister." Elsie said it over again.

Jasper kneaded his palms into his eyes. Couldn't blame her for caring more about her family than anyone else. None of his family was in danger, so he guessed he had free range to care about anybody and nobody. Suppose he left her right now. Pilfered their suitcases for money, walked until he found a ride back to the city, and didn't tell anyone what was happening. They would survive if they survived.

The sun was turning gold. "Alright, listen." He looked her in the eye. "This thing can't come out in the day. We have a few hours left to find everyone and run. We need to watch out for Morlen, but we can take him if we're smart."

He held her hand as she stood and led her back towards the castle. At the woodshed, he handed her a rifle, which she held palms-flat, as if scared to touch it.

"Um," she said.

"You never held a gun?" he asked. "It's simple, just point and shoot."

Gingerly, she curled her fingers over it. With an eye cocked, she examined the trigger, poking at it like it was a strange new technology. He showed her: pull that back, hold it like this, keep your hands here when you're ready to fire.

"Oh, so it isn't *just point and shoot.* I knew there was more to it," Elsie said.

In the kitchen, he handed her a meat cleaver and oil lantern. Her fingers splayed out, juggling them all together.

"Quite a lot to carry!" she remarked.

"No complaining," he said. She sniffed.

"You're a real brute, you know. I cannot understand why Leo replaced Charlie with you."

"Please, Elsie." He sucked in a breath.

"*Miss Lambert,*" she said.

"No." He took a second lamp and knife while she arranged herself, frowning.

In the great hall, sunlight shone in big rays through the arched windows. The table was set with full plates of food. A few glasses had fallen. Frankie's body lay a few feet from the kitchen steps. Proulx was farther, flat on the stone. There was no blood. Elsie's incisors dug into her lower lip, suppressing a cry. It took them both a while before they could press on. Pieter Van Hoensbroeck's portrait was sliced in ribbons.

Which way to go? He listened for scratches, voices, anything, but it was silent. The apartments were empty, undisturbed like the dormitories. Elsie squirmed as she glanced over her own packed bags. They had to pass the bodies in the hall to get to the central tower. Jasper feared checking it, growing surer by the minute that something would be up there. Nothing in the bedroom. Standing on the chair, he stuck the barrel through the trap door before peeking into the cell.

"Since when was that there?" Elsie balked next to her old bed. "How did you know about that?"

"No questions," he said. There was nothing up there except the half a chain dangling from the stone. The others could be anywhere. Imprisoned, hiding, already dead. They climbed down and passed the chapel. The compartment under the pulpit was uncovered, nothing in it. They walked towards the courtyard, peeking into each room they passed. It was quiet, with no one alive, no one in the walls, and not even the sound of rain.

"Elsie." He spoke barely above a whisper, but it still felt too loud. "About your translation of the journal."

She looked surprised. "You care about that?"

"Yes. Did you ever get a sense of what was happening in it? Of what happened to Van Hoensbroeck?"

She tilted her head. "I suppose a bit. I know it wasn't very good. Don't make fun of me."

"I won't."

"Well, what I gathered is that Van Hoensbroeck hates his uncle. Hard to tell why, precisely, but the uncle is stealing money, and he can't stop it. He often calls him the devil. But he's following the uncle, or the uncle's following him. Hoensbroeck is very tormented; it seemed he was involved in something downright evil. I think he was planning to kill his uncle; there was a sentence that said as much, but that could have been an idiom. Flo gave me a whole lecture on idioms." She bit her lip when she mentioned her sister. "Anyway, I didn't get far. My dictionary went missing."

The courtyard's dead grass fried in the heat as they circled it, looking for prisoners in the windows. Jasper listened at the exits for voices that could be carried through the empty rooms. Elsie thought she heard something from the right, so they went back in, opening every door they passed. Finding no one, they tried the next hall, and the next. He had to tell her to be quiet as she shouted for her family. In the library, the piles of books cast long shadows, and they had to admit they'd lost the trail, if there ever was one. Snaking through the stacks, Jasper asked, "Wasn't a search party supposed to come from the town?"

"They came yesterday. No, the day before." She paused. "We were supposed to be gone. I don't know if they're coming back. How come you can ask questions and I can't?"

Out of the library, Jasper stopped at the base of the third tower. Elsie's eyes popped up the stairs and back at him.

"We're not going into that horrid room are we?" she asked, shivering when he nodded yes. "The monster—the monster was there that day!" She jumped as if a spider had landed on her.

The laboratory door was open only a crack. He tried to see through it as he listened. Silence, darkness. Extending the rifle he nudged the door. Nothing reacted to the creak. He pushed it wider.

Glass shattered and inky black acid spilled from above. The rifle was dissolving; Jasper tossed it and pushed Elsie back. Acid ate through the rock, leaving a plate-sized hole at the laboratory threshold. The door swung open, now shredded in parts where the potion had splashed. Beyond it, the tunnel wall was open, and the part of the desk he could see was cluttered with equipment and books. There was some liquid in the cauldron. He stepped forward, leg up over the hole, but was stopped by Elsie's gloved hand clenched around his arm.

"What are you doing?" she squealed.

"We should see what he's up to. And if anyone is in there."

"What if there's more?" Elsie pointed to the top of the door where the acid had fallen. Jasper didn't think Ansehelm would risk destruction inside the laboratory. But maybe he had concocted a more precise trap.

"Give me your rifle," he said. He had to hold it from the edge of the butt to reach from where they stood, but he was able to push the door open wider, angling to see as much of the room as possible. Whatever else was bubbling up in there, it was devoid of people. He turned around to see Elsie pointing through to the tunnel entrance.

"Where does that go?" she asked.

"The tunnels under the castle," he said.

"Tunnels…" She held her shoulders and snapped, "How do *you* know that?"

Taking a moment to choose his answer, Jasper said, "That's where the monster was keeping me."

A red-ribboned scroll paper had fallen to the laboratory floor. The map. Close to the entrance; if Jasper leaned, he could pick it up with the rifle.

"What's that? What are you doing?" Elsie asked.

"Map." He edged it closer, trying to hook the barrel through the middle of the scroll.

"Map? Of what?"

There—he had it. He swung the barrel, but the scroll was not as secure as he thought, and it dropped into the gorge.

"Shit."

Satin knuckles smacked the back of his head. Jasper spun around, swiping at her hand though it was already away from him.

"Excuse my language," he said. She stared, mouth-scrunched, full to the brim with petulant intensity.

"You did *not* answer my question," she said. "What map?"

"It's a map of the castle with those tunnels on it. Thought it might give us a clue where the others are," he said. He tried to think of where they hadn't searched yet, where Ansehelm would keep prisoners.

"How would you possibly know that paper was a map with secret tunnels on it?" Elsie asked.

"I saw the monster with it." Jasper headed down the steps, rifle first, only to be stopped by her fingers digging into his arm.

She swooped down on him from the landing above and said, "You're *lying!*"

He wrestled his arm away. "We have to go. And don't be so loud."

"You appear quite informed about the monster, and the murderer. Quite informed, indeed. You opened a secret door in *my bedroom*. You're talking about tunnels, you recognized a paper from that strange room, you're alive when everyone else is dead—"

"That a problem for you?" Jasper said.

"Perhaps it is!" Elsie sneered. "Mother always thought you were no good. No one ever saw you before coming here. My brother is pitifully senseless, so who knows what kind of trash he might have dragged in."

Jasper wondered what she would say if he pointed the rifle and forced her to walk right into the hole before the laboratory door. How truly low and disgusting that would be.

She *was* right that he was lying.

"Look, the truth is complicated, and it'll just distract us from finding your family," he said.

Her eyes narrowed.

"I wouldn't be running around this place with you right now, helping you find the others and keeping you safe if I was just going to betray you," Jasper said. "Because I could have left."

He let her simmer for a beat, then headed down. She followed behind, footsteps soft. He thought he saw her lifting her skirt out like she was heading to a ball. He glanced back, and no, she wasn't. She held the lantern and cleaver, watching him as closely as anything else. As if he were the fiend. If she and her family weren't so hostile, he wouldn't have had to lie. *Stupid and selfish.* He kneaded his fingers over his throat, coughing when he pushed too hard.

"Be quiet," Elsie said. They had reached the bottom, and as he turned to tell her off, he caught, from the back of the armory, shadows dancing over the empty racks. Sound trickled through the room. Voices? Footsteps? At least one pair. A shadow grew long over the wall, like a bayonet. He grabbed Elsie, whispering *run.*

They bolted into the halls, stopping around the bend of a corridor. Jasper worried about the sounds they'd made during the sprint. Leading Morlen right to them—he'd panicked and not been careful. They had to keep moving. When they were sure they weren't being followed, they resumed their search, opening doors to check as many rooms as possible. Of course, that meant more sound. All of it so loud against the eerie silence.

Back near the courtyard, on an upper level of anterooms, it seemed to be getting cloudy again. But no, it was the sun setting. They had to leave—he grabbed Elsie's shoulder just as she tried a door.

"It's locked," she said. She had dropped the cleaver and jostled the door with both hands.

"We have to go," he said. "If we're here after dark—"

She held her skirt up to kick at the handle. "What difference does it make?"

"The monst—"

"Because if we leave now, we'll be on the mountain at night—" *Kick.* "—being eaten by lions and tigers and bears."

"There aren't li—"

"There are *bears.*" *Kick.* He told her to stand back and threw his weight into the door. A few thrusts, and it cracked open, sending him stumbling in. The Lamberts he saw first, lying on the floor in their evening wear—Cordelia, William, and Florence. They appeared asleep, bound with rope by their hands and feet, bodies draped on the thin rug covering the floor. Elsie ran shrieking to them.

The door had opened on one end of a long room, solemn wood table stretched over it. Narrow and windowless, the only natural light came in from the hall. Its walls were lined with portraits—one had been knocked down, glass and frame splintering over the image of Pieter Van Hoensbroeck. A silver pitcher and cup stood alone on the dark wood. Matching chairs lined the table except at the head where, near the door waffling on broken hinges, there rested a throne. It reminded him of the one in the third tower, intricately carved with a curved back and arms cushioned in green velvet. The Lamberts had been placed below. On the other side of the room, Thorley and the maids were piled together in the same state as the family, backs leaned against cabinets. They would not wake, none of them. Jasper felt breath coming out of their nostrils.

Elsie had her mother under the arms, dragging her towards the door inch by inch.

"How is she so heavy? *You*, help me!"

"Where are we going to bring her?" Jasper asked. "You gonna leave your father?"

They needed to wake them up, somehow. Smelling salts—Verna would have them. She leaned against Maja, already in her dressing gown, hair undone and spilling over her face. No medicine on her. Perhaps Thorley carried them.

Jasper found a vial rummaging through the butler's pockets and lit a few candle sconces to see in the growing dark. It was cologne. Elsie jostled her mother's shoulders, then Florence's.

"*Wake up*!" she screamed in their ears.

"Elsie, shh," Jasper said.

"Do not speak to me that!"

Florence shot up with a gasp, eyes glinting with fright. "What happened?" Elsie asked at the same time Florence said, "Where's Leo?" Elsie turned to Jasper.

"I don't know. Last I saw him, he was alive," he said, kneeling to free her hands.

"Where?" Florence said.

"Florence, what *happened*?" Elsie begged. Maja shot awake next, bending forward with a pained gasp as Verna slumped on the floor behind her. Jasper helped her out of her binds, then set about freeing the others as Elsie and Florence untied their parents. Next to wake was Irene, then Mr. Lambert. Through the hall windows, Jasper saw the sun had just set. He took the cleaver from outside the door and tried to hand it back to Elsie.

"We need to leave," he said. She was hugging her father. He dropped the weapon near her and helped Maja stand. Dottie, Thorley, and Mrs. Lambert were up now. Disoriented, all of them blinked and shivered. Elsie embraced Cordelia as the others registered Jasper. They seemed surprised. Trembling, Mr. Lambert turned to him and asked,

"You're alive? Do you know where my son is?"

"No. He's not dead though," Jasper said. "We should leave now."

"We need Leo," Cordelia said. William stood only to slump into the throne. He held Elsie's hand, speaking mostly to her.

"That creature brought us here. He wants me to give him this castle, and *money*. To force my hand, he took Leo. I—" He looked down guilty. "I agreed. I expected to have my son back. And *you*, darling. I did not know what had happened to you."

Dottie struggled to stand. She was mumbling Proulx and Frankie's names. Jasper held her hand, trying to guide her and the others towards the door. Mr. Thorley rubbed his throat. "He made us all drink some substance, and we fell asleep," he said. Jasper was telling them they had to go, but they lumbered groggily around the room. Mr. Lambert was still lounging at the head of the table.

"He forced me to give him this castle and…" William took a deep breath before the next words. "…ten thousand dollars a year."

"He'll kill Leo, kill us all!" Cordelia cried.

"Not if he wants an annual allowance," Florence said.

"Not if we leave!" Jasper said. Why weren't they running?

"We'll get Leo back. We *must*," Elsie said. She and her mother looked out the open doorframe, through the hall window at the sunset.

Irene's eyes flicked to Jasper. "Did you see Ned?"

His heart sank. "Yeah."

"And the others? Are they…?"

Jasper shook his head. Dottie let out a soft cry. The last of the servants huddled together.

"*We* should leave," Jasper whispered. The others shot him looks through wet eyes.

"And abandon the family?" Mr. Thorley said under his breath.

"He needs them, he doesn't need us," Maja said, furtive glances to the others.

"The longer we stay in the castle, the more danger we're in. If they won't leave without Leo." Jasper shrugged.

"How did *you* survive?" Irene asked. He held up his bloody arm.

"He's been feeding off me."

Dottie shirked back. "*Feeding?*" Their expressions twisted in repulsion. At least they were beginning to understand: Ansehelm was a butcher, and he would kill them no matter they did.

Verna hadn't woken yet. Thorley bent to check on her, and as soon as his hand touched her, he jumped back with a yelp.

"She's cold," he said and pressed two fingers to her wrist. Now it was clear how wooden she was, lips frozen in a part. Mr. Thorley's anxious humming told them there was no pulse. He lifted her hair up, and Verna's dead eyes stared back.

Shrieks sounded up, the Lamberts turned their heads. *What killed her?* Elsie whispered. Maja quivered, cupping her hands to her chest as she puffed shallow breaths. She looked at her shoulder, the one Verna had leaned on, like it was on fire.

"It—it bit her," Dottie said. "But she was alive. When we fell asleep, she was alive."

They stared at Verna's body as Jasper took a step towards the door. "We should—"

With a scream, Maja leapt for the exit but never made it past the threshold, stopped in her tracks by the figure at the door.

CHAPTER TWENTY-THREE

ALL EYES ON THE MONSTER, they backed against the walls. Jasper froze in the middle of the room, struck by Ansehelm's transformation. His muscles had filled out under smooth skin, and thick black hair strung down his back. The scraps of fabric that had covered him were replaced by a suit that, though it looked centuries old, was stainless. Iron still clamped his neck, but he held his head high. He had a squat, triangular face, morosely pallid, with jutting cheekbones ending in a short chin which his sneers spilled over. Uncanny how they mixed with his new youthfulness: a trick of the light, and he could be taken for a man of eighteen. His eyes drilled into Jasper with ominous glee. He peeled his lips back, showing off freshly grown teeth. The fangs hung the length of his gums.

Ansehelm shifted his gaze to Elsie. "You are here, I see," he said. Her parents and sister drew her in to them, all against the wall behind the throne. She held the meat cleaver across her chest. Jasper raised his rifle.

Maja had not been able to retreat far from the entrance. Ansehelm sunk his teeth into her neck, holding her to him like a leg of meat. No one moved as she screamed. Fingers already poised to shoot, Jasper fired. The bullet lodged in the monster's side, but it did not so much as pause his meal. Veins pulsed up under his skin, glowing bright red as the blood surged in. Not long before Maja was dropped dead on the floor. Ansehelm popped the bullet out of his side, frowning at the hole it had made in his waistcoat. The dent in his flesh smoothed over on its own, leaving no trace of what had happened. In a second, he snatched the rifle, breaking it over his knee. Sulfur curdled in the air as the pieces rattled on the ground. With one hand Ansehelm picked Jasper up and threw him at the back wall like a child would a toy.

Jasper hit the wall, falling over a cabinet and onto the floor. Pain cracked through his bones.

Facing the others, Ansehelm reached around to the back of the iron collar. He pinched the metal and tore it apart, throwing the shackle in spilled gunpowder. He kicked Maja's body to the side and sat at the head of the table, curling his fingers over the arms of the throne. Huddled to the side, the Lambert family watched him with dismay.

A squeak escaped William Lambert. "Please. I've agreed to everything," he said.

Ansehelm glared, leaning away as if the man's presence offended him. He produced a document from his suit.

"Sign." Ansehelm pushed the paper down the table. His lip curled as Mr. Lambert shuffled over in his tailcoat, slipping a reading glass over one eye. Trembling, William nevertheless surveyed the contract.

"My word," he said under his breath. "These terms are…*unreasonable.*"

With an irritated growl, Ansehelm snatched Elsie's wrist, doing nothing more than pulling her towards him. That was enough to get her father to scribble his name on the line. William backed away when it was done. Ansehelm breathed out, an unpleasant matter finished, and let Elsie go. He fixed his eye on William Lambert.

"You will leave, you will never speak of me or even this castle, but you will make money for me," he said. "Send it once a year. If you never miss a payment, I will have no reason to visit you or your family. Be careful that my existence is kept a secret. Do not think I cannot hurt you in your city, should you break any of our terms. And when you are gone, I will take money from your children, and their children, and so on. We will see whether your family line or I die first."

Mr. Lambert choked down a cry. "Where is my son?"

"You will have him back if you behave," Ansehelm said.

From where he slumped on the floor, Jasper blurted out, "You don't have him."

For a moment, Mr. Lambert showed a spark of hope. From his throne, the monster smiled.

"Well, then, Jasper, where is he?" Ansehelm's teeth glistened. "I thought you two would have stayed together."

Eyes turned on Jasper for a moment, then back to the monster.

"Please," Mr. Lambert said. "Let us go. That was our deal."

"Go." Ansehelm waved at the door. The Lamberts did not move. Irene took a cautious step forward. Ansehelm snapped at her, "Not you."

Irene's hands flew to her mouth. Florence met her eye, briefly. Bracing himself on the cabinet, Jasper stood. It hurt to move, but he could do so without screaming. The knife he'd carried had fallen when he was thrown and nicked his leg. He doubted any blade would do much against Ansehelm. The rifle grip, splintered in a wooden point, was strewn on the floor not too far away. Bones sloshing, he stumbled towards it.

"But," Cordelia asked, "where is Leo?"

"Perhaps I want to keep him here as insurance," Ansehelm said. "Perhaps Jasper killed him. Did you?"

Jasper held the broken rifle on unsteady legs. The others looked at him, this time more piercing, more curious.

"No," he said. "Why don't you let all of us go? We'll leave now. You won't be bothered."

He pointed the splintered wood like a spear towards Ansehelm. The pinpoint eyes glimmered.

"Then what will I eat?" he said, settling into the chair.

Jasper heard shrieks all around him. He kept the wood pointed as he inched towards the door. Ansehelm held his gaze. He was almost out. He lifted his hand, about to summon the others to follow, when, in a blink, the monster had filled the exit. Jasper brandished the wood point, and Ansehelm shirked away, anger simmering into a smile.

"I do not wish to hurt you, Jasper." Ansehelm looked past him at the others. "When I have so much to thank you for. Or did you not all know?"

Again, the eyes on him. Needling in. Jasper's blood ran cold. Numb, he was a statue as Ansehelm told the story. How he had found, fed, and freed the vampire. How he had crawled around under their noses, letting them be vulnerable, ignorant of what was happening until it was too late. How he had even taken pleasure in it. Stolen. Lied. As the story went, the others forgot who they were afraid of, hanging on Ansehelm's every word. They turned on Jasper. Through his shocked nerves, he could feel white-hot shame balling up inside him. Excuses ran through his mind. How could he have guessed the truth? He thought he was dealing with a frail, dying, old man. Anyone would think that. Ansehelm was a liar. All of it died before reaching his lips. He didn't even move when the monster snatched away the broken rifle.

As he concluded, Ansehelm nestled back in the throne, turning to the Lamberts to say, "And he did all this while fucking your son."

Jasper choked on dry air.

"*Slanderous!*" William bellowed. Cordelia Lambert's brow furrowed. She said quietly, "I don't understand."

"Slanderous," Ansehelm repeated with a laugh. Jasper could feel them all curdling in disgust. Their hatred was growing. They would kill him as soon as they had the chance.

Florence took the meat cleaver from her sister's hand and jammed it across Ansehelm's eyes. The blade did not sink deep, but it was enough to send him roaring, eyes oozing as they bolted. Still in shock, Jasper was late to scutter for the exit. Dottie and Thorley whizzed past him and made it into the hall. The others were converging on the door, Florence leading the way. She was almost out of the room when the monster pounced on her. He ripped the cleaver out and sunk his teeth in, drinking until he could look at them with healed eyes.

She moaned as he let her fall, still alive. Cordelia lunged to tend to her, but Ansehelm blocked the way. They were still trapped. Florence clutched the bleeding punctures on her neck. Her legs had fallen over Maja's body. Jasper was only a foot away from where Cordelia reached for her daughter, Elsie and Irene shuddering behind her. William had not yet made it around the table. Nostrils flaring, he leaned over with a fist clutching the contract.

"Let us go!" He shook the paper. Ansehelm scowled with his daughter's blood on his lips, and William Lambert exploded.

"You promised we would not be harmed, and my son would be returned. I upheld my end of the bargain. You cannot change the terms. You cannot harm *my* children. We will not be treated this way! You need my money, well, you'll get nothing." He stomped his foot on the ground and ripped the contract to shreds. "I will not allow myself to be bullied by you *lowlives*. Filthy, scheming servants and evil freaks of nature. You have no idea who you're dealing with. The banks won't let you touch a cent. The law is on my side. They'll root you out! They'll send an army! If you do not deliver my son and let my family leave *right now*, you'll be *sorry*!"

His panting echoed in the room, fizzling out into silence. With his long face clenched, Jasper recognized something of Leo in him.

One of Ansehelm's freshly regrown eyes twitched.

"I have lived one thousand years, and you people only grow worse," Ansehelm said through his pearly, pointed teeth. "Arrogant, petulant, overfed, over-educated, too convenienced, materialistic, upset over *shoulds*. Like my damned nephew. For centuries, I watched men become mockeries of themselves before *him*. I thought he was the worst it could get, but now I find you people are more loathsome than ever. Bargains. Armies. I treat you as prisoners, when what you are is food."

He snapped Florence up by her neck and drained her until she was dead. With a screech, her mother collapsed on the ground.

"*You can't, you can't, you can't,*" William sputtered.

"I have!" cried Ansehelm. "What stopped it? An army?"

William ran to hug Elsie. Irene, holding Mrs. Lambert's hand, looked up red-faced, and spat.

Ansehelm tilted his head, fingers curling in and out from his palm, deciding how he felt about that.

"So much endured to emerge for *this*," he said. His voice faltered just then, and he stared into a void, nails dug in so deep a bead of blood—Florence's, Maja's—dripped from his fist. He blinked, relaxed his hand, and surveyed the humans again. When he looked over Irene, she whimpered, so he kept his gaze on her.

"What are you doing?" he asked.

Mouth agape, she stammered, "The sign of the cross."

"Is it?" he shook his head. "You do it wrong. You have no humility, I can tell."

He stepped forward and stomped his foot down. The floor reverberated thunderously to Jasper, who wobbled on throbbing legs. The injuries were getting harder to push through. He had splintered his legs when he fell on the cabinet and didn't know if he had broken bones or only sprains. Standing was becoming unbearable; he slid, back against the wall, to the floor. Spiky pain jutted over his sides. His right hand still hurt. He could barely hold his head up and stared down at himself. Sweat and pus seeped into his clothes. And blood. Ansehelm's nose twitched.

"Even the servants. Pretentious and puerile," he muttered. From his waistcoat he took out a bottle filled with some mixture that smelled of mint. "Now I have to keep you another night. Perhaps we will not have a repeat of *this*."

Giving Florence's body a kick first, he poured liquid into the lone silver cup. The Lamberts and Irene huddled together in the middle of the room, cowering as Ansehelm ordered them to drink. He held the cup out to Elsie, who buried her face in her father.

"If you do not want to drink, then I will kill more of you."

Jasper saw Mr. Lambert's shoes as he was grabbed by his collar.

"Take him." William tossed Jasper between the creature and his daughter. Ansehelm caught Jasper by the hair, eyeing his bloody clothes before letting him drop.

"Drink, or I will take someone you do *not* want dead." Ansehelm smiled. He held the cup out again. Elsie whimpered, and her father took the drink in her stead. On the floor, Jasper could see Cordelia's sobbing profile. He turned and saw shadows by the entrance.

Bang, and a bullet pierced William Lambert in the head.

CHAPTER TWENTY-FOUR

ROBERT MORLEN LOWERED the musket with a big, yellow-toothed smile. In its place, he raised a crossbow loaded with a wooden stake right at Ansehelm. One boot pinned down Leo Lambert, who squirmed against rope binds on the floor.

"Now *he* inherits it all, and I have him." Morlen tapped his shoe on Leo's back. "So if you want him, give me what I want."

Ansehelm's fangs glinted as his jaw hung open, face melting into deep anger. One eye was on the stake. Venom in each word, he asked, "What do you want?"

"You know!" Morlen screeched. "You know damn well! Immortality. You eat humans. You live forever. You told me all about it when I found you but wouldn't tell me how to get it. So I tried myself. I consumed the dead and the living, but none of it *worked.* Then I found it out. I need your blood. So give it to me, or I'll kill them all, and your little scheme'll fall through." He shook the crossbow.

"You wish me to give you my blood in exchange for the son? So that you can become a vampire and live forever?" Ansehelm's shoulders bent like a perched crow. "Is that it?"

"Yes!" Morlen said. Ansehelm said nothing. The seconds ticked by. The stake jostled nervously in its holster. Leo whined through the rope gag, eyes darting to his father and Florence. He got louder, rolling himself, pushing against the boot. Keeping his focus, Morlen kicked him in the head, but Leo only thrust harder. It knocked Morlen off balance, and in that moment, Ansehelm had the crossbow. He grabbed Morlen, who shrieked more in sorrow than fright, and tossed him with the others.

"You demand *my* blood?" Ansehelm careened over him. "Pretentious wretch. You want immortality? Why perpetuate something so worthless? I would give a worm eternal life before you. Pathetic. Here, you will watch someone else get what you want, and then you will be their first meal."

Morlen whined from an open-mouth frown, his rotting face so desperately sad it made Jasper shudder. That was what he was looking at when Ansehelm bit his neck.

The sting was faint. Jasper's pulse beat in his ear as it pumped blood for the vampire to drink. It felt like being held by a statue and smelled of the earthy tunnel dirt. Mind blank, he sensed sorrow just out of reach—not a real feeling but the silhouette of one. The world grew gray, soundless. He could not be sure if he was dead already or not.

Warm blood dripped on his tongue like the ping of a lantern through the night. Salt. Metal. Heat. The taste roared over him. His senses shot back, and he saw his mouth around a wrist hard as stone.

Ansehelm's veins threaded over his face, a web turning from red to purple to white as Jasper drank. Disparate images bubbled up: dense woods, a speeding river, bare feet on straw by a fire. Memories that were not his. They popped away as quickly as they came. This close, Ansehelm's pinpoint eyes were bright, and Jasper could see now that the glow came from underneath them, like magma about to rise. He thought he saw in them a flicker of affection.

The wrist pulled away. Jasper licked the blood off his lips, squeezing the last droplets down his throat. Wails and hisses cracked in his ears. From the floor he looked up at the rest of them. Robert Morlen was puffed up like a cat, bent over William Lambert's legs. Leo had crawled to his mother, she and the others untying him as fast they could. As he waited to be freed, Leo's eyes flicked over the room. They stopped on Jasper. Blue, like fresh, violent water. His face was still bruised, and he was covered in dirt. Morlen must have kept him down in the tunnels. Jasper remembered washing himself in the sun just hours ago, and it felt like a happy memory.

The pain started. Like his insides being boiled. Jasper rolled over onto his hands. Morlen was shouting, "Give it to *me*! Give it to *me*!"

Ansehelm picked up the silver cup with his drug, attention on the remaining Lamberts. It spilled as Morlen dove at his legs, biting and scratching in pure rage.

Free, Leo jumped for the crossbow strewn on the floor and fired. The wooden stake hit Ansehelm's leg, and he fell with a howl, still trying to rip Morlen off him.

A blur of feet flew past. Jasper picked himself up, pushing through roiling cramps to flee. They made it out of the room, Leo holding the empty crossbow and his mother.

Irene trailed them pulling Elsie by the hand, the slowest besides Jasper.

Snarling from behind. Ansehelm was in the hall. Jasper saw him in streaks of white as he leapt for Elsie. But Leo and Cordelia, realizing who he was after, managed to grab her first and thrust her out of harm's way. Losing her grip on Elsie's hand, Irene stumbled and knocked into the vampire. The three Lamberts were already farther ahead. Ansehelm growled, Irene cowering under him. He broke her head on the floor, paying no mind to the blood pooling out.

Jasper lagged behind, hearing his leg bones crunch as he scrambled. He couldn't feel anything above the horrendous nausea. He kept expecting to be next—for the sudden pain, perhaps torture, then unconsciousness. But Ansehelm focused on the Lamberts, now scurrying down the stairs. He arched, ready to jump, as Robert Morlen crawled out with the splintered rifle wood and buried it into his leg.

Howls resounded behind Jasper as he hurried to catch up with the others. They were on the ground level now, halls growing dark.

"Leo," Elsie asked, panting, "where are we going?" They had run straight and were approaching the armory.

"We have to hide," Cordelia said.

"There are men at his house—Morlen's," said Leo. "He told me some of the townsmen are keeping watch. They'll get us out."

"Do you know how to get there?" Elsie asked.

"I do," Jasper said. "Through the back. In the woods."

No one looked at him, but they heeded his directions, sprinting into a cool night. They did not stop for a moment, even as they ran further under the looming mountain shadows. A half-moon lit them through the overgrowth. On the other side of the gate, Jasper couldn't remember clearly where to go, but every impulse told him not to stop running.

The others followed unquestioning—anything to put distance between themselves and the castle. They jerked through the woods, Leo holding his sister and mother, until they saw a light.

A lantern hung outside Morlen's brick hut over an anxious guard. He pointed his rifle as the group flew out from the trees. Only then did they stop. Elsie dropped to her knees in exhaustion, lavender skirt billowing out over the grass. Jasper bent and clutched his sides.

"What in God's name?" the guard said.

"He's after us!" Leo cried.

"Morlen?"

No one answered.

"He looks sick." The guard pointed at Jasper.

"Don't worry about him," Leo snapped. He held the crossbow at his side, which the other eyed suspiciously. But the guard lowered his gun and waved them in, taking Elsie's hand as Leo took Cordelia's. Jasper was the last in, and he slumped against the door as the guard lit a few scattered candles. The hut was cramped, and cold. They rested on what they could, stools and crooked chairs. Elsie and Cordelia hugged each other with wet faces. Leo, hunched over, stared unblinking. The corpses had been moved, but the smell lingered in Jasper's nostrils. His feet brushed the table where he'd seen Shaw's body.

"You the family from the castle? The Lamberts?" the guard asked. Leo nodded, running a hand over his face. The guard pried for the story, but they didn't know what to say, except who was dead and that they had to get away. The guard only had one horse, he said.

Jasper touched his jagged legs and felt bones in the wrong places. His fingers were ashen blue. It was freezing. When he shivered, cracks in his spine shifted. Was it broken too? He couldn't tell—that pain was dull compared to his stomach. He let out a long moan as his insides churned.

"What's wrong with him?" the guard asked.

The others fixed onto him. Cordelia squeezed her son's arm.

"Why did you bring that thing here with us?" she hissed.

Leo's brow fell, a cold pique in his eyes. Like he wanted to squish Jasper under his shoe.

Jasper looked to Elsie, even Cordelia, but they only gave him bitter glares. Leo slammed his fist against the wall, the sound booming through the hut. On a table, Morlen had left a few whittled wooden stakes. He loaded the crossbow with one, pointing it at Jasper.

"You're one of them." His voice was low.

"No," Jasper said.

Blue eyes and the bow locked on him. For all the mess of dirt and blood and scratches, Leo held himself high. With each step his rage surged. Jasper could smell the dust of the cut wood like gunpowder.

"Hey, now, what's going on?" asked the guard.

"*He*," Leo spat, "is a monster." He narrowed in on Jasper. "We saw you drink that thing's blood."

"He forced—"

"You were working for him this whole time."

"He lied to—"

"I'm sick of you!" Leo's chest swelled. "My father and sister would still be alive if it weren't for you."

Jasper lifted himself off the floor, dredging all his pains up with him. A new instinct told him to run from the stake. Maybe, he thought, he should just let it happen—be shot and get a quick release. But no. It was less that he didn't want to die and more that he didn't want Leo to get any satisfaction.

"Blame me," Jasper muttered. "Yeah, I let him loose. I didn't know what he was. I didn't know about Morlen. I didn't think anybody was gonna die, and I didn't want them to. But you know what? It was funny when he scared you people. And, Leo, it was your idea. Why don't you blame yourself?"

His fingers were already on the knob. As the stake hit the wall, he stumbled out and reeled into the thicket. It took a moment before he realized he was not being pursued. The woods seemed clear, and their lanterns bright; he was sure they could see him. He could see them. Leo paced back and forth, in one window and then the other. Though he couldn't distinguish the words, he heard voices, crying and murmuring through the brick. He tuned them out to the hooting owls, and when he stepped back, branches wove across his vision like threads of a net.

CHAPTER TWENTY-FIVE

NOTHING TO DO NOW but find a place to die. He shuffled deeper into the forest, washed in the scent of pine and sweet night flowers. The moon led him to a cliff-edge clearing, more forest draped below it, and all around mountains chained into the distance. Collapsing, he pressed his cheek down in silky grass. The three towers of Kasteel Verlossen arched just over the tree line behind him.

Jasper's short peace was broken by a storm shredding his insides. Bursts of agonizing pain tore over him as, one by one, every organ from spleen to heart to throat exploded and dissolved. He leaked sweat and piss, vomiting up acid as his organs popped. Each time he expected to die, but he just wouldn't. It all kept happening. Even when his brain felt like it had melted, he remained conscious, and his screams sounded, unbroken, up the mountain peaks.

Impossible to tell whether it had lasted an eternity or no time at all. The anguish subsided, though its memory lingered, and he moaned over phantom aches. Then, a crunch. He felt his bones shift. Touching his legs, he found they had realigned. His spine curved effortlessly back and forth. His body felt calm. Hollow. He flicked the dirt off his hands and saw they were smooth. No scratches, no bruises. Not even a chipped nail. His tongue hit the back of his teeth. *There* were the fangs.

He shivered, awed, not afraid. The fangs did not seem out of place. They felt like his teeth; a new, yet natural, addition. He touched the tip of them with his finger. Not as sharp as the ones in the pouch. But maybe they were—his hands were different now. His skin was harder, somewhere between rubber and rock, perhaps less sensitive to the prick. He didn't feel cold; in fact, he was entirely comfortable. No heat came from him. He breathed, sucking air into lungs that were somehow still there, but what came out was as cool as the forest. Unchanged by its sojourn in a dead body. He stepped over the clearing, light on his feet. Dried blood on his pants smelled like food that had just spoiled. Thirst and hunger twisted into one impulse. There was some new need inside him.

Before he saw them, he knew they were near. One was a living, bleeding thing. A human. The other was Ansehelm. He flew out from the trees and tossed Robert Morlen at Jasper's feet. The man wept, limbs broken like twigs meant for kindling. Ansehelm looked Jasper up and down, satisfied.

"Here. Lucky that you are being given your first meal."

Shock had not hit Jasper until then. He seized up, sputtering weak protests, "I... I don't..."

"You will eventually, so do it now," Ansehelm said. There was a power emanating from him that Jasper could feel, like picking up a scent. He was astonished he could have ever thought this thing was a human. When he looked at Morlen, he understood things too, the knowledge coming without logic. He sensed how badly the man wanted to survive. A desire so intense he wasn't even fighting, just curled in on himself. Crushed. Bleeding. The smell was inviting.

"I'm not a murderer," Jasper said.

"A murderer is a human who kills other humans."

"I'm—"

"You are *not*," Ansehelm said, his voice dropping, "human."

Jasper ran his tongue over the new teeth as the idea of drinking blood congealed in him. His protests were hollow; he knew he could bite into Morlen right now without regret. He felt that he should be upset. But what was the use of that? Clutching *shoulds* and trying to force what wasn't. He thought he was someone who accepted the nature of things, but was he? Maybe where some people forced others to bend, he only forced himself. Absorbing blows, twisting the facts. Looking away so his fantasies could thrive.

Morlen shrieked with primal, blubbering fright as Jasper leaned down. His blood was exquisite. Jasper wasn't prepared for how good something could feel. Nothing had ever come close. He sucked at the punctures his fangs had made long after it stopped flowing, in case there was more. Ansehelm beamed in delight.

"Wonderful," he said. "I worried you would keep arguing."

Jasper wiped his mouth and licked the last speck of blood from his thumb. He looked at Ansehelm under the moon.

"Who chained you in the tower?"

Ansehelm cocked his head; he thought it was a silly question. Jasper met his eye.

"Goddammit, tell me."

"Pieter Van Hoensbroeck. He *hated* me." Ansehelm's lip curled up, and he looked at the mountains. "I promised him alchemical secrets and immortality but gave him nothing. Same as this one." He kicked Morlen's body. "I was smarter with you. Or perhaps you were stupider."

"Maybe you have a bad strategy." Jasper anticipated a threat as he said it, but the vampire laughed.

"My fault is I like to play with my food," Ansehelm said. "Van Hoensbroeck was a descendant of mine. Great, great, and so on grandson of one my brothers. His pompousness was an insult, so I took him for all his money and followed him across the globe to get more. I should have remembered that I was not all-powerful. His entitlement rubbed off on me." He shuddered. "Pieter was prepared to kill me, but by the time he had the opportunity, he had grown to so deeply despise me that he chose to torture me for eternity instead. He pulled my teeth out and chained me there to suffer at his hand whenever he felt like it. It is difficult to hurt a vampire's body, not impossible. You should learn that. Especially if you are deprived of blood. You grow *weak*."

"But you can't starve to death?" Jasper said. "You're immortal."

"It is not true immortality, because one can be killed. Especially young ones." Ansehelm's fingers folded in front of him. "Well. I made you, I will be responsible and tell you what you need to know. You can be killed by a wooden stake through the heart. Avoid them altogether." He showed off his leg, scarred gray from the night's altercations. "Worse is sunlight. You cannot expect to see the sun again unless you wish to burn to death. Now, you must consume only blood. Water will not hurt you, but it will not help. Animals will sustain you if there is nothing else, but not for long. Human blood nourishes—it is what we are meant to drink.

"A single human has all you need for one night, but if it is a hassle to kill, as it sometimes is, you can drink less and thus leave them alive. It takes some training to control your thirst, but the living human produces new blood, which is a convenience. If you keep one, you could feed off it for years, but you must remember not to allow it to bleed out, and to provide it with water and food. You look at me like this is obvious, but you will forget and curse yourself when it dies."

Jasper balked. "I could never do that to—"

"Then if you plan to kill every night, make sure you are careful," Ansehelm said. "Too many angry humans and you will have a problem. You are not invulnerable; you cannot take whatever you like, constantly satiating yourself. I worry about this for you, with your modern inclinations."

Jasper took the bandage off his arm. Scarless. He let the blood-caked cloth drop to the ground, saying, "You sure satiated yourself."

Ansehelm snarled. "Sometimes one must take control through threats. I knew it could all be blamed on him." He gestured at the corpse. "And I had not drunk human blood in centuries. I am not yet fully recovered, and there is still much to do to rectify the situation. That reminds me: do not kill that lover of yours. *I* need him now."

Jasper nodded. It hadn't occurred to him at all, killing Leo, but now the idea of it festered in his mind. Destroy the Lamberts, ruin Ansehelm's plans. Squeeze some money out for himself. He flicked his fangs with his tongue. "I thought you hated modern greed."

"One day, the world became a place where I needed money, and so I take it," Ansehelm said in his defensive growl.

"You've been in a tower for three hundred years. The world is different."

"Not truly," Ansehelm said, "from what I have seen so far. The same as Pieter's time, anyway."

"There's new technology—"

"Please do not talk about it. I am sure I will see all of the *technology*." He stuck his tongue out.

Jasper put his hands in his pockets, looking down at his filthy pants and boots. He remembered putting these on in his apartment in the dark before dawn, his mother and the boarders sleeping around him. He had tried not to wake them. Later, as the sun came up, he had met Leo, smiling at him from the glossy black car.

"When you pulled the wires out of the automobile, you didn't think anything of it?" he asked.

"Is that what it is called? Automobile?" Ansehelm repeated the word with a sneer. Jasper shook his head.

"Why be immortal, then, if you hate the future?" he asked.

Ansehelm threw his hands in the air. "Why be? I *am*. Should I let myself die because of a philosophical quandary? This is the type of foolishness I cannot tolerate with you people!"

Scuffing his shoe on the ground, Jasper kicked a pebble. It went further than he expected, and he heard it fall down the cliff in pristine clacks. Ansehelm growled under his breath, still incensed. He picked Morlen's body up by the ankles.

"I will take this, so it is not found," he said, and, to Jasper's amazement, floated up off the ground.

"Can I—?" Jasper gaped. The corpse dangled above the grass as Ansehelm levitated.

"You will, eventually, if you last long enough."

"Oh." A thought bubbled up. "The potions—"

"No more of that. I will not teach you. I have reached my tolerance with you, Jasper. Go do what you will, but do not come back to the castle. And again, do *not* kill that man. I need him."

"I'm not going to kill Leo," Jasper said. Ansehelm was half turned away, lifting higher towards the tree line. "You're just gonna leave me?"

"Yes," Ansehelm said, and floated down to face him one last time. The faintest sympathy shimmered behind his eye. "You must be able to tell that I am not a true friend. It was not a lie when I said I hated your former masters, but I do not like you, either. I do not wish to answer your questions anymore or speak in this language with you. When you are cut off from your native tongue, you will understand. It will happen. The world changes, and changes, and changes. I barely recognize it, and I have only lived one millennium." He looked right at Jasper then, expression plain. "Your world will *all* fade one day, but there will still be humans to drink. You will not understand what they care about or why they believe the things they do. How they act, what they strive for, will to you be absurd. Even other vampires, separated from you by place and time, will be foreign. Had I known that when I was young, I would have turned all my brethren. If there is someone you wish to take with you, Jasper, turn them now. Ih fîrhazze ëz dīn Sprâhha bisprehhan zuo muozan."

Ansehelm dissolved into the forest.

‡‡‡

Jasper's thoughts rolled over each other, none at the forefront for long. The half-moon shone over a different peak.

He was dead, but he wasn't. He took a step, nothing new, except he did not feel his tendons stretch. There was no swirling in his gut or muscles shifting—sensations he had not even been aware of until they were gone. An almost discomfiting absence. All he could feel was a cackle of electricity, humming up and down, as if there were wire currents coiled within him.

He could walk back into his home on 47th Street like nothing had happened if he wanted to. No one could stop him. He could leave again just as easily. Brimming with energy, he felt that sense of strange, frightening excitement from the dream. He would be able to fly. If Ansehelm wouldn't teach him magic, he could learn some other way, because he could go anywhere and do anything.

Almost. He was a monster. He had to give up the day. But if he were only a little careful, he would live forever. An eternity of doing whatever he wanted, starting now.

He just stood. Hands in his pockets, like a kid hanging out on a street corner. All the thoughts clamored in his mind until a realization sounded, loud over the din, that he wanted so much he did not know what to do.

Looking out, he could see every detail of the forest. Not like by day or lamplight, but a different vision of distinct dark hues and contours, of spectacular movement. Rich like living art—he wanted to immerse himself in it. At least he could know the one thing, that he wanted to keep taking in this view. So, he did not move.

It would not last forever, and then what? He thought of getting money, seeing his family, seeing men, all the old desires. He weighed them against each other to see if anything inspired him, but they only left an odd taste in his mouth.

Was there anyone he wanted to take with him?

Two decades of indignities fired up inside him. No exhaustion or hunger to bury them under now. He hated it, wished he could change back. Shame balled up like iron. For letting himself be tricked. For putting up with his own maltreatment. For the way he had not hesitated to drink that man's blood. Those were *shoulds* again. Things were what they were. He was a monster, stupid, and a pervert too.

He had never expected real love from Leo, just a little understanding. Even if they despised parts of each other, they could have let those contempts slide off in the name of camaraderie. That was what Jasper had done for Leo; it wasn't too much to ask in return, was it? Some grace.

Maybe he would find some now, dead, with all the time in the world.

There was a hint of blue in the sky, but he noticed it like a lightning flash. He could smell dew. *Almost* immortal. Frantic, he looked around, hoping a hiding spot would appear. The open sky was ominous, threatening dawn at any moment. He dashed under the canopy, cracking through the forest floor in his new strength. He was running towards the castle, and Ansehelm's order surged in his mind. Could he risk it? It had nothing to pump, but his heart still raced as he combed for a safe place to wait out the day. He heard himself panting, panicked.

"Jasper!"

He stopped in his tracks, locking on her immediately. Dottie called to him from behind a boulder.

"Come here!" She waved her arms. An instinct told him to do so. He hopped over so quick it startled her, and he sensed the little spike of fear. Her blood smelled fresh. She took his hand, shivered, and led him around to a split in a rock outcrop.

"A cave," she whispered. "He can't find us here. Are the others with you?"

"No." He squeezed in after her, watching her feel her way along when he saw so clearly. A spider's web lay in front of her hand; he brushed it aside before she touched it. Where the cave was wide enough, Mr. Thorley huddled, hugging his knees. He called to her as if she were miles away when it was only a few feet.

"It's Jasper." She touched Thorley's hand and sat, stumbling a bit. She explained, "I heard someone running and thought it could be one of us."

"Thank you," Jasper said.

"It must almost be dawn," said Thorley. Dottie nodded, "It is."

"Where are the others? What happened?" Thorley asked.

"I don't know where they are," Jasper said.

"But what happened?"

He told them about Florence and Mr. Lambert. And about Morlen, up to a point. He had gotten separated from the others during the escape, he said.

"When the sun is up, we'll go to town. It's not safe now," Dottie said.

"Won't be more than an hour," said Thorley.

What would he do? What if they tried to get him to leave, asked for reasons?

In the dark, the humans could not look at each other, their expressions free. Mr. Thorley's was set in deep worry; an odd smile flickered on Dot. A centipede crawled over her, but she either didn't notice or didn't care.

"Jasper, you'll defend us should anything happen," Thorley said. "As you did release the monster on us?"

"I'm sorry," he said.

Thorley's expression changed to a crinkled pinch. "You didn't... You weren't *with* Leo Lambert?"

"Yes, I was."

They looked startled, snapping their heads towards him, but unable to truly look. Dottie sniffed. Jasper could sense her discomfort, but she shook her shoulders to clear it out. She didn't want to dwell on it. He watched as she balled part of her skirt in her palms, then smoothed it back down.

"That thing, that monster," she said. "I know how this sounds, but trust me when I tell you it's a vampire."

"Oh?" Jasper said.

"Don't give me that tone. You don't believe me. But it's true, I mean, how else do you account for all that we've seen?"

Mr. Thorley snorted, but Jasper could tell he believed her more than he let on.

"How would you explain it, Clarence?" Dottie snapped.

"I don't think we stand a chance against the undead." Thorley tried to make it sound like a joke; he was sweating. Fear made his blood smell stronger.

"I know how to kill it," Dottie said. "We need to do it ourselves, in the daylight." The cave's sliver of an entrance was growing brighter. Jasper felt a dip; his strength was draining.

"I'm injured," he said. "And exhausted. I need to rest here for a few hours."

"No," Dottie said. "It's not safe in here. Too dark. It's only safe in the day."

"I *want* to rest here," Jasper said.

"We'll carry you," said Dottie. She was smiling at him, her eyes on his. She could see them now, surely, looking at him with a simple compassion. *Don't argue!* He wanted to shout. Why couldn't they leave him be?

Even if they left him now, they might come back. And if they found the others, they would tell them what Jasper was. The whole pack of them could root him out of the cave.

He drank Dottie last, though afterwards he thought, that had been crueler. She had known what was coming, and spent her last moments curdled in fright.

‡‡‡

Jasper woke the following night, unscathed. He wanted more blood. Was it normal to feast so much yet wake up hungry? Would it happen every time?

The corpses surrounding him didn't bother him. The memory of those in the pit still did, a human trauma welded into his brain. Everything from before he had been turned swished hot and frenzied in his mind: one long, unremitting panic. But these bodies were no more disturbing to him than any other fact of nature.

Sad how Dottie had gone. He was sorry about it. He stood so her eyes, cloudy and stuck wide open, faced him. As if by staring into them, he could scrounge up some last connection. *See you in the afterlife,* that was something people said. Maybe it was true, but it wouldn't happen to him, because he wouldn't die.

Was there anyone he wanted to take with him?

The thought of seeing his sister felt obscene now, to show up with fangs and blood on his tongue. His mother— he did not want to see her at all.

Was there anyone?

No.

Right now, he was hungry. Different than human hunger, like there was something *wrong* deep within him, and until he had blood, he would not for a moment be at peace. Was this how Ansehelm had felt for centuries, chained in the tower? It would be torture.

His skin was lichenous in the moonlight. Outside the cave, smells came as distinct as sounds and visions. Leaves, sap, juice from wild berries, the musk of living wood, the rot of shit and dead things. Metal-salt: that was blood.

With a swivel of his neck, his eyes landed on a squirrel, just slipping under a log. He could tell by the scent it would not be as good as a human. If he wanted *that*, he'd have to find one first.

 To one side was the hut and the castle, and somewhere below that, the town. He didn't know who was where, whether alive or dead, or what Ansehelm had done. The thought of dealing with any of it—even with one of the men from the town, even if he only had to hear about Morlen or Shaw or the Lamberts, was excruciating.

Broken legs in that castle room, all their disgust bearing into him. They thought him worse than vampires or cannibals.

He didn't want to be a threat, but he craved their blood. Didn't want to hurt anyone, but he might have to defend himself again. They would burn him alive in the sun. The last of the survivors—and there must be some left—they knew about Jasper. He was weaker than Ansehelm, and they hated him more. They would hunt him.

He had not been a threat, not to anyone. Hadn't meant any harm. That was all he could say for himself, and he wasn't sure it was worth much at all.

He lunged and scooped the squirrel into his mouth, reaching under and pulling it from the log in a single second. Instinct told him how to move. Of course, the squirrel was not enough, but there were plenty in the woods.

Leo could come through the trees brandishing a wooden stake.

Warmed on rodent blood, he headed back towards the cliff where he had transformed. The moon was fuller. It shone like the spark of a lighting match that had been frozen and hung it in the sky.

A waving path dropped down the rocks into the woods below. He tested it: far too steep for a human, but his feet knew just where to go and, where before he would have bent and fallen, he seemed to float, as if walking on air as much as earth. Briefly, he tried to levitate as Ansehelm had, but no luck. One day, he thought.

In the forest, the dark-bright colors and earth smells contoured around him. He stalked through, grabbing creatures that passed by, slowly filling the empty crags inside him. A monster in the woods. He didn't know how long he'd stay, or where he'd go from here. So much could be done now, beyond any dreams he had before. But it was safe deep down the mountain, hidden under canopy.

There were animals here he had never seen before. Deer. A bear, brown, big as a carriage, plodding around the woods. A pack of coyotes that glared at him through the trees. None came close, sensing that he was dangerous. They all trusted their instincts. They wouldn't hurt him. He roamed freely, nothing to block his way. No agendas, no voices calling him.

Hunting a bird up a tree, he stopped to rest on a branch. The bark massaged his new body as he drank. He let one leg swing down, gazing at the mountains and sky. No soot to block the stars. His clothes were tearing, they wouldn't hold up much longer. Didn't matter. There was no one around to care.

He could do anything he wanted, but if he went out into the world, he would have to talk, lie, steal, buy, sell, kill, pretend to be alive when instead he could sit here in seclusion and without an echo of obligation.

He would let himself become all creature. Churning through dirt with the worms. Tranquil as the dead. If he was doomed to loneliness, he could at least be at peace. Jasper put a hand on his chest. Calm. No heartbeat.

END

THANKS FOR READING

I'm glad you made it here and I hope you enjoyed *Leech*! Thanks for reading, and I would deeply appreciate it if you took the time to leave a review. Not only do reviews help me as an independent author, but I'm eager to hear your feedback.

Please leave a review on:

Goodreads at www.goodreads.com

Storygraph at app.thestorygraph.com

Or wherever you purchased from

Stay in contact:

Visit **www.23ghosts.com**

Follow on Instagram **@23ghostsbooks**

ACKNOWLEDGMENTS

Leech began as a short story, written in response to a call for classic gothic stories from a small online magazine. As I started, it quickly became apparent that this idea was bigger than the 4000-word limit the magazine allowed. I still didn't think this was going to be my first novel until it was, and after years of work I'm glad it's out here in the world. There were so many different versions, documents and notebooks filled with drafts, sketches, outlines, wistful ideas, and attempts to impose structure. Throughout that there were editors and friends who helped shape this into its final form.

I couldn't have done this without Kendra's help: thank you for always being there to read, give feedback, and talk through it. You're an amazing friend and writer.

Thanks to everyone who listened to me go on about this story and bitch about the writing (and publishing) process. Especially Maria.

Thanks to my parents for their help, and for always supporting my writing.

Special thanks to everyone who let me talk about my book in large social settings.

I'm so grateful to have many wonderful friends who offered their support and enthusiasm about the project. Thanks for getting excited with me!

ABOUT THE AUTHOR

Gabriel Ryves is a writer and occultist who's always been fascinated by what lurks behind locked doors. He lives in New York.